Christie Barlow is the author of thirteen bestselling romantic comedies including the iconic Love Heart Lane seri[...] *Dream*. She lives in a ramshackle cottage in a quaint village in the heart of Staffordshire with her four children and two dogs.

Her writing career came as a lovely surprise when she decided to write a book to teach her children a valuable life lesson and show them that they are capable of achieving their dreams. Christie's dream was to become a writer and the book she wrote to prove a point went on to become a #1 bestseller in the UK, USA, Canada, and Australia.

When Christie isn't writing she enjoys playing the piano, is a keen gardener, and loves to paint and upcycle furniture.

Christie loves to hear from her readers and you can get in touch via Twitter, Facebook, and Instagram.

facebook.com/ChristieJBarlow

twitter.com/ChristieJBarlow

bookbub.com/authors/christie-barlow

instagram.com/christie_barlow

Also by Christie Barlow

The Love Heart Lane Series

Love Heart Lane

Foxglove Farm

Clover Cottage

Starcross Manor

The Lake House

Primrose Park

Heartcross Castle

The New Doctor at Peony Practice

Standalones

The Cosy Canal Boat Dream

A Home at Honeysuckle Farm

NEW BEGINNINGS AT THE OLD BAKEHOUSE

CHRISTIE BARLOW

One More Chapter
a division of HarperCollins*Publishers* Ltd
1 London Bridge Street
London SE1 9GF
www.harpercollins.co.uk
HarperCollins*Publishers*
1st Floor, Watermarque Building, Ringsend Road
Dublin 4, Ireland

This paperback edition 2022
1
First published in Great Britain in ebook format
by HarperCollins*Publishers* 2022
Copyright © Christie Barlow 2022
Christie Barlow asserts the moral right to
be identified as the author of this work
A catalogue record of this book is available from the British Library

ISBN: 978-0-00-841311-8

This novel is entirely a work of fiction. The names, characters and incidents portrayed in it are the work of the author's imagination. Any resemblance to actual persons, living or dead, events or localities is entirely coincidental.

Printed and bound in the UK using 100% Renewable Electricity
by CPI Group (UK) Ltd

For Kim Smith, Sam Newey and Ashley Costello.
Three awesome women.
And the inspiration behind the story of New Beginnings at the
Old Bakehouse.
Without them this story would have never been written.

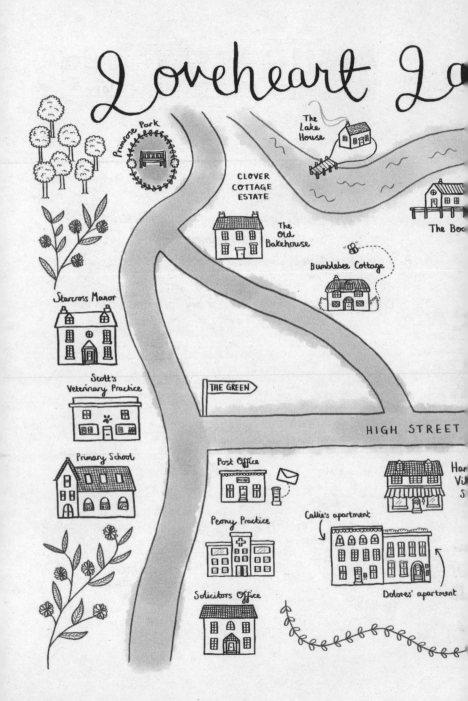

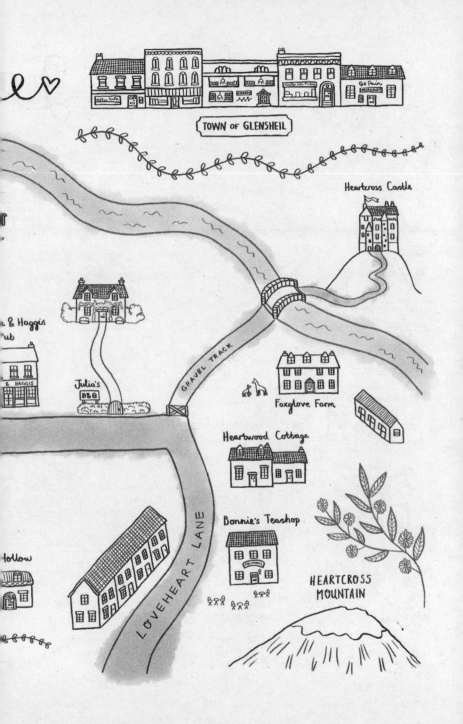

Chapter One

Thud!

Molly McKendrick, standing behind the counter at The Old Bakehouse, brought both hands up to cover her heart. She looked over to the window and smiled. There was Cam standing outside on the snowy pavement, wearing his traditional toque hat and his apron tied around his waist. With a huge beam on his face, he gestured towards the snowy windscreen of the van. Molly threw her head back and laughed. Cam had drawn a love heart in the snow with their initials etched at the top and bottom.

'You big softie,' she mouthed at him, still smiling.

Just as Cam was about to walk inside, he playfully threw a snowball at the window, causing Molly to jump again. Shaking her head, she watched him stamp the snow from his boots before entering the shop. It was good to see Cam in a better mood as she'd begun to worry about him in the last few weeks. His mood had seemed to change overnight and he'd become pensive, and at times a little short-tempered.

As the door opened and Cam stepped inside, Molly shuddered at the cold blast of air and walked towards the window. Outside was a typical winter's evening, the beam from the streetlamp highlighting the hypnotic sight of snowflakes flurrying to the ground. The dusting of snow over the village green marked the beginning of the festive season.

'It's a beautiful winter wonderland out there,' said Molly.

'It's blooming freezing is what it is,' replied Cam, hanging up his hat and apron on the peg behind the counter ready for tomorrow. He joined Molly at the window and playfully touched her cheek with his cold hand.

'Get off me,' she said good-humouredly. 'You're freezing!'

She tried to wriggle away from his clutches but Cam slipped his arms around Molly's pregnant waist and rested his head on her shoulder.

'Christmas is coming and I am getting fat,' she joked, smiling warmly at Cam over her shoulder.

'You are not fat, you are utterly gorgeous, and blooming ... blooming!' he replied.

'How is it you always say the right things?' Molly pressed a gentle kiss to his lips before turning back and watching the snow fall. 'This is my favourite time of year. Log fires, hot chocolate and family film nights. Everything is just so perfect. Us, this place and our soon to be extended family.'

'I couldn't agree more,' Cam replied, checking his watch. It was exactly six o'clock and he turned the sign on the back of the shop door to CLOSED. 'It's not been as busy today with the weather like it is, but I still need to cash up.'

Cam had managed The Old Bakehouse for the last four years – a change in career from dentistry to resurrect a business close to the heart of the community, one that was founded by his Great-Uncle Ted – and he had never looked back.

Molly – the local vet – had gone into partnership with Rory Scott, the vet from the Clover Cottage estate, and was currently enjoying some time off during her pregnancy. With their first son George just starting school and another baby on the way, Molly had been helping out in the shop for the past couple of weeks to relieve some of the pressures on Cam.

'If that snow keeps falling, the shop may be quieter. People won't want to venture out in this. Not that I'm complaining,' he added quickly before disappearing into the back of the shop whilst Molly straightened the jars of chutneys and jams on the shelf. He returned a few minutes later carrying the most delicious, calorific-looking hot chocolate, layered with cream and pink and white marshmallows, and handed it to Molly. 'Just for you,' he said, giving her a tired but adorable smile. 'I know how much you are craving hot chocolate at the minute.'

'This is the life,' Molly murmured and patted her

stomach. 'I think I'm using cravings as an excuse. This baby is due out in only a few more weeks and goodness knows what is baby and what isn't.' She looked down towards her bump that was growing bigger by the day. 'But I'll worry about that at a later date.' Cupping the drink with both hands she leant into Cam's chest. 'And why can't I be craving fruit or vegetables? Just my luck!'

'Make the most of it,' he said, lightly kissing the top of her head then taking a glance towards the window.

'What are you thinking? You've suddenly got a worried look on your face,' Molly said.

'I don't want you driving out in this, especially in your condition.'

In recent weeks, after hours, Molly had been loading up the van each evening with all the leftover perishable goods and making the journey over to the homeless shelter on the outskirts of Glensheil whilst Cam bathed George and put him to bed. It was their way of giving a little back to the community. Molly knew that whenever the temperature dropped outside, the line-ups for the shelter started early and a stream of people – both young and old – shuffled their way through the doors, so she always aimed to get there when the shelter opened a little after six-thirty. Their faces chapped from the cold and their hands trembling around the warm bowl of soup, they were grateful for a place to shield from the bitter chill outside.

Every one of these people had a story to tell. Their lives had not panned out the way they would have liked. Some were friendly and some weren't but without fail she'd turn up every night with any leftover food from The Old Bakehouse and she knew the volunteers at the shelter were extremely grateful.

'I'll be absolutely fine,' she replied. 'Honestly, don't worry.'

'I know we are doing our good deed, and – never mind the weather – that place isn't without drama.' He raised an eyebrow.

Molly knew exactly what Cam meant. Some of the shelter's visitors were struggling with mental illnesses and addictions and sometimes there were situations that escalated out of control, but that hadn't stopped Molly.

'Let me go instead,' continued Cam. 'Like I've just said, those roads will be treacherous and you are eight months pregnant. I don't want anything happening to you.'

'You big softie. Honestly, don't worry, it's a straight run. I'll be there and back before you know it and never mind me – you're the one I'm really worried about.'

'Me ... why?' asked Cam, surprised.

'Because you have been up since the early hours and I know you are going to pull your face when I say this, but you really could do with some help in the shop.' Molly had begun to wonder whether Cam's recent irritable mood was down to the fact he never stopped. 'You are baking all the bread and pastries and making the jams and chutneys. An apprentice is what you need.'

'But it's a family business.'

Molly could have predicted Cam's words. She knew how much the business meant to him, and how much he wanted to make his grandmother proud. After all, this was the icing on the cake: her cherished grandson moving into The Old Bakehouse and opening up the bakery shop again after all these years. But Cam was going to run himself into the ground if he didn't acknowledge the fact that he needed help.

'And we are your family, that little boy through there and this baby right here. We need you to be fit and healthy, not run into the ground. We just need to find you the right apprentice or a shop assistant, someone who complements the business, not complicates it. It may take time but as soon as this little one is born, I'm going to have my hands full, and at some point I need to go back to my vet's surgery. I can't leave it in Rory's capable hands for ever.'

'I know it's not easy and I do appreciate your help. I can only imagine how, after dropping George at school, you want to put your feet up.'

Molly knew it was far from easy. With the combination of the baby kicking and heartburn throughout the night, she couldn't remember the last time she'd had a proper night's sleep.

'That is so, but though you know I'll help out as much as possible, and Dixie works on a Monday, your grandmother isn't getting any younger either, Cam. At least promise me you'll think about giving someone a job. As a business we can afford it. Can't we?' Molly knew she'd tagged the question on the end to gauge Cam's reaction. Were his recent mood swings down to worry over the business? Was it in financial difficulty?

Cam looked at her. 'Of course we can afford it, but it just has to be the right person.'

'I agree with you. And what's this...' She pinched his chin playfully. 'That stubble is fast becoming a beard and your hair needs a trim, and those bags under your eyes are rather on the dark side, and you drink a bucketful of coffee to keep yourself going each day. Sooner or later something has to give and I'm hoping that it's not going to be you.'

Every morning, the kitchen at The Old Bakehouse was a hive of activity from three a.m. when Cam started work. He baked all the loaves and pastries from scratch before the rest of the village began to stir and he was ready to greet customers with his beatific smile when the doors opened for business. Cam was the life and soul of the bakery, thriving on the everyday chat with the villagers.

'Why don't we advertise, just to see what the response is like? It couldn't hurt.' Cam's jaw became rigid and Molly knew he needed a little more persuasion. 'Just think about it. It would take me literally five minutes to write up a job advert and post it.'

'I know, it's just hard because no one will love this business as much as me.'

Molly knew the reason why Cam was reluctant to let anyone in. He'd had a previous business and worked hard to set up his empire, but then it all went to his ex-wife in the divorce settlement. That's when he started over fresh in Heartcross and opened up The Old Bakehouse.

'History will not repeat itself; we are a family now and I won't let you down.' Molly knew they were only words, and Cam's past hurt ran deep, but all she could do was prove it to him. 'You aren't asking anyone to be a partner, you just need a decent shop assistant and maybe an apprentice baker who could learn the ropes and help to lessen your load in the meantime. It's the perfect plan. We could interview them together.'

Molly knew very well the pressures of running your own business; it had been exactly the same for her in the early days of starting up her veterinary surgery. She was reluctant to share or let go of the reins and micro-managed everything. It was only since becoming a mother that her priorities had changed and she'd finally admitted she was burning herself out – and, in her eyes, that's exactly what Cam was doing now. If only he could see it himself.

Molly didn't need to say anything else to Cam as she could see he was mulling over the idea as he glanced around the shop. He wasn't one for making rash decisions. He was one for thinking things over, and in his own time hopefully he'd suggest it as though it was his idea in the first place.

'I'm going to load up the leftovers onto the van and get over to the shelter.'

'Are you sure you don't want me to go?'

'You get George ready for bed.'

'Okay, and maybe I'll run you a bath for when you get back.' His eyes flashed with that knowing look.

'Offering to run me a bath … making me a hot chocolate … I know exactly what you are thinking.'

He grinned at her then, a smile that implied she knew

him inside and out. She gently pushed the empty mug against his chest. 'The sooner I get to the shelter, the sooner I'll be back. Now go and see to George.' Molly pressed a swift kiss to Cam's cheek and grabbed her coat from the hook at the back of the shop.

As she began to take the leftover baked goods from the shelves and load them into large wicker baskets for the shelter, she began to think about how lucky she was. She'd been adopted as a very young child by Di and Doug but her life could have taken a very different path if she'd stayed with her biological parents, who'd had her when they were sixteen.

Their lives had been fuelled by alcohol and drug abuse and she had no clue what had happened to them, if they had stayed together, or even if they were still alive. Even though she'd been curious at times to know more about them, she'd never felt strongly enough to do anything about it. She loved her life just the way it was.

Her thoughts turned back to all those people who'd be queuing up outside the shelter on this cold frosty night. Tonight, the temperature would hit minus five and, as soon as the shelter doors opened, the homeless would be grateful for the warmth, a bowl of hot soup and the company of others. No time was a good time to be homeless, but the winter months always brought extra challenges.

'I'm just heading out,' she shouted to Cam who appeared in the doorway giving George a piggyback. 'You pair are a vision of total gorgeousness,' she chirped, pinching George's cheek lightly before placing a noisy kiss on it, leaving George playfully wiping it away.

Cam looked towards the window, his eyes full of concern once more. 'Please let me go tonight? I really don't like the thought of you venturing out in this.'

'Honestly, I'll be okay,' she replied, slipping her arms into her coat then attempting to do up the buttons. 'Oh my!' She looked down at her stomach. 'I think I may have put on a little too much weight,' she acknowledged, but she was grinning as she wound her scarf around her neck and pulled on her hat and gloves.

'You look as fat as Father Christmas,' George said, pointing at Molly's stomach.

'Don't you be cheeky, you little ragamuffin. Now you be good for Daddy and go and get your bath.'

Six-thirty was always bathtime, seven o'clock a bedtime story, and at seven-thirty George was tucked up in bed and Cam and Molly finally got to spend a couple of hours together before Cam went to bed.

'Right, I'm off!' She jangled the van keys.

'Are you sure? Because I can go...' Cam asked, once again looking out of the window.

But Molly held up her hands to curtail further discussion, leaving Cam sighing in defeat. She walked over to him and breathed in his familiar scent before kissing him on his cheek and waltzing towards the door. 'You just make sure there's a nice warm bath waiting for me.' She tipped him a wink before opening the shop door and hurrying towards the van.

The falling snow was bitterly cold so she quickly sprayed the windscreen with de-icer before climbing behind the wheel. She fired up the engine, gave a shiver then turned on the radio. With the toasty seat-warmers switched on and the heat ramped up she indicated and pulled away from the shop, waving at the boys, who were watching from the window. The snow was coming down with a bold grace and Molly drove carefully towards the track leading up to the bridge that linked the village of Heartcross and the town of Glensheil. It was only a few years ago that the worst weather in a century had hit this tiny village, with devastating effects: the bridge had collapsed, leaving the villagers stranded.

The Scottish weather was unpredictable – it could turn overnight – and that's why Molly was keen to provide as much support as possible to the homeless shelter. She didn't like the thought of anyone sleeping on the streets at any time of the year, let alone in weather like this. She glanced up at Heartcross Castle as she passed. A couple of days ago the trees were heaven-blended browns and sweet umber caramels, but now each was frosted with a lacy brilliant white. There wasn't a soul in sight as Molly drove over the bridge but smoke spiralled from the chimney pots of the houses. No doubt everyone was cosied up by their log fires, shielding themselves from the cold.

It was only a ten-minute drive to the shelter, which had been a part of the community for as long as Molly could remember. It offered more than the basic needs of the homeless; it was also an institution that provided hope and strength for people to believe in themselves so they could change their lives for the better. The shelter was situated in the square next to the splendour of the town hall, which was a fine piece of architecture and one of the most photographed landmarks in Glensheil. Molly turned right and slowed down as she followed the narrow side street that led around the back of the church towards the square.

The shelter was just up ahead and immediately Molly clocked the long line of people queuing in hope of a bed for the night. She knew the old, battered mattresses with springs poking in one's back couldn't be the most comfortable – nor was the hardness of the floor beneath a thin sleeping pad – but to those people queuing it was luxury and a lifeline they needed. Molly knew that there were more people than beds, and it broke her heart to think that some of them could possibly be turned away, especially in conditions like this.

Parking the van as close to the shelter door as possible, she spotted some of the regulars, and as usual there were a few faces she hadn't seen before. The running of this shelter was a testament to Sam Evans, who'd been a volunteer since what seemed the year dot and was now the woman in charge. It was a giant task to provide food and warmth to all these people and keep the shelter running but Sam made it look easy.

Right on time the doors to the shelter opened and with their duffle bags and belongings slung over their shoulders and sleeping bags tucked under their arms, the men, women and families began to filter inside. Molly swung the van doors open and placed one wicker basket on top of the other, determined to carry more than one inside at a time. As soon as Sam spotted her, she came to help. She was a slim woman, with steely grey hair pulled back in a tidy bun. She wore a red check shirt, a pair of denim dungarees accompanied by cherry-red Doc Martens boots, and a thick green cardigan that hung from her shoulders like a blanket. Molly's guess was that she was in her mid-sixties, though she'd never thought it right to ask.

'It's going to be a busy night,' said Molly, unintentionally wrinkling her nose as she stepped inside the shelter. The smell of sour body odour mixed with cigarette smoke got her every time.

All around she could hear chatter, the raised voices in the background mingling with the sounds of chairs scraping and a TV playing somewhere.

'The bad weather always brings more people in off the streets but, thankfully, we have more volunteers here tonight, to help with the food,' shared Sam, nodding towards the kitchen.

'There are three more baskets in the van if you want to take these ones through to the kitchen. I've thrown in some honey and jams in. They're weeks within their sell-by date, so they can be used at any time.'

'Molly, we can't thank you enough; you and Cam are both so kind.'

'Anything to help, you don't need to thank us.'

Every time Molly walked through these doors she was in awe of Sam, who gave up her time on a daily basis to bring a little comfort to the lives of the people that wandered in off the streets. Some she knew from old as they'd been coming for years, and she knew that Sam was fond of many of them. Having a heart of gold, Sam would give them all a permanent home if she could.

Sam walked towards the kitchen balancing the wicker baskets in her arms and it wasn't long before Molly was by her side unloading the rest of the goods onto the long aluminium counter. She greeted the volunteers who were helping to prepare the meals, laying bowls out in a long line on the cafeteria-style counter. In the main room the homeless were given a warm drink as they settled themselves.

'This is the busiest I've seen it in a long time,' observed Molly, peering through the hatch from the kitchen to the vast main room, with its bare walls, tiled flooring and long rows of tables with folding chairs. The serving staff setting up tonight's meal provided a smile and light conversation while numerous people claimed their place to sleep and others wrapped their hands around polystyrene cups of warmth. Molly caught the eye of a man she'd seen a few times – Stan. He smiled at her then tipped his flat cap. His wizened face was a map of wrinkles hidden behind layers of grime and his hair hung as a tangled mop of brown and grey under his flat cap. His coat looked like it was once high-end but now, worn and dirty, it hung from his thin, fragile limbs. Molly guessed Stan must be in his early seventies, and wondered what his story was as she swallowed down a lump in her throat.

Being pregnant, Molly knew her emotions were heightened, but all she wanted to do was take Stan home and let him have a warm bath and a comfy bed to sleep in. Of course, she knew she couldn't. Molly didn't know how Sam kept her emotions in check because she herself could instantly start crying just thinking about everyone that walked through those doors. There was a certain sadness that bled through the room, yet a comforting feeling now the residents were safe, warm and off the streets for the night.

'When I arrived earlier, I discovered a huge pile of fresh clean blankets folded up on the step,' shared Sam with a smile on her face. 'I was so relieved, knowing the numbers of people seeking shelter would increase tonight with the temperatures so low.'

'Where did the linen come from?' asked Molly, stirring the big pot of soup that was bubbling away on the stove.

'Starcross Manor. Flynn sent me a text to say the hotel had them going spare. Honestly, that man is a saint. That text couldn't have come at a better time, and that's what I love about this community, we do look after each other,' she said. 'And all this...' Sam was close to tears as she looked over all the fresh bread that Molly had brought. 'They will all have full stomachs tonight.' Sam took a knife and began slicing the bread, laying it out on plastic trays.

One of the volunteers helped Molly lift the big pot of soup off the stove and place it at the serving hatch. Already, the residents were forming an orderly queue, with Stan right at the very front.

'We are being spoilt tonight, look at that bread!' Stan's eyes were wide and thankful.

As the volunteers began to serve, the residents were soon sitting down and tucking into a warm meal. There wasn't a spare seat in the room.

'I don't like this part...' Sam looked up towards the clock. 'It's time to shut the doors. I'd prefer to leave them open all night, but we are already full to capacity. Could you free the latch on the way out and shut the door behind you?' Sam's voice faltered.

Molly touched her elbow and nodded. 'Of course,' she replied, picking up the empty baskets.

'And that bread is going down a treat.' Sam smiled. 'And don't think we don't know that Cam bakes extra bread each day, just for us. Thank you.'

There were no more words needed as the grateful look on Sam's face was touching enough and Molly's chest heaved as she walked towards the door. She wished she could do more. Taking one last look over her shoulder she glanced around the room and caught the eye of Stan, who gave her a wink. As she stepped outside onto the pavement, the ice-cold air immediately hit her as she slid the empty baskets into the back of the van. The snow wouldn't be letting up anytime soon; it was still coming down thick and fast, and the weather for the foreseeable future was forecast to be much the same.

Just as Molly unlatched the door, she felt a presence standing right behind her and gasped as she nearly jumped out of her skin.

'Sorry, I didn't mean to frighten you, Mrs,' came the Scottish twang of a young girl with her hood pulled up over her head. Her bare white knuckles clutched a duffle bag that was thrown over her shoulder. In her other hand she clenched a grimy pillow.

From underneath her hood, all Molly could see was a wide pair of hazel eyes staring back at her. For a second, she was transfixed. There was something in the look of the girl's eyes that immediately triggered thoughts from Molly's past. Molly shuddered as she could suddenly see every detail and feel every feeling from when she was a small child. For a moment she closed her eyes, trying to shake off the image.

'You didn't, it's okay,' she replied, smiling warmly at the girl, who quickly averted her gaze, not meeting Molly's friendly eye. Evidently the harshness of street life was already teaching this young girl to stay isolated in every possible way, that even a stray glance could mean trouble she'd best avoid.

The girl turned to walk away.

'Where are you going?' asked Molly, the bitterly cold snowflakes now stinging her cheeks.

'I don't want any trouble,' the girl replied defensively as she spun around. 'I just wanted a bed for the night. You're locking up. I've missed the time.'

Even though she had an oversized jacket thrown over her tiny body the girl was shivering.

'Not on my watch you haven't.' Molly smiled warmly, opening the door wide.

The girl hesitated.

'Go on, get yourself in there and get yourself a warm meal,' encouraged Molly.

As the girl pulled down her hood, Molly was taken aback by her age. She'd known she was young but now Molly could see her properly she looked barely out of her mid-teens, though it was difficult to tell. She smiled and nodded her thanks before walking past Molly into the warmth of the shelter.

'I'm Molly, by the way.'

'Bree,' the girl answered, but didn't wait around to make any further conversation.

Molly cradled her bump as she watched Bree disappear towards the main hall. Despite the shelter being full, Sam welcomed Bree at the door and pointed her toward the queue for food.

Feeling a pang in her heart Molly watched her for a moment. She felt sad that such a young girl was out on the streets fending for herself. There were so many questions swirling around in her head. How does a young girl end up on the streets with no family to care for her? How was she going to turn that situation around? And where would she be sleeping tomorrow? Molly looked down towards her bump. 'We are so lucky,' she whispered, pulling the door shut behind her as her phone pinged.

Rummaging in her pocket, she saw it was a text from Cam.

Worried about you, are you on your way back yet?

Just leaving now, I'll be fifteen minutes max.

She punched her reply then quickly pulled on her gloves. As the engine started and the wipers swished away the falling snow from the windscreen, Molly turned up the heat. She took one glance back towards the door before pulling away. For some reason she couldn't stop thinking about Bree, whose wide hazel eyes were firmly implanted in her mind as she pulled on to the road and carefully began to drive towards home.

Chapter Two

The next morning, the door to The Old Bakehouse flew open and in strolled Dixie with the biggest beam on her face. 'Food, glorious food,' she sang. She wafted her nose in the air. 'Freshly baked bread ... I'll never tire of that smell.' She walked over to the shelves behind the counter and inspected the loaves, then glanced at the paper-wrapped muffins, colourful fruit tarts and glazed flans.

'Where is he?' she asked over her shoulder.

'Who, Cam? He's through there,' answered Molly with a smile, knowing full well that Dixie meant George.

'Of course I don't mean Cam!'

'Charming!' Cam's voice bellowed from the bakery kitchen.

Dixie popped her head around the door to see Cam pulling out a tray of freshly baked bagels from the giant ovens. 'As much as I love you, I did mean my great-grandson.'

'G-Ma!' George appeared in the doorway and stomped his way over to Dixie with his arms open wide.

'Here he is. My favourite boy in the world and an overload of cuteness. And what are you wearing on your feet?'

Proudly, George looked down at his brand-new bright red wellingtons. 'My new boots!'

'I'm not going to lose you in the snow wearing those, am I? And wait until you see what I have outside for you.' George clomped his way over to the window and squealed as he saw Darling the dog tied to the lamppost with a bright yellow sledge right next to her. 'I thought we'd travel to school in style this morning.'

George threw his arms around Dixie's legs and hugged her tightly before running off and returning with his coat and school bag dragging behind him. Three mornings a week Dixie walked George to school. She was indeed the proud great-grandmother. Molly zipped up George's coat, pulled his hat down over his ears and slipped his hands into his gloves. 'Have fun!' She kissed him on his cheek whilst Cam high-fived him, but she noticed that George was pulling at Dixie's pocket.

'Did you bring me any sweets?' asked George.

Dixie gave him a look that Cam had seen many times when he was a small boy. He couldn't help but smile. It was the look that meant: *Be quiet, don't tell the parents.*

'Please do not tell me you fill my son full of sweets on the way to school,' said Cam to Dixie, who was looking considerably sheepish.

'Not all the time, and it doesn't do you any harm.' She gave Cam a cheeky wink. 'Right, young man, are we ready?'

George hugged Molly then Cam, who handed him a white paper bag with a warm bagel inside. 'Take this, you can eat it on the sledge.' With his backpack hoisted up on his back, George headed outside with Dixie, much to the delight of Darling, who began yapping the second she saw them.

Molly wrapped her arms around Cam's waist and they watched as George sat on a blanket that had been placed in the sledge, with his legs stretched out in front of him. They chuckled as Dixie began pulling the sledge and George squealed with delight, clutching his bagel. The sight of Darling prancing in the snow as she attempted to walk beside the sledge was comical enough to make anyone smile. They set off up the road leaving tracks on the freshly laid snow and soon were out of sight.

'I hope I'm as sprightly at that age,' said Molly, who already felt exhausted and had only been out of bed for just over an hour.

'You were quiet last night and a little so this morning.' Cam narrowed his eyes at Molly. 'Are you feeling okay?'

'Of course, just pregnant,' she replied with a smile, as she began piping the insides of the doughnuts with jam. 'I'm not sure how anyone can ever say they enjoy being pregnant or that they feel radiant and blooming. I can't sleep properly with the constant night-time kicking from this one; I'm exhausted and feel blooming awful.'

Cam gave Molly a hug. 'You are doing amazing. Only another few weeks to go and then the real fun begins.'

'Ha, and then that really does mean no sleep.' But Molly knew the real reason why she had struggled to sleep last night. She'd tossed and turned thinking about the girl she'd met in the doorway of the shelter – Bree. There was something about her she couldn't quite put her finger on. She seemed very familiar but Molly didn't know why. It was unnerving her a little.

Molly knew that the shelter would close after breakfast until it opened up again this evening and so Bree would be back on the street for the day. Sam had been campaigning to extend the opening hours but with no official outcome so far. Molly had often seen homeless people walking down the street or sitting in doorways in the day but had never thought about what they did with the rest of their time. Where would Bree go? Would she sit around waiting all day for her luck to change or for money to fall from the sky and instantly change her situation? How do you actually turn your life around when you're in that position?

Last night the shelter was full of people, all with different lives, different mindsets and different ambitions. She knew some might fit the stereotypes but also knew that many didn't and that most homeless people were on the streets simply because they'd had a run of bad luck and were depressed and embarrassed about their situation. They needed a chance to get back on their feet and back into society.

Bree looked too young to be faced with this life all by

herself. Every time Molly thought of those wide hazel eyes staring back at her she felt a tremor of emotion, an image from the past she just couldn't shake off. With the weather this cold and bitter she knew even daytime spent on the street would be freezing.

'You're daydreaming again!' Cam playfully nudged her arm.

'Hey!' she said, squeezing the piping bag. Jam squirted over the counter.

'You are meant to get that in the doughnut, not everywhere but... You doughnut!'

'Ah, funny,' she replied, rolling her eyes. 'And who are you calling a doughnut?' She aimed the piping bag at Cam and pressed it with full force. She giggled as Cam quickly moved out of the way and strawberry jam trailed across the counter.

'You are lethal with that thing,' he said, throwing a cloth at her. 'I'll be banning you from the bakery kitchen if you carry on. Now back to work,' he ordered with a smile.

Molly saluted. 'Yes, Chef!'

Cam carried on checking the ovens before he began baking a batch of croissants. He looked across at Molly. Her cheeks were glowing and her pregnant bump touched the counter. Cam couldn't quite believe their second baby was about to be born in a matter of weeks. Molly was his world and he loved her with every inch of his body. She was kind, generous, always thought of others, and he knew he was a lucky man that their paths had crossed.

Turning away, Cam was stricken with a sudden surge

of guilt. When George was born, they'd promised each other that they would always look after one another and be honest and open about everything. But he'd been in a dilemma for a few weeks now, unable to tell a soul what he was grappling with, knowing that there was a possibility he was about to shatter his family's lives. Cam had always championed honesty, and feeling that twinge of guilt his thoughts turned to the letter he was hiding in his apron pocket. He knew he should tell Molly his news as the date of his scan was getting close, but at this stage in her pregnancy he didn't want to worry her. Cam had always found personal stuff difficult to talk about – it was just the way he was – and there never seemed to be a right time to broach the subject. And truthfully, he felt scared. He always thought his future was mapped out with a happy ever after for the family he cherished with all his heart, but there was a possibility this scan could change everything. All he had to do was try and keep everything together for another week and then the wait would be over and he could tell Molly the – hopefully good – news.

Trying to keep his emotions in check, he concentrated on beating the eggs in the bowl in front of him, hoping Molly wouldn't notice the tears in his eyes.

They worked in silence for a couple of minutes until Molly switched on the radio and began to sing along, using the piping bag as a microphone, causing Cam to look over in her direction and laugh.

'You're looking way too serious for your own good,' she

remarked, placing the piping bag down on the counter and holding out her hands. 'Come and dance with me.'

Cam shook his head in jest. 'You are mad, you are.'

'I know.' She grinned, grabbing hold of him. 'Come on.'

Cam twirled her around and she laughed and danced them towards the shop window, where she stopped mid-twirl. 'Look at the weather.' Even from inside they could tell there was a cutting chill in the air and a heaviness about the sky. The snowfall had stopped for the time being but it wouldn't be long before those flakes began to fall to the ground again.

'We are entering the world of Christmas; the winters in Scotland can be brutal,' replied Cam, taking a brief look out of the shop window. He let go of Molly's hand and opened the shop door. He quickly looked up the road. There was no one in sight.

'Usually, we have a queue of villagers waiting outside but I suppose they don't want to venture out in this.' Cam pointed towards the regular orders that were piled up on the trays at the back of the shop. 'I think I'm going to load these up in the van and do my good deed for the day by attempting to deliver them. It'll save people venturing out in these conditions.'

Molly slipped her arms around his waist and snuggled into his chest, 'That's what I love about you, you're always thinking of others. Maybe take some extras out on the van, just in case people fancy something else. Those pies smell delicious.'

'Good plan. Will you be okay holding the fort?'

'Yes, of course, and Dixie will be back shortly after she's walked Darling, who might have to be nicknamed Prancer in this snow. That dog really would prefer to be curled up in front of the fire.'

Cam chuckled. 'That's exactly what I'd like to be doing today. I'll load the van up then bring in some extra logs for the fire. If we keep that door ajar and the fire stoked, the warmth should filter through.'

'Sounds like a plan,' replied Molly, loading up a couple of boxes of freshly made doughnuts for the van then once more looking out of the window.

'You look lost in thought,' observed Cam, taking a sideward glance towards Molly.

'I'm just thinking about the shelter.'

'What about it?'

Molly stopped what she was doing. 'All those people with their only possessions packed inside their rucksacks and no home to call their own.'

Molly knew that there was a possibility her life could have spiralled out of control if it hadn't been for Di and Doug. Though she'd long ago buried any feelings she might have about her biological parents, out of love and loyalty for Di and Doug, and had no burning desire to investigate her past, she couldn't help thinking that if it wasn't for her adoptive parents she might easily have been in the same position as Bree, sleeping in shelters.

'We're very lucky,' replied Cam, staring out of the window, his hand now tightly clutching the letter in his apron pocket.

'We are indeed. A gorgeous husband ... a healthy son and a new baby on the way. And two businesses, not to mention a beautiful home. We have everything – and a wonderful future.'

Lost in thought, Cam didn't answer, causing Molly to glance up at him. Noticing he was suddenly preoccupied, she poked him gently. 'Earth to Cam.'

He spun round. 'Sorry, what did you say?'

'I was just saying how lucky we are. Are you okay? You've suddenly gone very...'

With his hands still clutching the letter, he forced nonchalance. 'I'm always okay.'

Molly leant up and gave him a swift kiss. 'As long as you're sure ... because I have noticed you have been a little quiet of late.'

'Really?' replied Cam. 'I promise I'm fine.' Wanting the pressure off himself, Cam steered the conversation in a different direction. 'Anyway, how was the shelter last night? Packed to the rafters, I bet, in this weather.'

Molly sighed, slipping her arms around Cam's waist. 'Stan – one of the regulars – he's in his late seventies. He should not be sleeping on the streets at that age. He should be looking forward to Christmas, surrounded by his family and friends.' Molly's voice faltered. 'Sam and her volunteers work so hard. They make the world a better place.'

'They do and people like Stan will be grateful to them.'

'I know we do our bit – Sam knew we baked extra bread – but I just wish we could do more.'

Cam hugged her tight. 'I know, but you can't go

worrying about everyone and everything. We have to take care of us because…' There was something in the tone of Cam's voice that caused her to look up at him.

'Because…' Molly prompted.

'Because…' The words were on the tip of Cam's tongue but once again this felt like the wrong time to share his fears. The shop was about to open and he didn't want Molly getting upset. 'Because we have another arrival very soon.'

Molly looked down at her stomach and rubbed it gently. She thought of Bree. 'It just makes me a little sad, that's all, especially when it's cold outside and with Christmas coming, that people don't have family to rely on.' Molly took a breath. 'Let's load that van up and get the shop open, even though I think it's going to be quiet today.'

'More bread for the shelter later then.' He gave Molly a quick kiss on the top of her head then pointed to the window as he grabbed his coat and van keys. 'It's snowing again.'

'The postman has been early,' said Molly, attempting to bend down and pick up the post from the mat. She laughed. With a huge stomach in the way it was proving difficult but on the second attempt she successfully scooped up the pile of letters. 'And it'll be great to touch my own toes again soon,' she shouted after Cam, who'd begun loading up the van.

Sifting through the pile of post, she found most of it was the usual junk along with the local free newspaper, the headline boldly proclaiming, 'Winter Storms Are On Their Way.'

'Anything interesting?' asked Cam, picking up another tray of orders.

'Just weather warnings and—' Molly stopped mid-sentence, too busy staring at the cobalt-coloured envelope in her hand with the baker's hat gold seal of approval stamp on the front. Feeling a surge of excitement, her heart gave a little leap. She knew *exactly* what was inside this envelope. 'Oh my gosh! Cam! It's here!'

'Huh?' he replied, looking over his shoulder.

Molly waved the envelope in the air with enthusiasm but as soon as Cam clocked it, the smile immediately slid from his face. 'Come on, open it.' She thrust the envelope towards him.

'You open it if you wish. I'm a little busy.' Cam pulled in a deep breath and carried on loading up the van.

'What is up with you? This is huge!' A little perplexed and disappointed that Cam wasn't showing any interest, she tore it open. 'It's it! It's it!' she shouted after him, her voice rising an octave. 'I'm so proud of you! You've been invited to compete for the title of Baker of the Year!'

The Annual Scottish Baking Competition was held once a year in a magnificent manor house in Edinburgh. Three bakers came head-to-head, live on stage, where they would have to bake their creations under the pressure of time. Their brief was that a special element had to be incorporated into the recipe. Elite judges crowned the best baker. Cam's being chosen was a major compliment as the competitors were hand-picked to compete, based on their skill and reputation. With the prize money a whopping

£50,000 and the publicity that surrounded the competition usually resulting in some very lucrative TV and magazine partnerships for the winner, it was a very big deal. So why was Cam acting like it was nothing?

'This is the most prestigious award ever and you'll be following in your Great-Uncle Ted's footsteps. Here, take a look.' Molly held out the envelope towards a stoic Cam. 'I was only thinking about this the other day. This is big! How exciting is this?' She studied him closely, but still saw no hint of enthusiasm from her husband. 'Even though you don't look that excited. What's going on with you? Please tell me you are going to compete.'

Cam was silent.

'But you have to. Dixie and your Great-Uncle Ted would want you to compete.'

He raised an eyebrow. 'Now that is emotional blackmail.'

Molly pinched her finger and thumb together. 'Okay, maybe a little, but why aren't you standing there full of excitement? If you win this award then it opens up a whole world of opportunities and that prize money could help to pay the wages of a new apprentice.'

'Because...' Cam knew exactly why he wasn't going to compete.

She wound her hand around in a circle, prompting him to continue. 'Because...'

'Because...' He had things going on in his life that Molly didn't know about. Knowing that the appointment in the letter in his pocket could change the course of his life, Cam couldn't concentrate on anything else. Thinking on his feet, he improvised with 'I'm not sure I'm good enough yet.'

Molly let out a strangled laugh. 'Are you for real? Why would you think you aren't good enough? Have you seen this place? Your baking is to die for. At least take a proper look at the invitation.'

Reluctantly, Cam reread the invite then placed it on the counter. 'It's not just about being a baker though, is it? Look…' He tapped the invite. 'The special element this year is chocolate.'

'And? You fill pastries with chocolate every day.'

'It's not quite the same thing and not to the standard of what the judges are looking for.'

Molly knew that Cam was making excuses. 'So, get baking and perfecting your chocolate creation. With the weather like this there will be plenty of time.'

Cam still wasn't forthcoming but Molly noticed he stole a glance towards his Great-Uncle Ted's photograph hanging on the wall. His eyes looked a little bleary. 'He would be so proud of you. Look how far you've come.'

For a moment, they both looked over at the old black and white framed photograph of his grandfather's brother, wearing his apron and traditional toque hat. He was standing proudly outside the door of The Old Bakehouse on its first day of opening.

'Maybe next year,' Cam said, dismissing whatever thoughts had consumed him. 'I'll just grab the logs for the fire and be on my way,' he said.

Molly noticed the doors at the back of the van were still

wide open as Cam disappeared out of the shop. Shutting the shop door to keep the warmth in, Molly switched the sign on the back to OPEN. Outside, the snow was gently falling all around and there wasn't a soul in sight. She walked over to the photograph of Ted and stared at it for a second. His framed awards were proudly displayed underneath in a row. Ted Bird had won Scottish Baker of the Year for ten consecutive years. He was the master of his craft and rather famous all over Scotland in his day. There had been a number of magazine articles written about him and he'd appeared on TV numerous times, but he was all about keeping it real and all he wanted to do was bake. He was never interested in becoming a celebrity of any sort.

Molly thought about Cam. He was always the first one to encourage her and make her believe in herself and deep down she wondered if the reason why he was reluctant to enter the competition was that he doubted his own ability. Perhaps he didn't want to put himself out there with the best of the best and not do his great-uncle proud. Was Cam scared of failure? If he entered and didn't win, Molly knew that would dent his pride, and she also knew that he might be thinking that the only way to protect his pride was not to enter at all. Yet she also knew how rare it was for a baker to be invited to compete for the title, which meant that one of the judges of this prestigious competition must have visited the shop and sampled Cam's baking.

Cam appeared in the doorway. 'All the logs are stacked up, and I've thrown a couple more on the fire.'

Refusing to let the subject lie, Molly picked up the invite.

'You do know that you wouldn't have received this unless someone out there thought you were good enough, don't you?'

Cam took the invite from her and placed it back down on the counter. 'I do what I do because I love it, and I don't need to win a title to confirm that.'

But Molly wasn't listening. A sudden movement had caught her eye. Staring out of the shop window she fixed her gaze firmly on the open back doors of the van. She pointed. 'Cam, we are being robbed.' Then, almost without thinking, she reacted and rushed towards the door.

'Molly, no!' Cam grabbed her shoulders. 'Stay where you are.'

Cam flung open the bakery door and shouted 'Hey!' at the hooded figure that was shovelling food from the back of the van into a rucksack.

The figure stopped dead in their tracks, before flinging the rucksack over their shoulder and grabbing a handful of croissants. Molly watched as the figure then began to run like the clappers towards the green with Cam hurtling after them, his shoes sinking into the freshly laid snow. Gosh, they were quick.

Fuelled by adrenalin, Cam pushed his legs harder. There was no way he was letting the thief get away. The runner stumbled and Cam stretched out his arm and made a grab for the rucksack. The thief fell backwards and Cam put a firm grip on their shoulder and began to frogmarch them back towards the shop, but the culprit wasn't giving up easily and wriggled and writhed. However, there was no escaping Cam's grip as he bellowed across to Molly, who was watching aghast from the shop doorway, 'Call the police. I've caught him.'

He hadn't thought through what he was going to do next. Should he keep the person imprisoned in the bakery until the police showed up? Could he?

Molly nodded and rushed towards Cam's mobile, which was on the counter.

'Will you take your hands off me? You're hurting me!'

Hearing a female voice, Molly stopped in her tracks and Cam immediately released his grip. They both stared at the hooded figure in confusion, then Molly realised she recognised the coat.

'Bree? Is that you?'

'You know her?' Cam looked towards Molly.

They watched as Bree pushed down her hood and stared straight at Molly. 'You need to keep him away from me. You can't go around manhandling people.' Bree's voice was anxious as she edged backwards towards the door.

'Oh, no you don't.' Hurriedly, Cam swung the door shut and locked it, placing the key safely in his pocket.

'You can't lock me in; you've kidnapped me. It's me who should be reporting you.'

'Don't be ridiculous. I am not kidnapping you and you've got a cheek. You've just stolen from me,' Cam defended himself, looking towards Molly. 'Ring the police,' he repeated.

Molly hesitated. 'I think we all just need to take a moment and calm down.'

Cam couldn't believe what he was hearing and pointed at Bree in disbelief. 'She's just tried to steal our goods.'

'We don't need to get the police involved,' Molly said, trying to calm the situation. 'There's no harm done, it's only a few croissants.'

'And that makes it all right, does it?'

'No, it doesn't but…'

Just looking at Bree was breaking Molly's heart. She was standing there shivering with the cold. Her hands looked numb and her cheeks crimson from the bitter chill outside. The last thing this young girl needed was to be carted off to the police station and charged with a crime that would be on her record for a long time. She needed help, a warm by the fire and a good breakfast inside her.

'What are your plans for this morning?' asked Molly in a calm caring voice.

Bree was on the defensive. 'I thought I'd open up my million-pound empire, maybe fly to New York on my private jet; I've not quite made up my mind yet. The world is my oyster.' She shrugged.

Cam noted her sarcastic tone. His patience was wearing thin. 'I'm calling the police; let them deal with this,' he said adamantly as he picked up his mobile phone. But before he could dial the number, Molly took the phone out of his hand and placed it back on the counter before bustling him towards the back of the shop, leaving Bree standing alone, watching them closely.

'There is no need to get the police involved. She wasn't stealing the crown jewels; it's just a few pastries and croissants,' Molly insisted in a hushed whisper. 'She's hungry.'

'Are you insane? Stealing is stealing. We know that. It's wrong.'

Molly knew exactly what Cam was referring to. 'It's been over five years since your cousin tried to rip off Dixie and swindle her out of this place and Bumblebee Cottage. He's paid the price and is still paying the price. This is a totally different situation and not one we are talking about now.' She glanced back over her shoulder to see Bree running her finger over the jams and chutneys on the shelves. 'Look, I know you don't trust anyone, but in the grand scheme of things, this isn't a big deal. All Bree is doing is fighting for survival. She's a child that's hungry. Put yourself in her shoes. Where's your compassion?' Molly exhaled; she had been speaking metaphorically but she'd noticed the state of Bree's shoes, which looked like they had seen better days.

'She also knows the difference between right and wrong. What's going to happen if she goes back to all her friends and tells them we are an easy target? They could be flocking in their droves to rob us blind.'

'How many friends do you think she's got? Not many ... if any... Please just let me deal with this.'

'I can hear you both, you know.' Bree was standing with her arms folded as she looked between them but then fixed her stare on Molly.

And there it was again, that look in her eye that triggered something inside Molly that she couldn't shake off. Briefly closing her eyes, she tried to push the image away but it flooded her mind. There was her own tiny hand gripping on to a stranger as she was led out of a dark and dingy room. Molly steadied herself and put both hands on the counter.

'Are you okay?' asked Cam, noticing that Molly had suddenly paled.

'Yes,' she replied, taking in a deep breath. She didn't know what was happening. Why were these images and emotions surfacing all of a sudden? 'Honestly, you go and get the deliveries done. Leave this to me.'

Cam looked at Molly then back at Bree. 'Are you sure?'

'I'm sure.'

'Okay, but you tell her that if this happens again...' he said, taking the key out of his pocket and handing it to Molly.

Molly watched Cam leave by the back door and soon he was at the front of the bakery. She caught his eye as he climbed into the van and saw disapproval etched all over his face as they exchanged uncomfortable looks. She knew he wasn't happy, but once he calmed down and thought about it, he would understand that all Bree needed was a break. She didn't need the police to be adding to her troubles.

As he drove off, Molly decided she would do the decent thing. 'Come on,' she said as she gestured towards the door that led through to the main cottage.

Bree looked a little startled and began to walk

backwards towards the shop door and bumped into the window. 'What are you going to do to me?'

Molly held her hands up, causing Bree to flinch. 'Oh my gosh, I was just going to make you a hot drink and maybe something to eat. Honestly, that's all. Please don't be scared.' Holding out the key towards her, Molly said gently, 'Here, you can go if you want to. It was just the offer of a drink.'

There was a look of uncertainty on Bree's face, but she didn't take the key. They just stared at each other for a second and once again some sort of familiarity was triggered inside Molly. She was beginning to wonder if they'd met before, but she had a good memory for faces and when she racked her brain nothing came to light.

'Do you have somewhere to be? You must be hungry; let me get you something to eat,' Molly offered. She noticed Bree relax her shoulders and her grip loosened on her rucksack.

'Funnily enough, my diary is quite empty this morning.' Bree's mouth hitched into a slight smile.

'A hot drink and breakfast it is then. This way.' Molly slowly headed out of the bakery, trusting that Bree would follow. Cautiously looking all around her, Bree did.

'Why are you being nice to me? And don't you need to open up?'

'Because I am nice,' replied Molly, noticing that Bree had stopped walking. 'And the shop can wait.'

Bree placed her bag on the counter then unzipped it.

Taking out all the items she stole from the van, she sheepishly looked towards Molly.

'Wow, you can really fit a lot in that bag,' observed Molly.

Bree didn't say a word but pushed the items over towards Molly, who grabbed some white paper bags from underneath the counter. Molly wrapped them one by one and pushed them back towards Bree.

'Put them back in your bag, save them for later,' she said, giving Bree a warm smile. 'Honestly, it's fine.'

'And what about your husband?'

'Don't you worry about him, he's a big softy really.'

Bree hesitated for a moment then speedily stuffed the items back in her bag. 'And you're not going to ring the police?'

Molly shook her head. 'I'm not going to ring the police. Let's get you a warm drink and something to eat. Hot chocolate, tea or coffee?'

Bree's smile was wide. 'Hot chocolate is my favourite. Sam from the shelter sometimes makes me one as a special treat.'

'Good choice,' replied Molly, thinking that it was always her go-to, as she led the way on the red flagstone floor down a dinky hallway from the bakery to the cottage. The black oak beams ran across the length of the low ceilings and the hallway was cramped. Molly stepped over the array of George's shoes and the pieces of Lego that were scattered all over the floor and wondered for a moment how she was going to manage with another child when she had trouble tidying up after the first. She led Bree past coat hooks that were overflowing with coats and hats for every season, and a number of umbrellas that had toppled sidewards onto the floor. The walls were lined with paintings of dogs and foxes and Molly could see Bree looking over them as she walked past.

Opening the door to the living room, whose windows showcased the impressive snow-covered gardens of The Old Bakehouse, Molly ushered Bree into the tiny yet cosy space. Orange flames danced in the open fire giving a welcoming warmth to the room. The living room housed a dresser spilling over with books and framed photographs, a little navy two-seater settee with tapestry cushions that matched the curtains, and two wingback chairs huddled around the coffee table in front of the fire. Molly watched Bree as she took in her surroundings.

'Take a seat.' Molly gestured to the chair nearest the fire before poking it and throwing a couple more logs on to keep it burning.

'Are you sure it's okay for me to be here? I don't want to cause any trouble.' Bree settled in the wingback chair but Molly could see she was apprehensive, her gaze shifting towards the door every few moments.

'Yes, of course, you have nothing to worry about,' reassured Molly. 'Give me your coat so I can hang it up to dry. It must be sodden with the snow. You were up and out of the shelter early doors.'

'Couldn't sleep.'

Molly didn't need to ask why. Sam had often mentioned

that a night time at the shelter reminded her of when she was midwife on the labour wards in the hospital. The wails and people shouting through the night gave the place an eerie feel but the alternative was sleeping out in a shop doorway with no real shelter from the blizzard.

As she took the coat from Bree, the first thing Molly noticed was the stench along with the torn pockets and the missing buttons. 'I'll hang this up in the kitchen whilst I make you a drink. Take off your boots and warm up your feet.'

Bree looked up and met her gaze then, after weighing up the situation, she cautiously began to take off her boots.

There were lots of questions that Molly wanted to ask – why was Bree on the street? where were her parents? – but she knew if she started bombarding her with questions that Bree would bolt. But it didn't stop her wondering.

'What do you want from me?' asked Bree, looking at Molly.

'Absolutely nothing. I just want to make sure you are warm, dry and fed before you go back out there.' Molly took a swift glance towards the window. 'How old are you, Bree?' The question had been on the tip of Molly's tongue from the moment she'd met her.

'Sixteen,' came the reply. Bree wasn't making eye contact; she was staring at the orange glow that crackled and hissed from the open fire.

Molly moved Bree's boots closer towards the fire, helping them to dry out, whilst she disappeared into the kitchen, taking Bree's coat with her. The stench from the dampened coat was piercing, causing Molly to rub her nose. Without thinking too much about it she stuffed it into the washing machine and put it on a quick cycle before making Bree a hot chocolate that was laden with cream and marshmallows.

'It's a lovely place you have here,' said Bree a few minutes later, taking the hot chocolate from Molly and grinning widely. 'Wow,' she enthused. 'This is some hot chocolate. The last time I had one covered in cream was when...' She stopped in her tracks, then tried to hand it back to Molly.

'I'm sorry, I can't afford to pay for this.'

'Pay? You don't need to pay for it,' reassured Molly with a warm smile. 'Would you like a bacon and sausage sandwich? And you don't have to pay for that either.'

Bree looked astounded. 'You don't get anything for free in this world.'

'Kindness is free.'

'I don't come across that much.'

'Well, you have today. Brown sauce or ketchup on your sandwich ... or both?'

'Both!' answered Bree. 'One on each half of the bread ... if that's okay,' she quickly added.

Molly noticed that Bree's mood had lifted. She was smiling down at her drink and scooping up the cream and marshmallows with her spoon just like George did.

'Best of both worlds. You make yourself comfy,' replied Molly, disappearing into the kitchen. Taking a swift glance over her shoulder she noticed Bree tucking her feet underneath her, then resting her head against the back of the chair.

By the time Molly had returned, Bree's eyes were closed and she was sleeping.

Quietly, Molly placed the sandwich on the table before taking the throw from the wicker basket at the side of the chair and gently laying it over Bree.

Molly couldn't help but think she looked so young. Her heart sank as she noticed the holes in Bree's socks, and the broken laces on boots that had seen better days. The poor girl looked shattered, her face gaunt and her fingernails black. This was no way for a sixteen-year-old girl to be living. At that age, Molly wasn't particularly streetwise – she barely went out in the dark and preferred staying close to her family – but it seemed that Bree didn't have that luxury.

For a moment she watched Bree sleep, then she went to check on the shop. There were still no customers in sight but Molly unlocked the front door as anyone walking into the shop would make the old-fashioned bell above the door tinkle, alerting her to their arrival. Wandering back into the living room she tiptoed past Bree, opened the drawer of the dresser then quickly rummaged through the multicoloured buttons that had been abandoned in the old biscuit tin for years. The tin had once belonged to her mother and Molly used to play with the buttons inside when she was a small child. She usually played shop and pretended the buttons were money, or sometimes she just sorted them into pretty piles. She knew it was daft, but that small tin held so many happy memories for her. She finally found exactly what she was looking for – three large buttons that she could sew onto Bree's coat. Grabbing a needle and thread from her sewing box she placed them on the coffee table. Knowing the washing machine would soon finish its cycle, she had just enough time to go and find Bree a pair of thick boot socks. Molly knew she had many pairs and she wasn't going to miss a few so the next five minutes were spent piling some warm items of clothing on to the coffee table, including a brand-new hat and scarf set Molly had been given for Christmas last year. She knew Bree could make better use of them.

With Bree still fast asleep in the chair, Molly heard the washing machine beep. When she opened the door and pulled out the coat, the smell was a refreshing change from the stale stench of earlier. Molly knew it would take her ten minutes max to sew on the buttons then she would drape the coat over the Aga and it would be dry in no time at all.

———————

Ten minutes later, with the buttons sewn on and the coat drying, Molly heard the bell in the shop ring out. She stood up quietly, careful not to wake Bree, and tiptoed into the shop to see Cam standing by the counter pulling off his bobble hat and peeling off his gloves. 'Oh my God, the weather is getting worse. The streets are silent but I've delivered all the orders and everything extra I took out has sold.' He placed a bag of cash on the counter along with the portable card machine. 'Everyone was surprised to see me but very grateful.'

'That's good to hear, I can't imagine anyone wanting to venture out in this.'

'I saw Drew. He'd had the same idea and was driving down the streets beeping his horn and selling sausages, eggs and cheese from the van. Have we had any customers?' He looked towards the nearly full shelves.

'Not one. I think it's going to be a slow day with the weather like this, but the shelter will be happy for the leftovers later.'

Cam took a look over Molly's shoulder. 'Talking of the shelter ... what's happened to the girl? What did you say? I hope she's on her way. It's unacceptable, stealing.'

Molly's heart began to beat faster. Cam was back quicker than she'd thought he would be. She screwed up her face. 'Not exactly.'

Cam raised an eyebrow. 'What do you mean, "Not exactly"?'

Molly took a breath. 'Even you have just said the weather is getting worse, and where exactly would a homeless person go in this weather, with the shelter closed until later?'

'What are you trying to tell me? Because I'm absolutely freezing. I need a hot drink and a warm by that fire. I hope it's still burning.' Cam started to walk to the back of the shop but Molly stepped in front of him.

'What are you doing? I'm freezing. Look…' He held out his hand to show her that the tips of his fingers were white. 'I can't even feel my fingers.'

Molly mouthed, 'We have a visitor,' then nodded in the direction of the hallway.

'Why are you whispering? You're being very cloak and dagger.' His voice was far from a whisper. All he wanted to do was put the kettle on. 'And what did you say to that girl? You still haven't answered me.'

'That "girl" is called Bree, and she's through there in the living room, getting warm by the fire.'

Cam stopped dead in his tracks. He looked up the hallway, then straight back at Molly.

'Why would you invite someone into our home that was robbing us blind?'

Molly could tell by the tone of his voice that Cam wasn't happy. 'Because I just couldn't throw her out on the street in this weather. I mean, look at you…' She gestured towards his hands. 'Even you are cold after an hour – just think how that wee girl is going to feel. And where would she go all day?'

Cam was staring at her in disbelief. 'Look, I understand what you're saying but this is our home – our *family* home. We know nothing about her and you can't just invite strangers in off the street. For all we know she could have a pocketful of drugs.'

Molly huffed. 'Just because she's homeless doesn't mean

she takes drugs. How very judgemental of you. And for the record she had nothing in her pockets.'

'I'm just saying that we don't know anything about her. Did you check them then?' Cam was looking relieved.

'I did when I put her coat in the washing machine and then I've sewn on some buttons to replace the ones she was missing.'

'You've been sewing buttons on coats?'

'Don't look at me like that. She's only sixteen years of age – *sixteen* – and she didn't get much sleep last night at the shelter. Yes, she had a roof over her head, but the noise through the night kept her awake, and I can imagine she would have to sleep with one eye open.'

Cam briefly closed his eyes then exhaled. 'It's not that I haven't got a heart, it's just that this is our home and adding pressure at this time is not what I need.' The words had slipped out before Cam could stop them.

'What do you mean, "adding pressure"?'

All Cam wanted to do was drink a cup of tea and get warm by the fire. He was dealing with his own uncertainties and he knew he sounded unkind but his own fears for the future were preying heavily on his mind and that's all he could deal with right now.

'I've been up early, I'm freezing from being out in the snow, and all I want now is a cup of tea by my own fire.'

Molly looked at her husband and realised Cam really did look exhausted, like he had the weight of the world on his shoulders. 'I'll put the kettle on for you.'

'Molly, please can you ask her to leave?'

'Where will she go?'

Cam shrugged. 'Where would she normally go? She must have a plan. Look, I do get it's blooming cold out but there are places to go and people who help… Call Sam,' he suggested. 'You've been kind but now it's time for her to leave. We don't need this to escalate,' he said firmly.

'And what's that supposed to mean?'

'It means that I know you. Before you know it, you'll be suggesting she stays for lunch and dinner too. Then what's next, you give her a bed for the night? Molly, you can't get involved. *We* can't get involved.' Cam had more than enough on his plate at the moment and though one of the qualities that he loved most about Molly was her gentle, kind nature and the fact she was always there to lend a helping hand, he could also remember a time when he had had to have stern words with her, when she began to bring home dogs from the animal hospital she owned. He'd been thankful when she'd joined forces with Rory, the other local vet, as the two of them had worked out a system of care for the animals that didn't involve them sleeping under Cam and Molly's roof.

Molly felt a little frustrated with Cam. Why did he not see what she could see? Bree might appear to have a tough exterior but inside she was a young girl fighting for survival and stealing food to curb the hunger pains in her stomach. She was sixteen, with no one to show her the way.

'She has no one, and a little kindness goes a long way.'

'That's why Sam is doing the hard work she does so

well. That's why there is a shelter. That's their safe place …
and this is ours.' Cam's voice rose. 'Ring Sam.'

Their eyes locked as neither of them backed down.
Molly felt exasperated. Cam was not seeing the bigger
picture. Who was it going to hurt if Bree shielded here from
the cold for a while? She looked towards the window. With
the snow still falling Molly didn't want to send her back out
in the winter wonderland, but Cam was clearly not up for
discussing this further. She knew by the look in his eye he'd
shut the conversation down if she tried to argue again.

Hearing the slam of the back door, they both looked
towards the back of the shop. Molly threw her arms up in
the air in frustration and hurried down the hallway towards
the living room.

'Bree,' Molly called out, but there was no answer. She
quickly scanned the room then checked the kitchen, but all
of Bree's belongings were gone. Even the cold sausage
sandwich was no longer on the plate, and the pile of clothes
she'd put together was also nowhere to be seen.

Cam was standing behind Molly.

'She's gone. She must have heard you.' Molly let out a
sigh of frustration. 'Her coat would have still been damp.
And where is she going to go in this weather?'

Cam didn't want to fight anymore and tried to reassure
his frantic wife. 'She will know where to go. I'm putting the
kettle on – do you want a drink?' he asked, as he threw
some more logs on the fire.

Molly didn't answer. She'd hurried towards the kitchen

window and looked out over the green but Bree was nowhere in sight.

'Okay, ignoring me isn't going to help.' Walking back into the bakery Cam took refuge in the kitchen where he made himself a drink and tied his apron around his waist. Taking a moment, he breathed deeply and placed his hands in the pockets of his apron, the letter still there reminding him to hold everything together for a little while longer.

Sipping his tea once it had brewed, he saw no customers in sight as he stood in the window of The Old Bakehouse. He stared out over the snowy green. Dixie was in the distance shuffling along the snowy ground pulling the sledge with Darling sitting proudly on top of it. Even though Cam was feeling a little emotional, the sight of Darling lording it up on the sledge brought a smile to his face. His eccentric grandmother was full of character and treated that dog like it was royalty. She even usually dressed it for Sunday lunch with a brightly coloured bandana. He was in no doubt that Darling loved the attention.

Dixie was heading towards the shop and he knew the second she stepped inside she would sense the tense atmosphere between Molly and him, and, being Dixie, questions would be asked. Usually, Dixie could sense something before it had even happened and more often than not was correct in her premonitions. Dixie noticed Cam standing in the window and waved above her head, pointing to Bumblebee Cottage, then back at The Old Bakehouse. He put his thumb up in the air, knowing that the strange hand movements were code to communicate she would drop Darling and the sledge back at home before she came in for a drink.

Pulling out the order book ready for tomorrow, Cam glanced over the orders, but his mind was on other things. He didn't like fighting with Molly and hated that she would be thinking he was unkind . . . but that wasn't it at all. All he wanted to do was hold his own family close and keep the rest of the world at a distance until he knew what exactly the scan would reveal.

With the weather as it was, Cam had offered to make deliveries again tomorrow to the villagers so he noted it in the book. He then noticed there had been an extra order in the diary from Starcross Manor and decided to give the hotel a quick ring to double-check it was still needed, because, according to the weather forecast, the snow would still be falling over the next couple of days and it was possible potential guests would find it difficult to travel. He slapped his trouser pockets with his hand but his mobile wasn't there. Then he remembered leaving it on the counter. But it wasn't anywhere to be seen. Thinking Molly might have slipped it in the drawer for safe keeping he checked, but it wasn't there either. Puzzled, he walked back down the hallway and took a swift look around the living room. He could hear Molly still pottering around the kitchen. 'Mol, have you seen my mobile?'

'It's on the counter in the bakery, where you left it.'

'I can't seem to see it.'

Molly appeared in the doorway, drying her hands on a

towel. 'Honestly, you're worse than George, it's like having another child in the house.' She rolled her eyes as she walked past him and headed towards the bakery.

Cam followed Molly, relieved that her mood had lifted somewhat and everything felt a little less tense. As he stepped into the shop there was a blast of cold air as the door swung open and Dixie stamped her snowy boots on the mat. She beamed. 'George has been dropped safely at school and I'm reporting for duty. Even though a cup of tea would be a great start and maybe a warm croissant. The joys of your grandson owning a bakery.'

'Starting work? It's nearly taken you two hours to do the school run,' teased Cam. 'Help yourself to a croissant, there's plenty. With the weather like this, you may as well have the day off. I don't think we are going to be run off our feet.'

Dixie had already reached behind the counter and selected a croissant from the basket. 'And Molly, we've got a girls' night planned. A little short notice, I know. Martha is whipping out her crystal ball as she's got a feeling something is brewing in the village of Heartcross.'

'Er, a snowstorm?' Cam suggested, cocking an eyebrow. 'You don't need to be psychic to work that out.'

Cam grinned as Dixie leant forward and swiped his arm with her glove. 'Now there is no need for your sarcasm. Actually, she means a scandal. There's some sort of scandal about to come to light. She's adamant.'

'You lot are bonkers. You'll make any excuse for a bunch of old women—'

'Less of the old,' Dixie cut in, pretending to be hurt.

'Gossiping about everyone and anyone's business,' added Cam with a glint in his eye as he teased his grandmother.

'Martha is a fantastic clairvoyant; she's had the gift for years.'

'The gift of meddling,' continued Cam.

Dixie waved her hand, dismissing Cam's words. 'You boys just don't understand. And you don't like it because you might be talked about. That crystal ball doesn't lie. You men usually have something to hide.'

'Don't tar us all with the same brush,' Cam said with a laugh but Dixie was looking at him in a way that unnerved him. He gave himself a little shake. There was no way that Martha could uncover what was going on in his world ... surely? He hadn't told a soul but with that thought etched on his mind he began to feel a little jittery.

'It's a good job Molly has a sensible head on her shoulders and isn't drawn into all of that nonsense,' he said.

'You'll be up for it though, won't you, Molly?' questioned Dixie.

But Molly didn't answer. She was too busy bending down and searching frantically under the counter. Cam was right, the phone wasn't anywhere to be seen. She stood up and looked over at Cam. 'It was here, it was definitely here.'

'What's up with you? You look like you've lost a pound and found a penny,' said Dixie, unravelling her scarf and taking off her coat.

Cam and Molly stared at each other. They each knew what the other was thinking.

'She would not have taken your phone,' stated Molly. 'She wouldn't.'

'Who wouldn't have taken his phone?' asked Dixie, immediately sensing the sudden atmosphere between them both.

'So where is it then?' asked Cam.

'She didn't have the opportunity to. I was with her,' argued Molly.

'So where is it then? Because I know I left it right here.'

'It must be somewhere. You must have taken it with you or placed it down somewhere else.'

'I didn't. I've not had it all morning. Who else came into the shop?'

'No one, but honestly, Cam, I don't think that is the case.' Molly couldn't believe that Bree would have taken it. Molly had been kind to her and let her into their home. And Bree had been grateful. Molly had washed and mended her coat, given her extra warm clothing and food – she didn't want to think of Bree stealing from them. 'I don't believe she would have done it.'

'This is exactly what I was trying to say to you. We don't know her. Phones don't just disappear into thin air. We've already caught her stealing once today. She cannot be trusted.'

Molly was fully aware that Dixie was watching them closely.

'But we don't know for sure. She's a sixteen-year-old girl

who might have stolen a croissant to curb her hunger, but come on, accusing her of stealing a phone ... that's something completely different.'

'Who's a sixteen-year-old girl?' interrupted Dixie, still none the wiser as to what was going on.

'Molly, I don't want to argue with you.' Cam blew out a breath and scratched his head. He walked over to the landline and picked up the phone. He dialled his number. The phone rang out. 'It's ringing, but it's not here in the shop.'

They stood in silence listening and then Cam hung up and rung the phone again. This time his phone didn't ring out, it went straight to answerphone.

'That phone is full of valuable contacts. My life is stored on it.' Cam put his coat back on and grabbed his van keys.

'Where are you going?' asked Molly. 'The roads are treacherous.'

He hovered in the doorway. 'I'm going to drive around and see if I can spot her and get my phone back. She can't have gone far in this weather.'

'Spot who?' asked Dixie, now a bit agitated at continuously being ignored. 'Am I invisible?' She threw her arms up in the air, which caused Cam to look towards her.

'Sorry.' Cam pressed a swift kiss to his grandmother's bewildered face. 'I'll leave Molly to explain.'

Molly knew there was no point trying to convince Cam that driving around the streets was a pointless exercise. Once he had an idea in his head, it was best to let him get on with it. She really didn't want the row to escalate further in front of Dixie. She watched alongside Dixie as Cam shut the door behind him and went striding off towards the van.

'Would you say I'm a good judge of character?' Molly asked Dixie.

'I would, and you don't suffer fools.'

Watching the van disappear down the road, Molly turned towards Dixie and relayed the goings-on of the morning.

'And are you sure there's be no one else in the shop this morning?'

Molly shook her head. 'No one … to my knowledge,' she replied, knowing exactly how it sounded. 'The shop has been dead all morning.'

Dixie raised her eyebrows. 'The sensible thing would be to call the police or have a chat with Sam at the shelter. Get her take on it.'

'But I just can't see how Bree could have done it.'

'Opportunists are quick and this girl has to survive on the streets, not that I'm agreeing with Cam or anything. There's only one way to find out … Martha can take a look into her crystal ball.'

Molly smiled. 'If only it was that easy. . . But I'll be there. I could do with a good girly natter. And a scandal, you say?'

'There's something brewing – Martha has that feeling. In the meantime, try and get this girl out of your mind. I'm not interfering and I wouldn't like to think of anyone out on the streets in this weather, but Cam is also right. You have enough on your plate at the minute.' Dixie gestured towards Molly's stomach. 'My new great grandchild, for one thing.'

As the old-fashioned bell tinkled above the door Molly quickly grabbed Cam's apron from the hook and tied it around her waist. She brightened and trilled a good morning, but now all that was playing on her mind was what Cam might do if he did actually find Bree. She hoped he would handle the situation with care.

'Dixie, could you possibly pop the kettle on? I'm in need of a cuppa.'

As Dixie disappeared into the main part of cottage, Molly served the customer and moved the unopened junk mail from the side of the till before once again checking over the shop for the phone. But it was absolutely nowhere to be found. All Molly could do was wait for Cam to return and hope that she was right and a good judge of character, and that Cam was wrong.

Hearing her phone ping in the hallway just at that moment, she quickly hurried towards it. But it wasn't Cam, it was a message from Isla, and she quickly swiped the screen to read the text.

Granny has got one on her again! I'm sure Dixie will have told you that she's started up her career as a fortune teller again, but at her age, I've told her I can't see a future in it!

Molly laughed then replied.

Can't wait, I'm in need of some entertainment.

Tomorrow, 8pm. Don't be late. I need my friends here to keep the older generation under control!

A night with the girls was just what Molly needed. Her thoughts turned once again to Cam. Picking up the landline she tried his number again but it went straight to answerphone. All she could do was wait to see if he'd caught up with Bree.

'Tea is brewed,' shouted Dixie. 'And the weather warning on the TV is advising us all not to travel. We have a few days of severe blizzards swooping over the Scottish Highlands.'

Molly went to the doorway and found Dixie sat in the armchair, drinking her tea. 'Maybe Martha is feeling a little uneasy with the storm brewing and she needs the distraction of exercising her psychic powers,' suggested Molly with a smile.

'She's hell bent on the idea that something is brewing, never mind the weather.'

Molly had to agree with Martha; she too felt that was something was coming and it wasn't just a birth. Bree had ignited unexpected flashbacks of Molly's own childhood and Molly was beginning to wonder more about her life before Di and Doug.

'There's a scandal coming to light, mark my words. Martha is always right.' Dixie gave Molly a knowing look before taking a sip of her tea. Molly could only hope that this had nothing to do with her, but her gut feeling was telling her something absolutely different.

Chapter Three

It was fast approaching four p.m. and there wasn't a chink of sunlight in the sky. George was sitting on the settee reading his school book to Dixie whilst Darling was curled up on the armchair fast asleep, basking in the warmth from the fire. Molly and Cam were in the bakery for the last hour of the working day. There had been a steady stream of customers after lunchtime, which thankfully kept them both busy. Cam had driven around the village and town for a little over an hour, but hadn't stumbled across Bree, and with the atmosphere still tense, there hadn't been many words spoken between them all day. Molly hadn't made up her mind whether that was actually a blessing in disguise, but the problem remained that the phone was still missing.

Finding fresh courage, Molly addressed the elephant in the room.

'You are going to have to alert the phone company and report your phone missing.'

'I know.' Cam's reply was curt. 'The inconvenience of it all. I've tried ringing the phone a dozen times, but it's straight to answerphone every time.'

'Look, I don't want to argue…'

'But you still don't think it's Bree and I disagree.'

'I just can't see how it could be.'

Her words hung in the air.

There was nothing more to say. Either the phone would turn up or it wouldn't.

'Maybe Martha can look into her crystal ball tomorrow night and solve the mystery.' Molly was trying to lighten the mood but Cam looked far from impressed.

'You aren't going to that, are you?'

'Absolutely I am, why wouldn't I?' replied Molly. 'Apparently, Martha has a gut feeling that all isn't right in the village and the older generation swear by her psychic powers.'

'I'm not sure if anyone should mess about with the unknown.'

'Martha reckons there are secrets being kept in the village, so I'm not going to miss out on this evening. Goodness knows what it might turn up.'

Cam looked up. 'I don't think you should get involved.'

'You haven't got something to hide, have you?' teased Molly, noticing that Cam suddenly looked worried. 'I mean, if you do have something to tell me, it's best to get out in the open now, before I hear it from Martha.'

'Don't be daft,' he replied but didn't look in her direction. They carried on working in silence, placing the unsold baked goods in the baskets, ready to take to the shelter.

'Are you really worried about what Martha might reveal? It is just a little bit of light-hearted fun.'

Cam knew he was being defensive and that it was more than likely because he felt guilty about keeping his appointment at the hospital from Molly. 'Of course not. You go and enjoy yourself. It won't be long before we are juggling nappies and bottles. You deserve a little fun.'

Cam was saying the right words but Molly knew him and she still had that niggle that there was something on his mind, a feeling she'd had for a few weeks now. Deciding not to pursue the conversation for now, she stared out across the green. She was still thinking of Bree. With the weather still freezing outside there would be a high chance of Bree being at the shelter.

Molly turned round towards Cam. 'If Bree is at the shelter tonight, I'll talk with her.'

He nodded, not saying anything else as he began to brush the crumbs out of the bread baskets. Molly watched him for a moment but he didn't look in her direction. He was lost in deep thought and she just wished she knew what was on his mind.

'There's a huge order for Starcross Manor in the morning, so I need to get my head down earlier tonight. It'll be a two a.m. start but I'll do my best not to disturb you,' Cam said, breaking the silence.

Not wanting the atmosphere to carry on, Molly slipped her arms around his waist. 'Don't you worry about me, this one keeps me awake most of the night, and I was hoping' – she kissed him on his cheek – 'that maybe we could spend a little time together.' She had a glint in her eye. 'After all, when I got out of the bath last night, you were fast asleep.'

Molly was expecting the usual genuine smile, the squeeze of the hand, the hug that feels like it's going to last for ever, but Cam gently pushed her away, taking her by surprise.

'Not tonight, I'm feeling exhausted.'

That wasn't the response Molly was expecting. It had never mattered before how tired he was. Her mood slumped a little. Feeling rejected made her confused. Was Cam making a point and punishing her for speaking up for Bree? Would he actually do that? She hoped she was just being ridiculous. Her emotions were heightened due to the pregnancy, so maybe she was overthinking it, but Cam had never turned her down – ever.

'We can't have you exhausted.' Though she was feeling deflated she tried to smooth the way. 'Why don't you go through to George and grab your dinner with him? I can eat mine when I get back from the shelter.'

'That sounds like a plan. I'll just load the van up first and shift the snow from the windscreen. Despite the weather, the takings have actually been quite good today after a slow start.'

Molly watched as Cam slipped on his coat. Last night he was adamant that he didn't want her to go out in the snow, but so far tonight nothing had been said about the appalling driving conditions outside. She swallowed. Despite their disagreement Molly knew there was something else preying heavily on his mind. If only she could get him to open up.

'Okay, I'll be off then,' she said, once Cam had loaded up the van.

'No, I'll go,' he replied, looking towards the window.

Molly felt her mood lift a little with his offer. That was all she'd wanted to hear – that Cam didn't want her venturing out in this weather. But she still wanted to go to the shelter herself and catch up with Bree.

George appeared at the door, saying, 'Daddy, I've set up the train track.' He slipped his hand into Cam's. 'Come on.'

Cam hesitated. 'I'm just going to…'

'Honestly, it's okay. You go with George. I won't be long.' Before Cam could object, Molly popped a kiss on the top of George's head and slipped out of the door.

Sitting behind the wheel of the van, Molly began the slow drive towards the town of Glensheil. The Met Office had issued a severe weather warning advising people to stay inside, but that wasn't unusual in the Scottish Highlands. It was still bitterly cold and heavy flakes of snow were falling fast and chaotically, the gusting wind shaking the van slightly as Molly drove over the bridge. The van's headlights lit up the icy cold river, which was running wild, turbulent and unforgiving, and Molly found her heart was racing. The weather conditions were really turning and, when she reached the square, the queue for the shelter was longer than she had ever seen it before. Just as she cut the engine the shelter doors swung open and everyone began to filter through into the warmth.

Alongside Sam, two other volunteers were waiting by the door. As soon as they saw Molly, they began to help to unload the trays of food and take them inside.

Grateful to be out of the biting cold, Molly stepped into the shelter and was met by a dancing display of Christmas lights wrapped around the tree in the entrance hall. It was truly beautiful and wouldn't have looked out of place standing in the town square or a department store, dressed as it was in its splendour and sparkles. Sam was a wonder. Molly knew that all the funds for the tree and decorations would have come out of her friend's own pocket. She had a heart of gold and her Christmas Day would be selflessly spent serving up Christmas dinner to the masses at the shelter. It was like a military operation each year but Sam made sure that anyone who was living on the streets and wanted a Christmas dinner got one.

'Look at all this,' exclaimed Molly. 'You have been busy. It all looks so … Christmassy!'

'It took some doing, but I like this place to feel as much of a home and as welcoming as possible. Christmas is a lonely time for many and I just can't bear to think of all the people fighting for survival on the streets.' Sam's voice faltered as Molly followed her into the main hall.

Inside, the room looked like a very cramped, busy café in the middle of a city at lunchtime. The noise was deafening.

'Wow, busy night.' Molly quickly scanned the room

looking for Bree, but she was nowhere to be seen. 'And look at this room,' she added.

There were paper chains pinned to the walls, tinsel draped around the notice boards and a mantel swag of twinkly fairy lights and crimson bows hanging above the serving hatch.

'If it was up to me, I'd leave this place decorated throughout the year. It just lifts everyone's spirits a little,' said Sam.

Despite the cold wintry night, the mood seemed jovial. There was a sudden scraping of chairs as the serving hatch went up and hot drinks were served.

Sam continued. 'Luckily, Bree, the young girl you met last night, helped me with the decorations this afternoon otherwise I'd still be tangled in lights and tinsel. Cup of tea before you head off?'

Molly nodded. 'Lovely, thank you.' She wanted to hang around for a couple of reasons. Firstly, she wanted a breather from the atmosphere at home, and secondly, she wanted to see if Bree turned up.

'Bree was here today?'

'Yes, a little quieter than usual, which is unlike her. And I have to remember, as much as I want to take everyone under my wing, solve all their problems and give them their forever home, that I have to stay professionally distanced, even when I don't want to be.'

'I can't imagine how you do it.' Bree had only been in Molly's company for a little over an hour and Molly already had a strong urge to take her in and help her get her life on track.

'These young kids don't come without their challenges but I suppose that's just like anyone. Living on the streets is not the start you would want for anyone. I just have to be careful not to overstep the mark and invite them into my home. Sometimes, what you see on the outside is not what you get on the inside. Yet you can't judge everyone by the same standards. All those people in there,' Sam took a swift glance along the queue, 'are unique individuals. In this room are one-time millionaires, business owners, once wealthy musicians, doctors, alcoholics, drug users … and none of them chose this path. Unemployment, lack of affordable housing, poverty and mental illness are all causes – things that take lives off the rails and make it seem impossible to recover.'

'There's a former millionaire sitting in this room?'

Sam nodded. 'Sometimes, there's an incident in your life that you have no control over and the next minute you find you're fending for yourself with no immediate help to rely on.'

'Have you ever got close to any of the people you have helped?' Molly was intrigued. With the thought of Bree still very much on her mind she knew exactly the reason she was asking.

'Oh yes. Twice. And each time it was a very different story and outcome.'

Molly grabbed a cup and pumped the tea from the flask then added a splash of milk.

Sam continued. 'The first was a girl in her twenties.' She smiled warmly. 'I helped her to get back on track, invited her into my home and she stayed for me for a while. We got her a job; I bought her new clothes and acted as her guarantor on a flat, which was a big risk.' Sam raised her eyebrow and blew out a breath as she remembered.

'We?' questioned Molly.

'Me and my husband at the time...' Sam paused. 'It started causing problems for us, me being here. Taking on the world and thinking I can solve everyone's problems.'

'Oh my, please tell me you didn't get stung for the flat?' Molly was wide-eyed, but Sam was shaking her head.

'No, she is now the CEO of a cosmetic brand and very successful.'

'So, the help you gave her turned her life around?'

'Absolutely it did, and I have free make-up for life. However...' She took a breath. 'I was naïve and thought everyone would be just as grateful for our help, but the next time I lent a hand was a very different story. I tried to help another person who ended up robbing us blind and stealing our car. I never would have believed this person would be capable of doing this to us. My husband wasn't happy. He kept telling me there was something that wasn't quite right and I needed to step away from this person ... but it's difficult. Especially when you see the good in everyone, which according to some is my downfall.

'Niggles began to start, my husband constantly telling me I had no time for our relationship and that the shelter was taking over my life. Unfortunately, the tension grew and grew and it broke us in the end. I understand why – my personal and professional life should have not crossed over. My husband's gut feeling was right. Not that I've ever told him that. I learned my lesson the hard way and that's why, as much as I want to get involved, especially with the newbies and the younger ones, I can't. I have to keep my personal life very much private even though that can be very difficult at times. This place pulls at your heartstrings.'

Molly was listening to Sam's every word and thought of Cam. Sam's ex-husband's reservations were exactly the same as Cam's. Molly knew that Cam was a loving, caring man who didn't have a malicious bone in his body and today's reaction was because he was worried about bringing a stranger into their home. It wasn't as though she didn't understand those reservations but her gut feeling was telling her there was something about Bree, and that's why she was immediately drawn towards the girl. Maybe it was just the motherly instinct in her.

'Bree can't be very old,' Molly began. She knew the girl's age but wondered if Sam would give her any further backstory on the teen. She cupped her hands around the warm drink and took a sip.

'Sixteen,' replied Sam, passing the loaves of breads to the volunteers, who began to slice them.

'That's a very young age to be out on the streets. What's a sixteen-year-old girl doing without a home? Where's her family?'

Sam looked like she was going to say something, but hesitated.

'Sorry, I didn't mean to put you on the spot.'

'It's okay, but I really can't go breaking confidences. This place is their safe place – some stories I know, some I don't, but all the information I do know, it goes no further.'

Molly nodded at Sam's integrity. She understood and maybe it was best not knowing Bree's story. Yet … she was already beginning to worry about the fact that she wasn't safe inside the shelter with the winds and snowstorm engulfing the streets of Glensheil.

'Do you want to help serve up the meal, or do you have to rush back?' asked Sam, lining up the bowls and placing a ladle in the huge pot of stew that was bubbling away on top of the stove.

Molly took a quick glance inside the pot. 'Actually, I'd love to stay and help and I must say that looks and smells blooming delicious.'

'Drew popped across with beef from Foxglove Farm. Because of the snow some of his deliveries were cancelled so he asked if we could make use of the meat. There's even more in the freezer. These people are going to be fed like kings and queens for the next few days,' said Sam with a thankful smile, handing Molly a white plastic apron and a hairnet. 'Pop these on.'

The plastic trays that the residents ate off were all stacked on top of each other, and it reminded Molly of a high-school canteen. Sam rang the bell above the hatch, indicating that they were ready to serve, and immediately there was the sound of scraping chairs across the floor. Within seconds, there was a long queue of folk standing in line bumping elbows as they chatted waiting for their turn. Molly looked down the long line then swung a glance towards the door, but Bree was still nowhere to be seen.

'Where is Bree?' asked Molly, still worried that she hadn't turned up.

Sam shrugged. 'I have no idea. Remember, two ladles per tray and a slice of bread,' she said, changing the subject as the first person appeared in front of Molly holding out their tray.

With the ladle in one hand Molly began to serve. There were two things that she noticed about everyone that stood in front of her. Their grateful smile and the blackened fingernails that clutched each tray. There wasn't one person who didn't say thank you, though, as the long line of people just kept coming.

Without warning, Molly could feel her eyes welling up with tears. Trying to keep her emotions in check she thought of Cam and the way he'd reacted to a stranger being in the house. She understood his hesitation but all Molly witnessed here were polite, vulnerable people that just faced a different set of circumstances from what people considered the norm. She wanted to ask each one of them how was their day, but did they really want to be reminded about the day just gone? Molly wished she could make life's circumstances better for them all, which was exactly what Sam was doing by making sure the shelter was up and running.

Stan was next in the queue. His hair was brushed to the

side and he looked cleaner than yesterday. He smiled, revealing a crooked, chipped tooth at the front.

'How are you, Stan?'

He nodded. 'I've had a good day, thank you, Miss Molly. I've spent the day in the library reading one of my favourite books of all time, and now I'm here for my tea and a bed for the night. How about you?'

Molly was taken aback that he'd asked how she was, and was reminded of her disagreement with Cam. Of course she wasn't going to moan about that, or share information about her personal life, so she simply said, 'I'm doing just fine, thank you,' with a warm smile, putting an extra half ladle on his plate.

He gave her a wink as he noticed. 'Fine isn't a good word. When everything is fine, it really isn't fine,' he replied, giving her a knowing look before thanking her for his meal and heading on his way. She watched him walk over to a table and place his tray down. He then said a prayer before he tucked into his meal.

After the long queue of people had passed, and every morsel of food had been served up, Sam wiped her brow. 'Thank you, for helping,' she said gratefully.

'My pleasure,' replied Molly. 'Honestly, anytime. It's very humbling, especially knowing for some this is their only hot meal of the day.'

'For some, their only meal of the day,' replied Sam.

'You do such wonderful work here, Sam.' Molly was in continuous awe.

'We all do.' She flashed a smile towards the rest of the

volunteers. 'Teamwork is what keeps this place going.'

The volunteers carried on making huge urns of tea whilst Sam filled the sinks with hot, soapy water as the first empty trays were stacked up at the side of the hatch. Molly collected them and passed them to Sam. 'I'm going to have to be getting home. I need to give George his bedtime kiss and Cam will be wondering where I am. He didn't know I would be staying this long.'

Molly felt a twinge of guilt. Cam might actually be worried about her as he didn't have a phone to check if she'd left yet and the weather out there was fierce.

'You make sure you drive safely. Those winds are brutal and I can't imagine it's much fun driving across the bridge in your van in this.'

'It wasn't fun at all,' Molly replied, taking off her apron and hairnet then slipping her arms back into her coat. She noticed Sam quickly counting heads before turning towards the rest of the volunteers.

'More heads than beds. We have some emergency floor mats stored in the room upstairs but not many. The food has gone too.' She looked over her shoulder at the crowded room. 'At least everyone has been fed and watered. Can we bring the mats down and get those laid out in the next room?' She looked towards the volunteers, who were already nodding and heading towards the stairs.

Sam turned towards Molly who was standing there with the wicker baskets stacked up in her arms. 'I'll help you to the van and lock the door behind you. There's no more room at the inn.'

'But you can't lock the door.' Molly panicked; she was thinking of Bree. 'There might be someone who needs a place to sleep.'

'Health and safety. I have to. But people aren't stranded, there's an emergency number that can be rung from designated places within the town. There's always a back-up plan.'

After the van was loaded, Sam's phone rang from her pocket and as she hurried back inside out of the cold to answer it. Molly noticed that Sam dropped the latch on the door, which was now firmly shut behind her. She was just about to climb inside the van when she saw a hunched figure in the distance, hurrying towards the shelter.

'Bree,' murmured Molly. 'Thank God.'

Striding back towards the door, Molly hammered hard, calling out Sam's name, but the door remained firmly locked. Molly turned back towards Bree and waved. She looked different from this morning; her coat was fastened and she was wearing the hat and scarf that Molly had left out for her. Molly banged on the door again but tried not to panic as no doubt Bree had been in this situation before and would know what to do. It was only minutes earlier that Sam had mentioned the phone line and Molly knew she'd offer to give her a lift to wherever there was a free bed for the night.

'Bree!' Molly called out. The snow was swirling all around and Molly shook the flakes from her face. Waving towards Bree she opened the passenger door so Bree could jump in and shield herself from the snow, but Bree stopped in her tracks. She looked directly at Molly then quickly crossed the road, leaving Molly standing there perplexed. Molly shouted again, but her voice was lost amongst the wind and the sound of a car engine starting up across the square. From a distance, it seemed that Bree had picked up speed. Then Molly watched in horror as Bree stepped off the kerb onto the road without noticing the oncoming car. Molly gasped and brought her hands up to her mouth. The car slammed on its brakes and the horn sounded as it slid a short distance along the road before colliding with a wheelie bin standing on the pavement.

The driver wound down his window and shouted expletives at Bree, but she didn't look back over her shoulder, simply carried on walking. Slowly the car reversed and drove off.

Molly was mystified. Why was Bree walking off in the opposite direction? It was downright rude to ignore someone if they were shouting your name. But for whatever reason Bree didn't want to speak to her. Was she was deliberately trying to avoid her? Then a fleeting thought passed through Molly's mind. What if Cam was right? Because the only possible reason that Bree was going in the opposite direction was a guilty conscience, which Molly didn't want to believe. She took a second and thought about it. There was also the possibility that Bree felt upset by the conversation that she must have overheard between Molly and Cam, which had caused her to suddenly up and leave. Molly wanted to apologise.

Without thinking, she slammed the van door shut and

took off after Bree, striding carefully along the ungritted icy payment. She continued to shout Bree's name but Bree didn't look back as she disappeared down an alley off the main street. Still following, Molly buried her chin under her scarf, the ice-cold wind stinging her cheeks as she turned down the same dark alleyway, which was cluttered with flattened cardboard boxes, broken wooden pallets and wheelie bins that were covered in snow. The sound of dogs barking echoed in the distance and an argument drifted through an open window of a flat above. Molly could still see Bree in the distance, and at that moment she slipped on the icy ground and let out a squeal. She grabbed on to a drainpipe but before she knew it, her legs were taken from underneath her and she landed on the freezing cold ground with a bump.

'Damn,' she muttered, crossly, catching her breath.

Hearing the squeal, Bree spun round then stopped walking.

Placing her hands on the ground, Molly stood up slowly and brushed herself down. Her heart was thumping nineteen to the dozen as she breathed deeply. Cupping her hand around her bump she thankfully didn't feel any twinges but the cold wind was chilling her to the bone and now all she wanted was to be back home into the warmth.

'Are you okay?' Bree was walking towards her.

Disgruntled, she muttered, 'I would be if I wasn't following you up dark alleys in the freezing cold. Why didn't you stop?' Molly's voice was a little agitated as she dug her hands deep into the pockets of her coat and looked at Bree, who shifted her gaze to the ground. There was an awkward silence. 'What's going on? Are you upset with me after hearing the conversation in the shop?'

Bree's eyes widened and she looked confused.

'You didn't hear the conversation in the shop, did you?' Molly asked, realising she'd gotten it wrong.

Bree shook her head.

'So why are you avoiding me?' asked Molly.

Bree still wasn't making eye contact.

'As much as I would love to be a mind-reader, the temperature out here is freezing and I happen to be eight months pregnant and need to get going home—'

'Home. Wouldn't that be nice… Welcome to my home, my world,' interrupted Bree, throwing her arms open. 'This alley isn't a bad one to bed down in; it's quite sheltered from the wind and the doorways are deep.' Bree's voice was hard, matter-of-fact. She turned and began to walk away. 'Go home.'

'Where are you going now?' Molly grabbed her coat. 'You can't be wandering about in this weather. You'll catch your death.'

Bree stopped. 'I don't have much choice and sometimes I think that isn't such a bad option.' She hoisted her duffle bag up on to her back and copied Molly's stance, digging her own hands deep in the pockets of her coat.

Those words hit Molly like a high-speed train. 'You can't mean that, you have your whole life in front of you.' As soon as the words left her mouth Molly knew that they sounded lame.

What did Bree have to look forward to? Nights on the street or in the shelter. Wandering around all day with no place to rest or call home. 'Where are you going to sleep tonight?' Molly asked.

Bree shrugged. 'The shelter doors are closed now but there's a café at the bottom of Clarets Row that stays open until late. I can ring the shelter helpline from there, but there's no buses and it's a long walk to the next town.'

Molly shuffled from side to side. She could barely feel her fingers and toes. The tip of her nose was cold and hair was limp and wet with the flakes of snow.

Bree looked as frozen as she did and all Molly could think about was getting them both into the warmth as soon as possible. Sitting in a café whilst they worked out Bree's next move didn't appeal to her.

'It's okay, you can go.' Bree was looking towards the ground. 'I'm nobody's problem but my own.'

'You still didn't answer my question. Why were you running from me?'

Bree looked shifty, and Molly asked herself, was it guilt at taking the phone? Even if it was, Molly couldn't just walk away and leave Bree to walk into the cold night by herself. She knew Cam was going to be far from happy with the words that were going to leave her mouth next, but she hoped, if he was in her shoes, he would do exactly the same.

'You can come home with me,' stated Molly.

She swung a glance towards the doorways and shuddered. 'There's a couple of spare bedrooms and stew left in the pot. You can even have a warm bubble bath if you like.'

Bree's eyes widened. 'Really?' she said, catching Molly's eye then looking back down at the ground.

'Really,' replied Molly, hoping that Cam could see the bigger picture when she walked back through the door with Bree.

'I can't remember the last time I had a bath,' replied Bree. 'It must be way over twelve months.'

'I'll let you into a secret, I've not had a bath for a while either, because I can get in but I have a little trouble getting out.' Molly smiled, patting her stomach, and began to walk slowly back along the alley, watching her step as she did so. She took a sideward glance at Bree and noticed a small smile hitched on her face, but it quickly disappeared.

'What is it?' asked Molly.

Bree swallowed, she dipped her head, but looked up under her fringe. 'I'm sorry…'

'What do you need to be sorry for?' When Molly asked the question Bree looked guilty, her face pale.

Bree hesitated. 'I stole from you.'

Molly stopped walking and for a brief moment closed her eyes. Her heart sank. 'It's okay, we do need to deal with it, but it will be okay … promise.'

'But what about your husband? He wanted to ring the police over a few bread rolls.'

Molly wasn't looking forward to Cam's 'I told you so'. And without a doubt, after this revelation taking Bree back to the cottage was going to cause fireworks. Her thoughts were ticking over. It was simple: everyone deserves a second chance. Bree just needed to promise not to steal from them again. Molly even thought she could pretend the phone had been mislaid somehow, or even blame it on her baby brain; she was always picking things up and leaving them in random places. It wasn't long ago that she left the toilet rolls in the fridge and the milk in the airing cupboard. For an easy life, Molly would say she'd picked up the phone and left it somewhere. She was doing it for all the right reasons; it was about giving a young homeless girl a meal and a bed for the night, and if she told the truth, it was unlikely Cam would let her through the door. Surely a little white lie to keep the peace wouldn't hurt?

Molly held out her hand. 'If you give it back to me, then I will sort it out from there.'

Bree nodded, and took the hat from her head and the scarf from her neck. She bundled them up and put them in Molly's hand, leaving her feeling puzzled.

'What are you doing?' asked Molly. 'Put these back on, you'll catch your death.'

'But I stole these from you. You sewed the buttons back onto my coat and I repaid you by taking these off the table. I am sorry. I shouldn't have.'

Molly was taken back. 'This is what you stole?' she asked, looking at the hat and scarf then back at Bree.

'Yes, they were just sitting there on the table and…'

'Is this all you took?'

Bree nodded.

Feeling relieved, Molly gave a tiny chuckle. 'You didn't

steal these. I left them there for you to have.' She pulled the hat back down over Bree's head and wrapped the scarf around her neck. 'They were for you.'

'Really?'

'Really,' confirmed Molly.

Bree smiled. 'Thank you, they really help on nights like tonight.' She paused. 'What did you think I'd taken?'

Molly knew this was her chance to ask Bree about the phone but she also didn't want to make Bree feel uncomfortable about coming back to the cottage and flee into the night. Goodness knows where she would end up sleeping. And surely, if Bree had been honest about the stuff she'd taken off the table, she would have mentioned the phone.

With a swift change of subject, Molly looked up at the falling flakes and avoided an answer. 'Come on, this weather is so cold I can't feel my hands and feet.' She didn't meet Bree's eye but looked down to the icy ground and began to walk. They hurried towards the main street and the van was soon in sight. 'Cam will be wondering where I am. He's misplaced his phone so he can't message me.' She took a quick sideward glance at Bree, who didn't react to the comment, leaving Molly still thinking the phone must be at home somewhere.

Molly unlocked the van and they climbed inside. Bree glanced at the shelter through the window. From the outside, in the darkness, no one would have ever guessed that inside there were numerous bodies shielding from the cold, snowy doorsteps that they'd frequented on many occasions. She shivered. 'I could really do with a good night's sleep…'

'And tonight, you will,' replied Molly, switching on the engine. With cold air blasting from the heater, she got out and quickly scraped the ice from the windscreen. She too glanced towards the shelter. She couldn't imagine anyone getting much rest with that many bodies sleeping under one roof – but, thanks to Sam, at least they *had* a roof. Looking at Bree, she was suddenly reluctant to take her home, especially after Cam's reaction this morning, but there was no other choice and she was just going to have to convince him it was the right thing to do. It was the best option.

Molly climbed back into the van and began to drive. The squall of snow was a white sheet that obscured the view. The conditions were awful, the wipers swishing at top speed, the flakes continuing to bat against the windscreen. It was only a few miles to home and they travelled slowly through the town, snow and ice crunching under the tyres. Roadworks had reduced the traffic to a single lane and once they were through the first set of lights the cars in front began to pick up a little speed. There were only a couple of pedestrians on the streets, clutching their bags tightly and dipping their chins, trying to avoid the cold stinging snow on their faces.

Stopping at the next set of lights, Molly noticed Bree was staring through the window towards the long line of Victorian houses beside the road.

'I always wanted to live in one of those houses – Millionaires' Row,' murmured Bree.

'Millionaires' Row… Are you from around these parts?' asked Molly, surprised Bree knew the common nickname for the houses along this road. But Bree didn't answer, just carried on looking at the houses. Some were in darkness, but others were lit up and they could see televisions flickering and families huddled together around the dining table. Once again, Molly wondered about Bree's family. Why wasn't she in foster care? Why wasn't someone looking out for her? Molly was sad at the thought that she was all alone in the world.

It was just before eight p.m. when they crossed the bridge from Glensheil into Heartcross. Along the snowy gravel track there was no street lighting and so Molly was thankful when they reached the high street. Bree was resting her head against the window.

'This morning … why did you leave?' asked Molly. She was intrigued. If Bree hadn't heard the heated discussion between her and Cam, then why would she have walked out?

Bree looked at her.

'I heard a man's voice and assumed it was your husband. I didn't want to be around if he still wanted to call the police, so I left, but I shouldn't have just walked out without thanking you for the food and mending my coat. I'm sorry, I don't have anything to give you.'

'What do you mean? I don't want you to give me anything,' asked Molly, puzzled.

'I can't pay you for mending my coat. No one is usually

this kind to me, except for Sam at the shelter. She's cool for her age.'

Molly smiled. 'I'm sure there's a compliment in there somewhere. Really, it was just a couple of buttons from an old tin I've had since I was a child.' Molly saw her opening and took the plunge, asking, 'Apart from Sam, do you have any other friends?'

Bree shrugged. 'Frenemies. People who pretend to look out for you.'

Molly understood it must be difficult to trust anyone in Bree's situation.

'But there's Stan…'

Molly noticed Bree smile as she mentioned his name.

'He looks out for me. He's been a regular at the shelter since I've been there and he won't have anyone taking advantage of me. He's taught me how to be streetwise. He's my friend with no hidden costs.'

'I'm glad you have Stan looking out for you.'

'He also taught me to play cards, but I'm not too keen on that whisky stuff he drinks.' Bree stuck out her tongue. 'Yuk, it tastes disgusting.' She paused. 'But I've never met anyone yet who hasn't wanted anything from me, except Stan and Sam.'

It saddened Molly to hear those words. 'Sometimes people can be kind without a hidden agenda.'

'I'm not sure about that,' replied Bree.

Molly pulled up outside The Old Bakehouse and cut the engine. The top window at the front of the house was in darkness, which indicated that George was tucked up in bed. Next door, the lights were on in Bumblebee Cottage and Dixie could be seen through the window sat in her armchair watching the TV.

'Let's get into the warmth, I can't feel my feet,' said Molly, opening the van door and stepping onto the snowy ground. She unlocked the shop door, and the toasty warmth inside welcomed her. Molly slipped off her coat and Bree followed suit, pulling the hat from her head.

'Cam?' Molly called out. She was feeling a little apprehensive but there was no answer. After they had both hung up their coats and taken off their boots, Bree followed Molly along the hallway towards the living room. The door was slightly ajar and the TV was blasting out loudly. The logs were still burning away on the fire and the room was warm. As she pushed open the door, she saw an empty mug and plate on the table, and then Cam, stretched out on the settee, fast asleep. She reached for the remote control and switched off the TV before stepping out of the room and closing the door behind her.

'We'll let him sleep, he must be shattered.' Molly's voice was low, careful not to wake him, and she was relieved to know that she had some time to perfect the explanation of why she'd brought Bree home. 'Would you like to have a bath whilst I check the stew and make you a drink?'

Bree hesitated. 'Are you sure it's okay for me to be here though?' She was looking towards the living-room door.

'I'm sure, stop worrying.' Even though Molly was still worried about Cam's initial reaction, she was confident that once she explained the situation all would be okay.

'In that case, yes, please.'

'This way.'

Molly led the way down another narrow hallway. 'The bathroom is just here.' Most old cottages had their bathrooms downstairs and when Molly moved into The Old Bakehouse it took a lot of getting used to. On many occasions, she'd wandered upstairs to use the bathroom before she remembered.

Pushing open the bathroom door, Molly switched on the light to reveal a room that wouldn't look out of place in a country living magazine. It was modern elegance with its minimalist design but complemented The Old Bakehouse's rustic theme with its free-standing bath, wooden panels and traditional fittings. Original oak beams ran across the ceiling, and the white tiles in the shower subtly accentuated the cottage style. The colour scheme was light and bright, giving the whole room a fresh, clean look.

'Wow, it feels like I'm in a countryside hotel. Not that I've been in any hotels, of course. It's just how I've imagined it.' Bree stepped into the room and looked all around.

'Feel free to use any of the soaps and products. I'll just get you some clean towels.' Molly walked over to a free-standing oak cupboard in the corner, took out two large fluffy white towels and placed them on the wooden stool next to the bath. 'If you want to give me your pyjamas, I'll warm them over the Aga and bring them back in about twenty minutes.'

Bree looked down at the clothes she was wearing. 'These

are the only clothes I have other than a spare jumper and underwear in here.' She placed her bag down on the rug at the side of the bath. 'When you are living on the streets, you kind of don't get changed for bed. It's not like you whip out your PJs and settle yourself down for the night. I stay in the same clothes and when they need to be washed, Sam will put them through the washing machine at the shelter – or there's the laundrette, if I'm feeling flush.'

It had never occurred to Molly what the night routine of a homeless person might be and now she felt a little silly. After placing the plug in the bath and switching on the taps, Molly told Bree to wait there whilst she disappeared upstairs. She returned holding clean fluffy pyjamas and a bathrobe. 'Here, take these. I'm a little too big for these now anyway.' She patted her stomach. 'Get changed into those and if you leave your clothes outside the door, I can run them through the washing machine for you.'

Bree hesitated. 'Why are you being kind to me?' Her tone was little suspicious and Molly realised that under the circumstances Bree was right to have her wits about her and be careful who she trusted. It was survival of the fittest out on the streets.

'Because it's in my nature, and that's what us village folk do,' replied Molly with a warm smile. 'Now enjoy your bath and I'll make you a drink and some food. When you've finished I'll be in the kitchen.'

'Thank you,' said Bree, pulling her jumper over her head to reveal an off-white T-shirt that had seen better days.

Molly couldn't help but notice how undernourished Bree looked. Her arms were skin and bones.

As Molly closed the bathroom door behind her, she peeped back into the living room, where Cam was snoring lightly. She watched him sleep for a moment before quietly walking into the kitchen and looking all around. Just what she needed; the place was a bombsite. The empty plates and cutlery were still left on the table from Cam and George's dinner and there were spilt juice and breadcrumbs on the table too. Molly sighed. She knew that Cam was tired and sometimes it was a hard task trying to get George into bed when he had other ideas, but it didn't take two minutes to load the dishwasher and wipe down the table. Checking the stew in the slow cooker and seeing there was enough left for her and Bree, she switched on the kettle and, while that was boiling, tided round and then made up George's packed lunch for the following day.

After re-setting the table and making a cup of tea, Molly noticed a notepad on the worktop and glanced over it. She smiled. Cam had been writing out a job advert for an apprentice. She was thankful he was coming around to her way of thinking. Cam would enjoy training a young, enthusiastic baker and, once they were trained, it would take the pressure off him a little. The invitation for this year's Best Bake Competition was now pinned to the corkboard in the kitchen. With a warm mug of tea in her hand, she reread it, hoping that there was still time to persuade Cam to take part.

Hearing the creak of the kitchen door, Molly looked up

to see Cam stretching his arms with a warm smile on his face. 'There you are, I must have fallen asleep in front of the fire. You've been ages.' He slipped his arms around her waist and pulled her in close. 'Aw, and you've cleaned up. I was coming back in to do this after putting George to bed.' He placed a soft, grateful kiss on the top of her head.

'Of course you were,' said Molly, giving him a look that meant she didn't believe him.

'Honestly, I was. I was just taking five minutes after I settled George, which seems to have turned into' – he glanced at his watch – 'over an hour.'

'You must have been tired. I see you might be coming to your senses.' Molly leant across and tapped the notepad on the counter.

Cam picked it up. 'You were right; Grandmother isn't getting any younger, and we can't keep relying on her to work in the shop and take George to school. Maybe if I can recruit a hard-working apprentice, it'll make our lives a little easier.'

'That it will,' she replied, leaning up and kissing him on the lips.

'And how was the shelter?' Cam asked.

'All very Christmassy. Sam has worked hard all day putting up a tree and decorations and, as you can imagine on nights like this, the shelter was packed. There was no more room at the inn. All the beds were taken.' Molly knew that wasn't the answer Cam was looking for, though; he wanted to know had she caught up with Bree. This was the exact moment she needed to tell Cam that they had a visitor in the cottage for the night. She swallowed but before she could speak, he did.

'I've eaten,' he said, pointing to the table. 'You've laid out two sets of knives and forks.'

'I know, I've laid the table for two because we have a visitor for the night.'

'Huh.' Cam was perplexed. 'Who?' He looked around. 'There's no one here.'

Molly could feel her heart hammering against her chest. She wasn't sure how Cam was going to react when she told him their visitor was Bree, but unfortunately that moment was taken out of her hands as they both became aware of a presence and turned to find Bree standing in the doorway.

Cam's eyes widened and his mouth fell open. Molly exhaled. She couldn't take her eyes off Bree. She looked so different. Her long, wavy towel-dried hair tumbled to below her waist. There were no dirty smudges on her face and her hands and fingernails were clean. Taking in the aroma surrounding her, Molly realised Bree had sprayed on a little of her perfume, which was on the windowsill in the bathroom.

'You look lovely and very clean,' said Molly, smiling. She didn't dare look sideward as she could feel Cam's eyes burning into the side of her face.

'I didn't know where to put the towels, so I've left them in the bathroom, and here are my dirty clothes. I've hung up my bag in the hallway too, I hope that's okay.' She was holding her pile of dirty clothes and hesitantly took a step forward then looked down at her feet. She stretched out her arms and handed the clothes to Molly. 'And I hope you don't mind, but I borrowed these from the bathroom.'

Molly heard Cam's intake of breath. Bree was wearing his slippers.

'It was just that my feet were cold,' she continued, 'and I didn't have any clean socks.'

'Of course we don't mind, do we, Cam?'

Sensing more than tension brewing, Molly dared to look at him. She knew they might be heading for a full-blown row. Cam was staring at her, disbelief was written all over his face. His mouth was opening and closing like a goldfish, but no words were coming out.

'There's a warm drink for you on the table and if you'd like to go sit by the fire in the living room, you know the way,' suggested Molly quickly, not wanting Bree to be a witness to the row that was about to erupt any second. 'And I'll dish up dinner. You must be starving.'

Bree slowly glanced between them both before picking up the mug of hot tea. As soon as the kitchen door was shut, Molly braced herself.

'What the hell is going on here? That girl is wearing my slippers and dressed in your pyjamas.'

'Keep your voice down, Bree will hear you.'

'Keep my voice down?' Cam swung a look around the kitchen. 'The last time I looked this was my cottage. Why is she here?'

'Just hear me out because my guess is you would do exactly the same if you were faced with the same situation as me. The shelter was full and there was nowhere else for her to go. I couldn't leave her out on the streets – have you seen the weather right now? – and she hasn't eaten and she's starving.'

Cam leant against the table. 'Molly, you can't get involved. If you take one person off the street, what about the rest? Is our home going to become a refuge? Are we opening up another shelter here?'

'Of course not.'

'It's been a long day and all I want is to be able to relax in my own living room with my family and now it's filled with strangers.'

'Not strangers, just one girl who is in need of a little bit of help.'

'And why is she wearing your pyjamas and my slippers?' His eyes were firmly fixed on her.

'Because … because I've asked her to stay the night.' Molly could feel her pulse ramp up as the words let her mouth.

Cam looked exasperated. 'You've asked her to stay the night?'

'She was stranded and, like I've said, look at the weather. What was I supposed to do, Cam? Leave her on the street? How unkind would that be of me?' Molly raised her voice. 'That poor girl is sixteen years old and has nowhere else to go. If she stayed out there tonight, she could die. Do you want that on your conscience?'

Her own outburst took Molly by surprise. She was confused. Why couldn't Cam see her point? His kindness was a quality she adored. Why wasn't he seeing the bigger picture? 'The season of goodwill is looking bleak if you can't even offer a bed for the night.'

'Molly, you really are missing the point.' Cam's voice was firm. 'This girl is a stranger. We do not know her background or where she has come from. For all we know she could have gone out of her way to befriend you so that she can rob us blind in the middle of the night.'

'Don't be ridiculous,' huffed Molly.

'Dear Mr Police Officer, yes, we've been robbed, no one has broken in but my partner invited a random stranger into the house, let her have a bath, fed her, gave her a bed for the night and when we woke up—'

'Stop being facetious. What do you suggest I do? The shelter was full, the doors were closed.' Molly threw her arms into the air. 'Why are you being like this?'

Cam knew he was keeping the real reason from Molly. All he wanted was his own family close, in their own home. He knew he was being selfish but that's exactly what he had to be to get through the next week. 'My phone has already gone missing, and there are other shelters.'

'Yes, but they are miles away and how is she meant to get there? There are no buses or trains due to the weather. So, what would you do next?' Molly threw the question at him.

'Ring Sam, ask her for advice, because I bet she would not suggest bringing her home. Did you ring Sam?'

Molly felt like she was under a sudden spotlight but there was something about Bree that made Molly want to help her. Staring at Cam, she could see he was waiting for an answer. Deep down she knew he was right; Sam would never suggest bringing someone back to the house, especially after the conversation they'd had earlier about Sam's own experiences. But she wasn't going to admit that to Cam.

'Do you really want me to throw her out on the street? Is that what you're saying?'

'You should not have brought her back here in the first place. I want you to ring Sam and ask for advice.'

'Do you not think Sam has enough on her plate? The shelter is full and one night of helping out someone in need is not going to hurt.'

Their eyes were locked when suddenly they both realised Bree was once again standing in the doorway, this time with her empty mug.

The silence hung in the air.

Molly was feeling mortified, knowing this wasn't a pleasant conversation for Bree to be privy to.

'I can go. I don't want to cause any trouble.' Bree's voice faltered as she looked towards the window. Outside, the temperature had dropped considerably and Molly knew it must be close to minus five out there. Bree might be more streetwise than other girls her age but she was still a young girl standing there looking scared, vulnerable and in need of kindness, not to mention a good meal. 'If I could just have my clothes back.'

Molly and Cam looked towards the washing machine. The drum was spinning round.

'You are not going anywhere. I'm just about to dish up

the stew. Have a seat.' Molly gestured towards the table.

Bree hesitated and looked at Cam. She didn't move.

Cam looked at Molly. Her eyes were pleading and he knew he could never actually send a young girl out into the freezing cold night.

'Enjoy the stew, it's pretty good,' he said, giving Molly a look that meant this conversation wasn't over, before he left the room.

Hurriedly, Molly pulled out a chair before Cam changed his mind. 'Take a seat.'

'Thank you,' replied Bree. Still a little hesitant and with one eye on the door, she sat down.

Molly took the hot beef stew out of the slow cooker and placed it on the table. Bree didn't say a word. Molly felt the awkward tension in the room and didn't want anyone to feel uncomfortable. 'Don't worry about Cam. He's just not one for surprises. He's a planner and when something happens out of the ordinary... I probably should have run it past him first.'

Bree nodded, picked up a knife and fork, and began to devour the food in front of her. 'This is good. The beef is so tender. It melts in your mouth.'

Molly watched as Bree hurried every mouthful. Molly had barely touched hers when she realised that Bree had nearly finished. As Bree scooped up the last mouthful she caught Molly's eye. 'Sorry,' she said sheepishly as she placed down her knife and fork. 'I eat fast. Probably a survival technique.'

'There's some more in the pot, if you fancy it?'

Bree glanced over to the slow cooker. 'If that's okay? Yes, please.'

Molly was impressed by Bree's manners. They were impeccable; she always said please and thank you.

'Survival technique?' queried Molly, scooping more stew into the bowl before sitting back down opposite Bree.

'The past couple of years I've been passed from pillar to post, family to family. Usually, families full of lots of kids. Most of the kids weren't kind and I didn't like it much. I never settled; I didn't belong anywhere.'

Molly could hear the sadness in her voice. She couldn't imagine not being raised by a loving family. She treasured the life and memories of her childhood, the family dog, the Christmases and birthdays. Her adoptive parents were simply the best – but all that could have been so very different for Molly. Once again, her thoughts turned towards her own birth parents. How would life have turned out if she'd stayed with them? Perhaps she would have been in Bree's situation.

'What about school?' asked Molly. 'College?'

Bree tore up the bread in her hands and mopped up the remnants of stew still in her bowl. 'Didn't like any of them and never made any friends as I changed schools so often. Families usually want younger kids so no one really wanted to keep hold of me for that long.'

The words saddened Molly. Her school life had been so different. She'd attended the same school and built up friendships that she still treasured today. Her teachers were enthusiastic, helped her to achieve her dream of becoming a vet, and the stability was something she cherished and appreciated. Molly couldn't help herself, she leant across the table and gave Bree's arm a little squeeze. She couldn't imagine anyone being so lonely in their early teenage years. Here was a young girl sitting here with her whole life ahead of her. She was beautiful, with impeccable manners. How had her life spiralled out of control at such an early age?

'You're wondering where my parents are, aren't you?'

Bree was beginning to open up and Molly didn't want to push her.

'You don't have to tell me if you don't want to,' replied Molly softly, though she wanted to know anything Bree was willing to share.

Instantly, Bree's eyes brimmed with tears and she placed her knife and fork in her bowl. 'My mother ... died unexpectedly of a coronary a couple of years ago.'

There was a sadness bleeding through the room and Molly wanted to take Bree and envelop her in the biggest of hugs. 'That's terrible. I'm so sorry, Bree.'

'It's not your fault. It's just life. I cope. I have to.' Bree's tone suddenly turned clinical and she wiped the tears with the back of her hand and shut down any emotion. Molly was amazed to see how quickly Bree composed herself; it was like she was too scared to show any signs of vulnerability.

'It was just me and Mum and now it's just me.' Bree took a breath.

'And there's no one else, no other family?'

Bree looked up and held Molly's gaze. Molly was sure

she had more to tell but Bree just shook her head. 'No other family, just me and an uncertain future.'

'You have been through a difficult time – more than difficult. I can't imagine. But the future has a funny way of turning things around.'

'Not usually for the likes of me. I don't have anyone to confide in and don't have the money or opportunity to enjoy the simple things in life, like going for an ice-cream with your mates or even dating a boy. Who wants to date someone who lives on the streets? To be honest, I'm not sure what's out there for me.'

Molly knew that talking this way was pushing Bree out of her comfort zone but she felt privileged that the girl was confiding in her. 'How about we become friends then? I just love ice-cream and you can always talk to me.' Molly's offer was genuine.

'I think you are going to have more than enough on your plate.' Bree gestured towards Molly's stomach then took a sip of her drink. 'And if you want me to get out of your hair, I can go. I don't want to cause any trouble.'

Molly noticed that Bree was already closing down again. She was back to being guarded, defensive. Maybe it was another coping mechanism, changing the conversation and bringing it back to the here and now.

'You aren't going anywhere in this storm. Cake?' she asked. 'That's the good thing about owning a baker's shop, there's usually cake.' Molly took a lemon drizzle cake from the tin by the breadbin.

'My mum's favourite,' replied Bree, her face lighting up.

She pointed towards the cake. 'More than her favourite actually. Her favourite colour was yellow, and she was obsessed with lemon. "Squeeze the day," she would say, every morning, without fail.'

Molly turned around and looked at Bree. There was something about those words that took her right back to being a tiny girl standing in a dark dingy flat. That was that same memory in the forefront of her mind again. She was being led away and her mum was standing behind her. The only difference was that this time her mum was wearing a yellow knitted cardigan. Focusing back on Bree, Molly noticed that the girl was smiling fondly but the tears had crept back into her eyes.

'What a lovely way to start the day,' said Molly, meaning every word, but her mind was still firmly on the past. She pushed her memory to try and expand on the image in her mind but there was nothing else.

Bree began to eat the cake, but this time she took her time, devouring every morsel.

'I'll take Cam a piece through,' said Molly, switching on the kettle and looking up at the clock. The time had flown by and Molly knew that Cam would be going to bed soon. He had an earlier start than usual in the morning with the order for Starcross Manor. 'I won't be a second.' Molly walked into the living room but Cam wasn't there so she placed the cake on the coffee table and walked down the hallway, noticing there was a flicker of light coming from the back of the shop. She stopped in her tracks in the shop doorway, not quite believing her eyes.

At first she was speechless but then the words left her mouth in a hushed whisper. 'What the hell do you think you're doing?' She was mortified, and quickly looked back over her shoulder before hurrying towards Cam and yanking Brec's bag from his hands.

Cam had guilt written all over his face.

'Well?' Molly's heart was racing as she looked behind her again. Thankfully, Bree was still in the kitchen where she'd left her. 'You can't go rifling through someone's bag! What the hell is wrong with you?'

All of the contents – Bree's whole life – were spilt out over the counter. A hairbrush, a toothbrush, a little make-up that had seen better days, wet wipes, tampons and a purse. There was a pair of dirty tights and underwear and a lightweight thermal sweater.

Molly swiped her hand over the contents. 'Have you found what you were looking for?'

Quickly, Cam began to shuffle everything back into the bag, his face a shade of crimson.

The silence was deafening but Molly remained quiet. She wanted him to speak and even though she hoped he had a damn good explanation, her gut feeling was telling her he didn't. She knew he was looking for the phone.

Still staring at him, she felt the tension between them growing.

'It was a spur of the moment thing,' he finally admitted, looking sheepish.

'And you were hoping to find...' She knew she was talking to him in a tone that she often used with George, to coax information that wasn't forthcoming. 'Drugs or your phone?'

Cam hung the bag up next to Bree's coat. 'Both, if I'm honest.'

'And did you find either?'

Cam shook his head.

'Well, there you go. Do you feel better now after snooping through someone's belongings?'

'Of course not.' Cam exhaled. He didn't know what the hell had possessed him to do it. 'I'm sorry, I'm just feeling … I don't know what I'm feeling but it doesn't mean that she's not already sold it on. These sorts of people know people.'

Molly raised her eyebrows. 'Cam, have you heard yourself? These "sorts of people" are just people fighting for survival, people whose life circumstances aren't as good as ours. Sitting in that kitchen is a young girl who needs a place to stay for the night. The shelter was full so I offered her a roof over her head. That is all there is to it. Come on, this isn't like you.'

'I know and I do hear you, it's just…' Cam knew he wanted to share with Molly the turmoil he was going through but he just couldn't bring himself to say the words. 'It's just I don't want you to get involved in something that's going to come back and bite us on our bum. I know you always want to make the world a better place but sometimes the future is not what we planned.'

'What the hell do you mean by that?' Molly felt that

Cam was talking in riddles. 'And why's it a bad thing that I want to make everything okay in the world?'

'I'm not saying it's a bad thing but...' He took a breath. 'You can't always put everything right in the world all the time. Sometimes you just need to focus on what's at home. Us. Our family.'

'You are really overthinking this. She's just a girl who needs a bed for a night. How many times can I say the same thing?'

'Have you actually spoken to Sam? Does she advise that this is a good cause of action, bringing someone into your home? Feeding them, letting them have a bath?'

Now it was Molly's turn to look shifty, as she knew for a fact that Sam would advise against it and she was crossing the line. 'I just want to help her.'

'That might be so but promise me you'll talk to Sam.'

Molly nodded, 'Okay,' she agreed. 'You have forgotten to put her purse back in her bag.' Molly swerved the conversation in a different direction; she really didn't want to get into what Sam would advise because she knew Cam would immediately jump on it. Especially when Sam's advice would be exactly what Cam thought.

Molly picked up the battered old purse; the metal zip was bent and not closed properly. A couple of coins fell out on to the table. 'See, she's only got a few pence to her name. Could you imagine living like this?' She popped the coins into Cam's hand. 'We need to put those back.' The stitching on the purse was unravelled and Molly gave the zip a little tug. They both stared into the purse.

Cam let out a low whistle and pulled out a wad of cash. 'That's hell of a lot of money.' He fanned the notes in his hand, then counted them quickly. 'There's sixty quid in there. Where do you think she got this from?' He cocked an eyebrow.

Molly hesitated. She knew exactly what Cam was thinking and it wasn't looking good. She shrugged. 'Surely you'd get more for a mobile phone. Yours was top of the range.'

'Desperate times, desperate measures. There will always be someone out there to take advantage and a few quid is better than nothing, especially when the phone didn't belong to you in the first place.'

'We don't know that; this could be government benefit or something. We can't jump to conclusions.'

Hearing the slide of slippers along the hallway, Cam and Molly panicked and guiltily spun around to see Bree walking towards them. Molly still had the purse still in her hand, and quickly held it behind her back so that Cam could take it from her.

'There you are.' Bree looked towards them. 'I'm sorry, I don't mean to interrupt, but if it's okay with you I'm really looking forward to sleeping in a proper bed; it's been a while. Would you mind if I went to sleep?'

Feeling flustered, Molly took a sideward glance towards Cam before answering. 'Of course not, I'll show you to your room.'

'Thank you. I'll just get my bag. I hung it up after my

bath.' Bree walked over to the bag and took it off the hook. 'It has my toothbrush in it.'

Molly glared into Cam's eyes but didn't say another word as she left him standing there, and led the way down the hallway to a small flight of stairs leading to the first floor of The Old Bakehouse. She glanced over her shoulder to see Bree had stopped to admire the old black and white photographs of the shop from past times.

'Those photographs look so old. This place is like something else. Lots of history. I wonder what it was like living in those times. This place has such a good feel to it... It's homely,' said Bree.

Molly pointed at a photograph. 'This is Cam's Great-Uncle Ted, he was the founder of The Old Bakehouse and won Scottish Baker of the Year many times ... ten years running, in fact.'

'Big shoes to step into,' replied Bree, admiring the photograph.

'And Cam has more than filled them,' said Molly proudly. 'Come on, this way.'

Molly was in a dilemma. As soon as Bree opened her bag, she was bound to notice her purse was missing and what was she going to think? Most probably that it had been stolen. There were two options: tell the truth or try and sneak the purse back into her bag when she fell asleep. Wishing Cam hadn't put her in this position, Molly scraped up a brief smile. 'Here you go, this is your room for the night.'

Switching on the light Molly heard a tiny gasp and saw

Bree's eyes were wide as she looked around the room. 'I've never seen a bed like that before.'

The bedroom was a simple rustic room featuring a beautiful four-poster bed, the white walls, black oak beams and minimal decoration allowing it to stand out. The goosedown duvet with Egyptian cotton linen added elegance and charm, and was dressed with duck-egg-blue scatter cushions.

Bree stepped inside the room. 'Can I actually sleep in that? It's like a bed fit for a princess.'

Molly couldn't help but notice that even though Bree was streetwise and used to fending for herself, there was an innocent, childlike look on her face. She really was amazed and grateful that this was her bed for the night.

'You can, and there's a small basin in the corner of the room, you can brush your teeth there.'

A huge smile hitched onto Bree's face. 'I'm never going to want to leave,' she exclaimed, jumping on to the middle on the bed and making Molly burst out laughing as she kicked her legs in the air. The happy look on her face said it all.

Standing there, despite the tension with Cam, Molly felt warm inside seeing Bree smiling and with a glow about her. She was clean, fed and about to have a good night's sleep.

'Enjoy. Sleep well and don't worry about getting up early. Sleep in as long as you like. The snow is going to continue to fall, so you might as well stay warm and cosy. Cam gets up early to start baking and no doubt I'll be in the shop. Make yourself at home.'

'Thank you,' replied Bree, rifling through her bag and pulling out her toothbrush.

'You're welcome. Sleep tight.' Molly closed the door behind her, leant against the wall and took a breath. Thankfully Bree hadn't looked for her purse and hopefully she would just slip into bed, which would give Cam time to get the purse back into the bag.

Feeling Cam's presence at the top of the stairs, she turned and saw he was walking towards her holding the purse in his hand. He held it out towards Molly.

'What are you expecting me to do with this? You opened the bag, you put in back inside.' Her voice was a hushed whisper.

Molly knew she was testing the water but she didn't want to get caught putting the purse back when she hadn't taken it in the first place. But knowing Cam was up early, and that there was no way he could go sneaking into her room, she knew she didn't have a choice.

'I'm not happy about this,' she muttered, taking the purse from him.

'I'm not comfortable with *any* of this.'

Molly brought a finger up to her lips then pushed him gently towards the top of the stairs. 'Shush, she will hear you.'

But before Molly could say any more, she noticed the door of George's bedroom was ajar. Peeping through the gap in the door was a sleepy-looking George clutching his teddy bear.

Molly stretched out her arms. 'What are you doing there, couldn't you sleep?'

'No wonder, with all the kerfuffle going on,' Cam murmured under his breath.

'Which is your doing.' She looked at Cam before scooping George up in her arms. 'Do you want to come and sleep in our bed for a while?'

Cam threw up his arms in frustration. He knew exactly the reason Molly would suggest that and so did she. She was feeling tired too and the last thing she wanted to do was continue this argument in bed, especially with Bree sleeping in the room next door.

She plopped a kiss on George's cheek and handed him to Cam. 'I'll just go and switch off the lights downstairs and tidy away the dishes. We can all do with an early night.'

After switching off the light in the living room Molly stepped into the kitchen and was amazed to see Bree had cleared the table and put the dirty plates in the dishwasher. She placed her hands on the counter and stared up at the lamppost outside. The snow was still falling. Molly poured herself a drink of water. She estimated there were already a good few inches on the ground and by tomorrow morning it was more than likely that most of the village would be snowed in. She glanced at the notepad; Cam's job advert was scrawled on the top page. She ripped it off the pad and placed it on top of the laptop. Tomorrow she would advertise the job and hunt down the best apprentice he could ever dream of, which would hopefully improve his mood.

Molly sighed. She felt exhausted. Her back was aching and her ankles were swollen. She cradled her tummy; it wouldn't be long before the new arrival was here. She switched off the lights on the way back to bed and padded quietly up the stairs. George was snuggled under the duvet and Cam was wide awake staring up at the ceiling. Molly knew exactly what he was thinking but didn't say anything as she slipped into the bathroom to clean her teeth. After changing into her PJs she climbed under the duvet. Cam was still lying in the same position and he didn't look in her direction.

'You need to go to sleep,' she whispered. 'You have a big order in the morning and the weather is looking worse and worse. I think the school will be shut tomorrow – Dixie told me the teachers struggled to get into school today – but if Dixie is around to look after George, I can help with some of the deliveries in the village.'

Cam murmured thanks but his eyes were still wide open as Molly switched off the bedside light and snuggled under the duvet. She knew they were in for a long night with a fidgety George sandwiched between them and Cam listening out for every creak of the floorboards in case Bree was going to rob them blind in the middle of the night. Drained, she closed her eyes and pretended to go to sleep, praying the tension would lift by the morning.

Chapter Four

A shattered Cam had barely slept a wink, as with every creak of a pipe or slight noise he was up listening for footsteps, but Bree hadn't left her bed all night. He switched off the two o'clock alarm and looked across at Molly sleeping. For the first time in a long time, she hadn't tossed and turned all night. She looked peaceful and well rested so, being careful not to wake her, he slowly lifted a sleeping George from their bed and tucked him up in his own.

He wandered downstairs and began his early morning routine, which was the same as always: fire up the ovens in the bakery, proudly place his great-uncle's hat on his head and tie his apron around his waist before heading into the cottage to make a cup of tea.

Waiting for the kettle to boil, Cam looked at the invitation on the pinboard, the baking competition very much on his mind. This wasn't just any competition – it was the competition of all competitions, and winning it catapulted your name into the elite world of top bakers. And of course the prize money would always come in handy. But Cam could imagine the pressure leading up to the competition, and that pressure on top of what he was already feeling would be a recipe for disaster. He remembered how his great-uncle Ted locked himself away for hours – sometimes days – perfecting his craft and his grandmother and grandfather had to step in to run the shop for a couple of weeks before the big event took place in Edinburgh. Cam knew that the other bakers who had been hand-picked to compete for this this prestigious award would be doing the same thing and that's what worried him the most – knowing he didn't have the same time and focus to devote to the competition.

He knew that Dixie and Molly wanted him to take part, but the timing was all wrong: he would need a clear head and to live and breathe competition prep for the next few weeks, but that was impossible. He didn't even know how to get through the next few days. Feeling the letter still in his apron pocket he knew he was going to have to come clean to Molly very soon, and knowing it could blow her safe world apart was making him physically sick.

The bakery felt colder than usual. In the light of the streetlamp outside the shop, everywhere glistened. Cam shivered and switched on the heaters before checking the ovens were at the right temperature. The first thing on his agenda this morning was the order for Starcross Manor, then the everyday orders, followed by the pastries and croissants. Molly would help with the cupcakes and doughnuts once she was up but Cam was beginning to think that she was right: he did need help. Business was growing and he just couldn't manage the large numbers he needed to produce all by himself any longer.

Cam initially learned how to bake with a little help from celebrity chef Andrew Glossop, who at the time was based up at Starcross Manor. But all Ted's recipes had been handed down to Cam and up on the shelf amongst his own baking books was his great-uncle's recipe book, containing all of Ted's bread recipes, handwritten with Ted's own illustrations. These recipes went back years. Dixie had handed over this family heirloom to Cam when he agreed to reopen The Old Bakehouse. She called it the Bread-Baking Bakery Bible and claimed everything you needed to know about making the best bread and pastries in Scotland was written in there. She was right.

Cam's kitchen mirrored his great-uncle's. All the ingredients were laid out in huge aluminium tubs and industrial-sized bowls on the counters with a stack of clean towels and everything else he needed. He looked over the orders in the book and set to work. The next delivery of wheat from the mill was due to arrive tomorrow morning, but with the weather like this, it was probable the track on this side of the bridge would cause problems.

Heartcross was separated from the local town of Glensheil by a bridge and a steep, mountainous track approximately half a mile long. In the summer it was the most beautiful track to walk along, easily accessible by foot and cars, but it was trickier in the winter months even for four-wheel drives, so all Cam could do was hope that the wheat could be delivered.

———————

For the next couple of hours, Cam was full steam ahead. As soon as the orders were complete and the shop was stocked it took the pressure off a little. Once the bread was baked, Cam checked every loaf just like he'd watched his great-uncle do when he was a little boy. Everything had to be as perfect as it could be, and he had to admit that this was one of the best batches he'd ever baked. Once more he glanced up at the photograph of his great-uncle and thought about the baking competition.

He knew it would be a good advert for the business, but The Old Bakehouse's following on social media was already great. Cam often did a live baking session from the kitchen which had many people tuning in, and he was amazed how many likes a loaf of bread could generate on Instagram.

Hearing the timer ring on the oven, Cam pushed his current thoughts from his mind and pulled open the oven door. The tray of baguettes looked and smelled divine. It was an aroma he never tired of. It made him think about family gathered around the old farmhouse table most Sundays whilst his grandmother served up a bowl of homemade soup with fresh warm bread. It was a simple memory that warmed Cam's heart. It made him think about George, who was funny, inquisitive and loved to spend time in the kitchen with Cam.

He wondered what he would remember about his childhood when he was all grown up with his own family. Cam closed his eyes and prayed he would be around to share his son's future. He knew however hard his life was going to become he needed to stay strong, but it was easier said than done.

With a dozen French baguettes baked to perfection, he began to place them on the cooling rack before he slipped them into their wrappings. Hearing the door creak behind him, he nearly jumped out of his skin and spun around, holding the baguette like a weapon.

Bree was standing there. 'If a baker assaults you with a baguette could he be charged with assault with a breadly weapon?' she joked, grinning.

Wearing Molly's dressing gown and with Cam's slippers still on her feet, she stepped into the bakery kitchen. 'What a smell to wake up to. Usually if I sleep at all, I wake up to the smell of either rancid dustbins or the stale body odour of maybe twenty-five other people. Sometimes even vomit or urine. But after a while you kind of become immune to it.'

'I guess neither are very pleasant,' replied Cam, as he carried on and pulled the next batch of loaves out of the oven.

'It smells so bakeryish.' Bree wrinkled her nose and peered inside the barrels that were half-full of ingredients. Cam watched her as she moved on to peering into the ovens and looking over the freshly baked croissants.

'It must be nice having a purpose in life,' she murmured,

casting her eyes over the row of bread-making books that were lined up on the shelf.

Cam took a sideward glance at her. 'And your purpose?'

Bree shrugged. 'What is there for the likes of me? The only thing I can do is get through each day.'

Her reply was emotion-free.

'Life is what you make it. You never know what is around the corner,' Cam said, his own words resonating with himself. He carried on, now placing freshly baked croissants onto the small trays that slid into the glass counter.

'Usually around the corner is another person trying to avoid me, or someone who crosses over the road so they don't have to say hello to the likes of me. Then there are the mothers who put a protective arm around their children as they pass me, telling them not to look in my direction.' She glanced at Cam, who caught her eye but quickly looked away and carried on what he was doing.

Bree began to read the spines of the books on the shelf. 'You have a lot of books. This one looks interesting.' She reached up towards the shelf.

Can spun a glance round. 'Don't touch that book.' His voice was firm.

Bree stopped in her tracks and raised an eyebrow, her arm poised in the air.

'Is it special?' she asked.

'Look, Bree, it's very early and I need to get on.'

But Bree didn't take the hint. She turned and looked

over at the large bowls that contained more yeast mixture. 'How many loaves do you bake a week?'

Cam was looking directly at her. With barely any sleep he was feeling tired and a little irritable. He wasn't used to his space being invaded this early in the morning and he wanted to be left alone with his own thoughts.

'Why don't you go back to bed for a while?' he said, not wanting to make small talk.

But Bree ignored Cam's question. 'That yeast mix is getting pretty large, those bubbles mean it's looking pretty good.'

Cam raised an eyebrow. 'You know about bread?'

'If you let that yeast eat for a little longer, you may need to add more flour.'

Taken by surprise, he asked again, 'How do you know about bread?' He stopped what he was doing.

'My mother.' Bree didn't elaborate any further but turned and went back to bed, leaving Cam watching her disappear down the hallway.

A few hours later, Cam was standing in the shop looking at the fully stocked shelves and wiping his hands. Glancing up at the clock, he could hear movement upstairs then the sound of footsteps followed by the light being switched on in the hallway. Molly was up and he hoped once Bree had left this morning things could get back to normal.

'Morning,' Molly said as she appeared in the doorway. 'Did you sleep okay?'

Cam hadn't had a wink of sleep. 'Not the best,' he admitted.

'Has anything been taken? I see we still have a TV, my laptop seems to still be in the kitchen, oh, and the iPad is still on the hall table.'

Cam was washing his hands under the tap. 'Okay, so maybe she isn't here to rip us off, but you can't blame me for being wary of a stranger sleeping in our house when we have a child to consider. Did you manage to slip the purse back into her bag?'

'Oh, I did that at about four a.m. when I was woken by the sound of talking. I took the chance then.'

Cam blew out a breath. 'Thank you.'

'I'd say you're welcome but it still doesn't sit right with me.'

'I am sorry,' replied Cam, looking directly at Molly. 'I know it was wrong.'

'And why was Bree up so early?'

Cam shrugged. 'I'm assuming she couldn't sleep. Maybe sleeping in a different place doesn't help.'

'I think Bree will be well used to that by now.'

Cam caught Molly's eye. 'Are we okay?'

'I hope so,' she replied, walking over towards him and leaning against the counter. She folded her arms. 'I've got to ask you something though. Apart from the last twenty-four hours, is there something bothering you? I just sense there's something not quite right.'

Cam was standing there, his hands in his apron pocket. This was the perfect opportunity to share his worries but he couldn't. He took a breath. The whole situation was eating him up inside. But the longer he could keep her world free from worry, the better.

'No, nothing at all,' he lied, not meeting her gaze.

'That's good to hear. I keep telling myself that my hormones are throwing my woman's intuition into overdrive and I'm worrying about nothing.'

Thankfully, she didn't notice his face pale as she was now standing in the window looking out over the snowy green. 'Doesn't it look perfect,' she murmured. 'So romantic. I love this place in winter and I love this place in spring, summer and...'

'That's all seasons covered,' said Cam with a smile, joining her at the window.

'Do you remember the day Dixie gave you the keys to this place? It's one of my fondest memories,' she reminisced.

Cam cast his mind back; it was one of his fondest memories too. He remembered Dixie proudly presenting the keys to him, and how he was full of excitement yet trepidation. It had been snowing outside and he and Molly had cleaned the bakery from the top to bottom. At the time Cam had no clue how to bake a loaf, but Dixie and Molly believed in him every step of the way. This was his life and one he loved.

'And the carpet picnic...' she recalled.

Cam noticed that dreamy look in her eye. 'And the burnt sausage rolls,' he said, grinning.

They'd laid a rug and set up a picnic on the bakery floor where they watched the snow fall on the green and made promises that they would look after and love each other for ever.

Cam swallowed and briefly closed his eyes. He clutched the letter in his apron pocket, trying not to think about the worst-case scenario.

Molly started to chuckle, bringing him back to here and now. 'And Martha predicted you'd become a baker and make this place a success.' She gave him a knowing look.

Cam was shaking his head. 'That wasn't anything to do with psychic powers. That was to do with the village rumour mill and my grandmother telling everyone she met that I was taking over this place but not to say anything.'

'Okay, fair point. But let me tell you about Martha. Apparently, she's asked Isla about taking over one of her vintage campervans on a permanent basis.'

'Why would she want to live in a campervan at her age when she has the comfort of the farmhouse?' Cam didn't understand.

'Not to live! She's thinking more of setting up a little business to entice the tourists to have their futures told. Ten pounds per reading, ten customers at day...'

Cam looked horrified. 'This is a quaint village in the Scottish Highlands, not the promenade at Blackpool. People actually pay for this?'

'People are fascinated by this stuff and she's only charging us a fiver tonight.'

His eyebrows shot up. 'You have to pay for one of our best friends' grandmother to feed you a pile of claptrap? I'm in the wrong job.'

'I could see you with a shawl, beads around your neck…' She laughed. 'Don't knock it until you've had a reading. A night with Martha Gray! Many of her predictions have come true, from babies to businesses. Maybe I should ask her about the winner of the bakers' competition?'

Cam let out a strangled laugh. 'Will you ask her about the winning numbers of the lottery too? Because if these special powers did exist, she would be rolling in it.' He slipped his hand around Molly's waist and they stared out over the snowy green in quiet contemplation.

'I could ask her to predict the sex of this one.'

Cam smiled down at her stomach. 'She has a fifty-fifty chance of getting that right.' He pulled Molly in closer, resting his head on top of hers. 'I love you,' he murmured. He could feel the emotion surging inside him and the tears welling up in his eyes. Molly looked up towards him, and pressed a soft kiss to his lips. 'You aren't going all teary eyes on me, are you? You big softie.'

'Molly, I really do…' Feeling a presence, Cam trailed off and looked over his shoulder.

'Has he told you that he tried to attack me with a baguette?'

Hearing Bree's voice, Molly spun around as the girl

waltzed into the bakery and jumped straight on to the counter, causing Cam to have a mini heart-attack.

'Off there, health and safety,' he demanded, shooing her off.

'Whoops, sorry,' replied Bree, jumping down and tightening her dressing gown. Cam noticed she was still wearing his slippers.

'What's this? You haven't really tried to attack Bree with a baguette, have you?' queried Molly, wondering what had been going on in the early hours of the morning.

'Of course I didn't,' he replied then murmured under his breath, 'Even though I am very tempted.'

'Don't mind him, he can be a little grumpy in the mornings,' said Molly but Cam was staring at her deadpan. 'I'm only joking,' she added, patting his chest. 'Bree, would you go and switch the kettle on for me? The mugs are in the cupboard next to the fridge. I could murder a cup of tea and a croissant.'

Bree disappeared and Molly took a croissant from the pile in the basket, tore a bit off the end and devoured it.

'No wonder profits are down,' said Cam good-humouredly, mirroring Molly's actions and eating one himself. 'I have to say though, these are very good.'

'Are profits down?' asked Molly, wondering if that was the reason Cam seemed a little troubled at the moment.

'Only slightly this week, due to the weather,' he replied.

'I wouldn't like to be out in this today.' Molly shivered. 'Cam…'

He knew exactly what she was going to say before the

words left her mouth. 'We agreed one night. Bree leaves this morning.'

There was only one way this conversation was heading and Cam didn't want to go there. The last half an hour had been calm and tension-free and that's the way he wanted it to stay, but Molly had different ideas.

'But where exactly is she going to go after breakfast? A park bench? We can't send her out in this.'

Cam gave Molly an incredulous stare, disbelief written all over his face. 'That is emotional blackmail. There are places for Bree to go. Ring Sam and get advice. George is going to be up very soon. He's our priority. We don't need any extra stress.'

Molly didn't have time to answer as the phone rang out in the shop and she walked to answer it. Cam was half listening into the conversation, but was distracted by the sound of George hurtling down the stairs shouting for Molly.

'In the bakery, George,' shouted Cam, turning to Molly, who'd just hung up the call.

'That was Dixie,' she said. 'She's feeling a little under the weather so I've told her to go back to bed but she noticed on the Facebook page that the school is closed so wanted us to know. No wonder, in this weather.'

There was a loud whoop from behind them as George punched the air. He looked an absolute vision of cuteness bounding towards them wearing his dinosaur onesie and huge monster slippers with claws. 'School is closed.' He ran towards the window and placed both hands on the glass. 'Can we build a snowman?'

'With the amount of snow out there, you can build an army of snowmen,' replied Cam.

Molly could hear the sliding of slippers up the hallway and Bree appeared in the doorway holding a tray with three mugs of tea. Placing the tray on the counter, she said, 'I didn't know what everyone wanted but...'

George was staring at Bree then ran towards Molly and flung his arms around her legs.

She bent down, and slid her arm around him.

'George,' she said softly. 'This is Bree, she's a...' Molly hesitated. 'A friend of ours. She's just staying with us whilst the weather is bad out there.'

Cam raised an eyebrow and butted in. 'Just for last night,' he reaffirmed, giving Molly a look that meant: *we agreed, one night only.*

Molly bit her lip and glanced towards the window. How could anyone think of sending anyone out into these arctic conditions?

Bree took a step towards George. 'I'm Bree. Pleased to meet you.' She held out her hand to shake George's but then brought her hand to her nose and wriggled her fingers causing George to erupt in fits of giggles.

'And this is George,' introduced Molly.

With a cheeky look on his face, George mirrored Bree's actions, leaving everyone with a huge smile on their face except Cam, who had a feeling Molly wasn't going to ask Bree to leave any time soon.

'Where's your own home?' asked George innocently.

Bree looked up to Molly for guidance as she wasn't sure how to answer that.

'Bree's just in between houses at the minute,' replied Molly, saved by the bell as the phone rang once more. She picked it up and Cam could tell by listening to one half of the conversation and from the look on Molly's face there was some sort of disaster unfolding.

'Of course, Drew, we can be ready in fifteen minutes, not a problem.' Molly hung up the phone.

'What's the emergency?' asked Cam. 'Is there a problem up at Foxglove Farm?'

'Not the farm,' replied Molly, looking towards Bree then back at Cam. 'Over at the shelter. Sam needs help. The boiler has packed up and the shelter has no heating. With the weather conditions like this, there's no one who can get out to take a look and fix it. Sam's managed to negotiate a community hall to move everyone into for a temporary measure. It might be for a few days but all the mattresses and tables and chairs need moving and of course the people. The only vehicle that's going to be able to drive in conditions like this is Drew's tractor and trailer. To move everything and get these people warmed up should only take a couple of hours but he needs help.'

'All hands on deck then,' replied Cam, then stopped in his tracks as Molly started walking towards the coat hooks in the hallway.

'Where are you going?' he asked.

'To get my coat. I've just said Drew—'

'Molly, you are eight months pregnant and are not humping mattresses between community centres.'

'I'm not, I'm helping Isla, Allie and Felicity to make soup and tea. These poor people could have died of hypothermia in the night.'

Bree was listening to the conversation and shivered. 'It sounds like my family haven't had the best of nights.'

'Why would your family live in a community centre?' asked George, looking up at Bree.

'They aren't really my family, but the closest thing I have to family,' she replied with a smile.

'And I've got to somehow get this order over to Starcross Manor.' Cam cast a glance towards the breads and selection of Danish pastries stacked on the trays ready to ship out, 'We can't leave the shop unattended; we'll have to call on Grandmother.'

'Dixie's feeling under the weather, remember? I've just told her to go back to bed. We can't ask her to look after George if she's not well.'

'I could help?' Bree offered, giving George a cheeky wink that made him giggle. 'Judging by the snow out there, surely there won't be many customers.'

George was jumping up and down. 'We can build a snowman, watch a film ... eat sweets.'

'We could,' replied Bree, smiling at him.

'There we go, all sorted. We will only be a couple of hours max, won't we?' Molly said happily.

Cam looked at his wife in astonishment. Had she really just agreed to hand over the care of their son and

Cam's livelihood to someone they'd only met yesterday?

Molly continued. 'You could put Starcross Manor's order on the trailer and we can drop that off on the way. Kill two birds with one stone, so to speak.'

Cam didn't know what to say; he was flabbergasted that Molly would even suggest that Bree be left alone with so much responsibility.

'Would you like to take Bree and go and get some breakfast?' Cam was looking directly at George, who pulled at Bree's hand as they disappeared into the kitchen.

As soon as they were out of earshot, he rounded on Molly. 'Are you being serious?'

'Why not? Do you really want me to answer that? The list is endless ... and she's only sixteen.'

'I was sixteen when I started babysitting, and I'm sure Bree will be glad of the extra cash. It's not as though George is a baby either.'

Cam looked horrified. 'I'm beginning to feel invisible. Molly, we do not know this girl.' Cam emphasised each word in a hushed whisper.

'I didn't know half the kids I babysat for until I turned up at the house, and believe me, some of those parents didn't know anything about me, except my first name.' Molly pointed to the window. 'And how many people do you think are venturing out on this weather? My guess is the shop will be empty, and they will just sit and watch a film. We can help Sam to get the residents moved and we will be back before we know it. Honestly, you are overreacting. She's just a girl who needs a break, a chance in life.'

Cam still felt apprehensive.

'Drew is going to be here any second,' Molly added.

'Mol, we agreed one night.' Cam was hoping that Molly could see his point of view too. 'We have our own family to put first. One night is going to lead to another and then it'll be even more difficult to ask her to leave.'

They were at a stalemate and it was only broken when Bree slipped back into the bakery. She was dressed now with her bag slung over her shoulder and she was buttoning up her coat.

Cam saw her out of the corner of her eye and took a breath. 'Look, we do know that things are difficult for you, and you aren't having an easy ride but—'

'But I'm not your problem,' interrupted Bree. 'I'm no one's problem except my own.'

Molly noticed Bree bristle as her eyes darkened and she looked straight at Molly. And there it was again, Molly's memories taking her straight back to the past. Bree was standing by the door ready to leave and there was something about this scenario that struck Molly deeply. She'd seen that look in Bree's eyes. It was the same look that was in her own mother's eyes as Molly was taken away all those years ago.

Bree's eyes left hers and now she was looking at Cam. Bree wasn't scared of looking Cam straight in the eye and Molly knew her bravado was more than likely a survival technique. 'I am just a normal girl with a different set of circumstances than what is considered the norm, and because of that it seems you don't like me much.'

Cam stayed silent. It wasn't the case at all. He didn't know this girl and though he fully understood her life had been tragic, he was dealing with his own fears and uncertainties and all he wanted to do was keep his own family close and safe.

'You think people who live on the streets are all the same but it's you people in your posh houses with your lucrative businesses that are all the same. You think I'm unworthy of kindness, incapable of being responsible, unemployable. I'm not on the street by choice but you know what? I'd rather be who am I than have your stereotypical blinkered views. I bet you've rifled through my bag looking for drugs.' Bree clung on to the straps of her bag.

'It's not like that,' replied Cam. He knew Molly was looking in his direction but he didn't dare look sideward.

The air was tense and Molly didn't like to see anyone feeling uncomfortable. She knew she had to intervene.

'We don't think you are unworthy of kindness. Every day we bake extra bread and treats to take to the shelter for people just like you and we are both in awe of the work that Sam does.'

'I get that, and thank you. We do all appreciate it,' said Bree, dropping the harshness in her voice as she genuinely thanked them. 'But doing a good deed and giving someone a chance are two different things. I'll be off now.' Her hand was on the door handle.

'Bree, wait. Don't leave like this.' Molly didn't want her

walking out into the bitter cold and, she had to admit, she was somewhat impressed by how Bree had stuck up for herself. She was a feisty young girl and though the words she spoke were a little emotional, they weren't aggressive or expletive. She was calm and spoke the truth. All people did need in life was a chance, and the world would be a better place without stereotypical judgement.

Her words had resonated with Molly, especially knowing that only a few years back Cam himself had been down on his luck. He'd gone through a divorce, lost his family home, his dog who was his life had passed away, and he'd no longer had a job after signing over his business to his ex-wife. It was Dixie who'd provided him with a lifeline, a place to live and a business to resurrect. Not everyone was that lucky.

Molly looked over at Cam. In her head she was willing him to say something – maybe 'sorry', and that Bree could stay for a while – but her thoughts were not getting through to him. At that second an excited George ran into the shop frantically waving a DVD in the air. 'Can we watch this film, Bree?' George's monster slippers slid to a halt on the floor and his arm dropped to his side. 'Where are you going? I thought we were watching a film?' Wide-eyed, George walked towards Bree, and she crouched down. 'That's a really good choice of film,' she said, tapping the DVD case, 'but I have to go, buddy.'

'Daddy?' George turned and looked towards Cam. 'I don't want her to go. I want to watch the film.' George cast a sulky glance to the floor and shuffled his monster slippers from side to side.

Hearing the beep of the tractor they all turned towards the window and saw Drew had pulled up on the road outside The Old Bakehouse. There was a group of other villagers sitting on tartan rugs thrown over hay bales and hugging mugs of tea.

Molly looked at Cam then at Bree.

'I'll stay here then and give Sam a ring to let her know,' said Molly, looking towards Allie, who waving at her from the back of the trailer and holding up a flask of tea.

'Please, Dad,' pleaded George once more.

Cam was looking at George then at Bree. He exhaled. 'Have you any experience of working in a shop or looking after children?' he asked.

'Neither,' replied Bree, honestly.

Molly noticed Bree's eyes brighten and a small smile hitch on her lips, hopeful that Cam might give her a chance. 'I can do it; I won't let you down. We can do it, can't we, George? What's the worst that could happen?'

Cam didn't even want to think about that possibility.

George and Bree stood in silence, their eyes flitting between Cam and Molly like they were watching an intense game of tennis.

Cam exhaled. 'No more than two hours max,' he finally agreed and was met by a huge, warm smile from Molly.

'Trust me, it'll be okay,' she whispered, opening the bakery door. Drew was standing on the other side.

'Morning! Wrap up warm, it's going to be a cold couple of hours. Are you ready?' he chirped.

'I'm just getting my coat,' replied Cam, handing Drew three stacked trays of bread. 'If we can just drop these off at Starcross Manor on the way?'

Drew agreed and loaded the bread on to the trailer whilst Cam pulled on his coat and grabbed his hat and gloves then turned towards Bree.

'You do not leave this house, do you understand me?'

Bree nodded. 'Yes.'

'And…' He scribbled a number on a piece of paper. 'This is Molly's number. You ring if there's a problem with anything. The price list for bread is in the book behind the counter. Write down anything you sell on the pad.'

Bree saluted. 'I can do that.'

Molly grabbed her hat and gloves, popped a kiss on the top of George's head and said, 'Be good for Bree.'

Cam looked over his shoulder as he left the bakery. He was giving Bree a chance and he prayed she wouldn't let him down.

As they stepped outside into the minus temperature Molly huddled deep inside her parka. Cam jumped on to the back of the trailer and extended his hand to help her up.

'Thank you, all she needs is a chance,' she said, giving Cam a quick kiss on his cheek before sitting down next to Allie, who handed her a warm drink. Cam took a place next to Fergus.

'I wouldn't like to be living on the streets in this,' exclaimed Fergus. 'Sam was saying they nearly all froze to death last night with the boiler packing up. Isla's taken the Land Rover, which is loaded with chicken and vegetables, over to the community centre. Hopefully, it won't take too long to cook up a broth and warm everyone up.'

Molly buried her chin under her scarf and waved at George who was standing next to Bree and watching from the window. As the tractor pulled away, the wheels on the trailer spun momentarily before they regained traction. Up ahead there were no tyre marks on the road or footprints on the pavement as everywhere was covered with a fresh onslaught of snow. There wasn't a soul in sight.

'I've been trying to ring you all morning,' shared Fergus, handing Cam a mug of tea from the flask. 'Straight to answerphone,' he added.

'I can't find my phone,' Cam replied, casting a glance back towards the window.

He felt an uneasiness pass through him as the tractor turned off the main road and George and Bree disappeared out of sight.

Chapter Five

Bree high-fived George and turned the sign over on the back of the door. The bakery was officially open for business. She felt a little twinge of excitement as she looked around the shop. No one had ever given her responsibility like this before, and she was determined to grasp it with both hands and not to let anyone down. The bakery was the quaintest thing she had ever seen, with its floral triangular bunting draped across the walls, and the colourful jars of jams and chutneys. It was full of charm, an alluring place filled with crunchy baguettes, buttery viennoiseries and decadent pastries. It reminded her of a place where her mum worked when Bree was a child.

She remembered it well, a bakery and coffee shop, which was just a short train journey away. Bree used to accompany her mum to work every Saturday. The owner of the bakery became part of their family and as she grew older he allowed Bree her own little table in the kitchen where she would help to knead the dough and make chocolate. She looked forward to going to work with her mum and often returned home with a huge bag of goodies. The things she remembered most about her mum's boss were his welcoming smile and the huge scar across his hand. Thinking back, she remembered how her mother had abruptly stopped working there when Bree was around seven years of age. She'd witnessed a hushed, heated exchange of words between her mum and the baker and then they left and never returned.

Taking a croissant from the counter she tossed it towards George. 'Here you go.'

'Are we allowed?' he asked, looking at Bree, then the croissant.

'We are.'

George didn't need telling twice. He ripped the croissant in two and stuffed half of it in his mouth, the loose flaky pastry falling to the floor like confetti. Bree ran her finger across the jars of homemade jams and chutneys and she read every label. There were such wonderful mouth-watering flavours. With his croissant devoured, George was pulling at her top and waggling the DVD in the air.

'Come on,' said Bree. 'Let me get you a drink whilst you switch the TV on.' George raced towards the living room.

Whilst Bree opened the cupboard doors looking for a glass, she cast a glance over the pinboard in the kitchen. It was littered with drawings by George, important telephone numbers and an official-looking invite. Cam had been invited to take place in the most prestigious baking event of the year. Bree had often heard her mother talk about it to the guy in the baker's shop when she was just a little girl so she knew this competition was a very big deal.

'The special element is chocolate,' she read.

After making George a drink, she pinned the invitation back in exactly the same place she found it and wandered into the living room. George had dragged his duvet from upstairs and was now snuggled under it on the settee with all his teddy bears lined up beside him. The DVD was playing and George didn't even look up when Bree placed the drink on the table.

'I'll be back in a minute, just checking on the shop.'

Leaving George watching the TV, Bree wandered down the hallway and, as curiosity got the better of her, moseyed into the next room, which was the dining room. It was impressive, with oak beams running the length of the ceiling and double cottage lights on every wall with green velvet lampshades. The window looked out over the garden of The Old Bakehouse, which looked imposing covered in untouched inches of snow. Picking up from the dresser a photograph of a younger Molly with her parents, Bree studied the image. She thought back to her own mother, who worked hard and often had three or four jobs at a time to keep a roof over their heads. They had very little money but it didn't matter because they had each other.

Walking towards the bookshelves, Bree noticed they were filled with classics and as she glanced up at the photographs on the wall, she opened another door, which led her back into the bakery kitchens. Looking around her, she breathed deeply, taking in the aroma. The smell immediately transported her back to her early childhood and the bakery her mum used to work in.

Noticing Cam's baker's hat and apron hanging on the hook, she took the hat and placed it on her head and admired herself in the mirror. Then her eyes flicked up towards the shelf of cookery books. She was drawn to the book Cam had advised her not to touch and she carefully pulled it from the shelf. It was a medium hardback diary with page after page full of handwritten recipes. The writing was elegant yet scrawny, in old-fashioned ink pen. Next to each recipe were hand-drawn illustrations. Bree carefully turned the pages and towards the back of the book she came across a section with each page dated with the year and each recipe planned out. It was only after scanning the framed awards that were dotted around The Old Bakehouse that Bree realised what she was looking at. Each recipe in this section was the one that had won Cam's Great-Uncle Ted the Baker of the Year award. Bree couldn't believe the work that had gone into each entry. Ted had baked each recipe over and over again umpteen times before the actual competition and each time he'd recorded the consistency, the taste, etc. Bree thought back to Cam's invitation for this year's entry and the special element – chocolate. Her mother used to bake the best chocolate slabs in the whole wide world and for a second Bree felt a little saddened. They used to bake it together and since she'd passed away Bree hadn't been anywhere near a kitchen.

The old-fashioned bell chimed to signal a customer so,

leaving the recipe book on the counter, Bree popped her head into the bakery. With the weather like it was today she was surprised anyone had braved the cold.

In trudged an elderly woman stamping her snowy Dr Martens boots on the mat. She was wearing a crimson teddy bear coat that hung from her tiny frame. Bree guessed she was in her mid-eighties; she was short and as she pulled her hat from her head her bob sprang in every direction with the static. Her blusher matched her coat, which also complemented the varnish on her nails. Bree admired her boldness.

The woman coughed then narrowed her eyes at her. 'And who are you?' she asked, looking through to the hallway then back towards Bree.

'I'm Bree.' She thrust her hand forward. 'I'm in charge for a couple of hours,' she said with a smile.

'Really?' Dixie was surprised after the conversation the previous morning in the shop, but who was she to interfere?

'Do you live in the village?' Bree asked.

'Right next door.'

The penny dropped. 'You must be Dixie, Cam's grandmother. You were feeling a little unwell this morning. Is there anything I can get you?'

'News travels fast.' Dixie was still looking straight at Bree. 'And where has my grandson gone gallivanting in this weather?'

Bree noticed that Dixie was scrutinising her every feature.

'The boiler packed up at the homeless shelter, and some

of the villagers are helping Sam to transport the mattresses and people to another community centre a couple of towns away. Cam volunteered to help.'

'And my great-grandson?'

'He's through there watching a film. I was just about to join him,' replied Bree, nervously fiddling with a paper bag from the counter.

Dixie was still looking at her in a strange way and Bree felt a little uncomfortable.

'Are you okay? You're kind of staring…'

Dixie cut in. 'I'm sorry, I actually don't know what's come over me, I've just had one of those moments. A … what do you call them?' She flapped her hand in front of her then placed one hand on her heart. 'A déjà vu moment.' She was still staring at Bree in a peculiar way.

'Would you like me to get you a glass of water?'

Dixie shook her head. 'It's okay. For a second there you reminded me of someone. The resemblance is uncanny, those hazel eyes of yours…' Dixie gave herself a little shake. 'Are you from around these parts?' she asked.

'Grew up in a couple of villages but originally I'm from the outskirts of Glensheil,' replied Bree.

'And you said your name was…'

'Bree.'

Dixie didn't know of anyone with that name but there was something about the girl standing in front of her that seemed all too familiar. If only she could put her finger on it. 'I just never forget a face, which I know is quite a thing at my age.' She gave a little chuckle, then blew her nose into her handkerchief. 'And this cold is making me feel sorry for myself. I'm going to get back up under the duvet for a while and recharge my batteries. Will you let Cam and Molly know I called in?'

'Of course,' replied Bree and watched Dixie leave the shop.

With no other customers in sight, Bree returned to the living room to check on George and smiled. The film was still playing on the TV but George had fallen to sleep. His duvet was pulled up under his chin and a teddy bear tucked under his arm. Bree stopped the film and switched off the TV. Then she stepped back into the bakery kitchen, where Great-Uncle Ted's recipe bible was still on the worktop. She glanced over the chocolate bread recipe then looked around the kitchen. She used to have lovely happy memories of baking with her mum so without giving it another thought she gathered all the ingredients together and began to make the chocolate sauce, combining Belgian chocolate from the shelf with the rest of the ingredients.

Once the chocolate sauce was made, Bree rolled the dough into rectangles then, just as her mother had taught her and according to Ted's recipe, she covered the dough with half the chocolate sauce leaving one inch of room on all sides. She did exactly the same with the second piece of dough and used up the remaining sauce. Then, using a bench scraper, she carefully cut each log vertically in half making sure the seam was side down. Bree was enjoying herself. She sang as she baked then suddenly stopped and looked in the mirror. She couldn't remember the last time she'd actually sung out loud and she looked daft wearing the baker's hat but she smiled at her reflection. Feeling happy yet with a tiny pang in her heart she wondered what her mum would think, knowing that since she'd passed away Bree's life had spiralled out of control. It wasn't as though Bree didn't have ambitions – she had dreams, she wanted to be successful, hardworking just like her mum – but it was proving difficult with no proper base to call home.

Laying the next piece of dough horizontally, and then the other vertically, she repeated the pattern, weaving the dough then shaping it into a circle, tucking the excess pieces under the rest of the dough. After transferring it to baking paper, she brushed it with egg wash and slid it into the oven.

Swiping her hands together, Bree felt proud of her attempt. She had enjoyed every second of her time in the kitchen. It made a change – usually she would be pounding the pavements, trawling the shop windows looking for job vacancies that she had no chance of getting when they discovered she lived on the streets.

With the bread baking nicely in the oven and the kitchen cleaned, Bree carefully placed Ted's recipe bible back on the shelf and took in the aroma.

The chocolate bread smelled divine and she hoped it tasted just as good. With George still asleep, she made a cup of tea and dusted down the shelves of jams and chutneys then sat on the stool behind the counter, looking out over the green. For the first time in a long time, Bree felt a sense of importance, self-worth. She was aware that she was smiling. Today she was a bakery assistant and that might not mean much to some, but to her it meant the world.

Bree was just about to check on George when the old-fashioned bell above the shop door tinkled again. She jumped off the stool and stood to attention behind the counter, transfixed. Standing in front of her was the handsomest boy she'd ever set eyes on; he literally took her breath away. She felt her heart beat a little faster. Their eyes stayed locked until Bree had a moment of shyness and looked away briefly. Reminding herself to breathe calmly she slowly looked up again. The boy standing in front of her gave her a lopsided grin.

'I don't think we've met?' He extended his hand. 'Ash.'

He was undeniably good looking, with a mane of blonde hair swept back from the smoothest skin, a chiselled jawline and piercing blue eyes. He towered over her, his bright-blue eyes looking down on her, and there was a softness to his gaze that put Bree immediately at ease. She guessed he must be around eighteen. 'You must be the postman.' She stretched out her hand. 'I'm Bree.'

'Must be the uniform that gave it away.' Was it Bree's imagination or did he have a glint in his eye?

She held his gaze and shook his hand.

'Woah, your hand is freezing!' exclaimed Bree as she retracted her own quickly, hoping the boy hadn't seen the blush to her cheek, the slightest touch of his hand causing a little flutter in her stomach.

'Yeah, sorry about that, it's a little chilly out there this morning.' He grinned, reaching into the post bag that was slung over his shoulder and pulling out a pile of letters. 'Is Cam around?'

'He isn't. They will hopefully be back within the hour though, if you want to call back?' suggested Bree.

'I need to apologise,' Ash shared. 'Yesterday, I dropped the post off first thing in the morning and missed out some letters. It was just junk mail but when I came back there was no one around so I left them on the counter by the till, right there, and somehow, I accidently picked up Cam's phone, thinking it was mine. I thought I'd had my phone in my hand when I was sorting the post but it was in my pocket. It was only later when I heard it ringing that I realised it wasn't mine, but then the battery died before I had chance to answer. I did leave an answerphone message on the landline number, telling him I'd return it this morning. Can I leave it with you?' Ash delved once more into his bag and held the phone towards Bree.

'Of course, I'll make sure he gets it as soon as he gets back.'

'Thank you.' Ash handed the phone over, his cold fingers brushing once more against Bree's.

'Is this your normal round?' she asked, placing a croissant in a white paper bag and sliding it across the counter.

'Hopefully, especially if I meet nice folk like you.' He was grinning widely and Bree wondered whether he was flirting with her a little. 'It's only my second day on the job and, I have to say, winter is not the best season to begin work as a postman,' he said, rummaging in his pocket and placing a handful of coins on the counter.

'On the house,' said Bree, 'and take this.' She made him a cup of coffee in a polystyrene cup. 'I can't have you freezing on your second week at work, now can I?' she said, giving him a warm smile.

'Very kind. Are you from around here?' he asked.

'I'm from everywhere,' she replied, then realised how confusing that sounded as Ash raised an eyebrow and so she added, 'Kind of. I grew up in Glensheil. It's my first morning in the bakery. If you want to pop by again that would be great.' Bree didn't know why she had said that, because it wasn't as though she would be working there every day. It was just a one-off, but the little white lie gave her a little boost that made her feel she was worthy of having a job. There was something about Ash that she quite liked.

'No doubt I'll see you around,' he said, hoisting his post bag up on his shoulder.

'Hopefully,' she replied, suddenly feeling a little shy and thankful her voice sounded relatively normal, as in her head it had sounded like it had risen an octave.

As Ash left the bakery, he looked back over his shoulder, giving her a wolfish grin and holding up the paper bag with the croissant, causing her stomach to give a little flip. Again.

Bree watched him all the way until the end of the road, where he disappeared towards the high street.

'Bree!' George's voice sounded from the living room. He was awake.

'Give me two seconds,' she shouted, locating her bag and rummaging inside for her purse.

Bree was just about to take out some coins and pop them in the till for the croissants she'd taken this morning and Ash's coffee – she didn't want Cam and Molly to think she had taken advantage of them – but was distracted by the oven timer.

Quickly grabbing the oven gloves she opened the door to see the delicious chocolate bread baked to perfection. Bree was delighted with her attempt. She hadn't baked anything since her mum had passed away and she'd forgotten how good it made her feel. Carefully placing the loaf on the cooling rack, she took in the aroma. It smelled scrumptious, it looked scrumptious sitting there and she hoped it tasted as good as it looked. Feeling proud she wrapped her arms around her body and beamed.

'The TV is switched off.' George appeared in the doorway clutching his teddy bear in his hand.

'You fell asleep, but since you're wide awake, shall we watch the film now?'

George nodded. 'That smells good.' He wafted his nose towards the chocolate bread then walked towards the counter. He rested his chin on the worktop and inhaled, making Bree laugh.

'But don't touch, it'll be hot. Let's leave it to cool whilst we watch the film and then if there's time, we could build a snowman.'

Despite the lack of customers due to the weather, Bree classed the morning as a triumph. This was a different way of life than what she was used to and she was thoroughly enjoying herself. Usually, her morning routine would be to leave the shelter after a disturbed night's sleep. After a cup of tea and a slice of toast Bree would find herself wandering the streets, taking shelter in the library and hoping to find a job.

Without fail, Bree would also visit her mother's grave once a week. It wasn't much to look at as there was no headstone and it was just a mound of earth, but it was right next to a bench for her to sit on. In the summer months, the sun beat down and Bree would borrow a book from the library and spend copious hours sitting on that bench, feeling close to her mum.

As she turned on the TV, Bree thought about the bakery. She had overheard Molly and Cam talking about advertising for help and her thoughts began to run away with her. Maybe she could convince them she was the person they were looking for? Bree knew she would be a hard worker. Feeling a surge of excitement rising up inside her, she knew she had nothing to lose asking for a trial. If that was successful, then maybe she could start to save for a deposit on a rented flat. The more she thought about it, the more she'd mapped the next year in her head.

'I'm going to make you proud, Mum,' she muttered, glancing up at the sky out of the window.

With a spring in her step, Bree bounced on to the settee, making George giggle as his teddy bear catapulted into the air and she caught it. After switching on the film, they snuggled under the duvet. Whilst George was quickly engrossed in the movie, Bree's thoughts were elsewhere. She was rehearsing a speech in her head. She was going to strike whilst the iron was hot. As soon as Molly and Cam returned, they would see everything had run smoothly and she was going to be brave and hopefully convince them to give her a job.

'Do you think you'll babysit me again?' asked George, looking up at her with wide, adorable eyes.

'I have everything crossed,' Bree replied, holding up her hand and crossing her fingers. Even though she was a mixture of excitement and trepidation, she willed Molly and Cam to return so she could run her idea past them.

Chapter Six

'Gosh, we've been a lot longer than anticipated,' said Molly, stamping her feet at the front door of The Old Bakehouse. 'But what a morning! I know the temporary shelter is a few villages away from Glensheil, but thankfully all those people will have a warm place to stay today. Sam is just an amazing person, isn't she? I can't believe how selfless she is.'

The villagers had spent the morning transferring all the beds, tables and chairs to another community centre and whilst Drew transported all the homeless people on the trailer, Molly, Isla and Allie had set to work cooking up a warm stew for everyone to tuck into once they'd arrived. She'd never seen so many grateful faces as the residents stepped into the warmth.

But Cam didn't answer her. His eye had caught his mobile phone, which was sitting on the counter next to Bree's bag. 'That's my phone.' He picked it up and turned it over in his hand. His eyes were blazing as he waggled it in the air. 'I just knew she had it. I told you so.'

Molly stood by Cam's side and looked at the phone in Cam's hand. There was no denying it was his.

'She had it all the time. Please tell me you see what I see.'

'I can see what it looks like but…'

'Molly! Don't you dare try and reason this out. This is my phone.'

'All I'm saying is before we jump to any conclusions, let's ask her and listen to what she has to say.'

But Cam wasn't listening. 'This is my phone and it wasn't here yesterday.'

Molly felt her heart beating fast. She could predict exactly what was going to happen in the next few minutes. All she wanted to do was grab a cup of tea and put her feet up, but there wasn't a cat in hell's chance of that when World War Three was about to erupt all around her.

'Bree!' Cam shouted down the hallway.

Molly swallowed as Bree appeared in the door with a huge smile on her face.

'You're back! As you can see, everything has run smoothly and George is in the living room, safe and sound. But you were right, there were no customers due to the weather, and I think all the villagers were out in force helping Sam. Dixie popped in, but she was going to rest for a while. How was it?' Bree knew she was babbling, but she was super excited to show them the loaf she'd baked and suggest a trial period in the shop.

Cam was staring at Bree, and Molly could feel the tension bubbling away, knowing she somehow had to calm the situation before it got out of hand.

'That's good to hear everything has run effortlessly,' said Molly, trying to smooth the way, but judging by the look on Cam's face he was about to explode.

Suddenly feeling the tension herself, Bree asked, 'Is everything okay?'

'Can we just ask where you—' Molly started gently but Cam interrupted and cut to the chase.

'Just get your stuff and go.'

Molly noticed Cam's face was mottled crimson. She knew he was angry and wasn't going to listen to what Bree was going to say and she also knew this wasn't the Cam she'd fallen in love with. His behaviour was bordering on erratic. He'd been up and down like a yo-yo in the past couple of weeks and it really wasn't like him. He wasn't even giving Bree a chance to explain herself.

'Why? What have I done?' she asked. Her voice was shaky.

Trying her best to keep composed, Molly kept her voice calm. 'Where did the phone come from? Did you take it?'

There was silence.

Bree was looking puzzled and shaking her head. Her heart began to thump faster. She had that horrible feeling in the pit of her stomach that she'd felt so many times since her mum had passed. A horrible anxious feeling that she never wanted to feel again.

'Because if you did, it's okay. We can sort this out.' Molly shot a warning glance at Cam, who was agitatedly running his hand through his hair.

'Of course she took the phone. I want you to leave.' His words packed a powerful punch as he turned back to Bree.

'What? I didn't take your phone.' Bree looked between them both, but it was obvious to her to that whatever she had to say Cam was not going to listen, and she could see how it looked. She'd grown up fast since her mum had passed, and life on the street had taught her to walk away with dignity, not to fuel the fire. Do not get into any sort of confrontation, no matter who's right or wrong. She hadn't taken the phone but she didn't need to explain herself to anyone because even if she tried, it was obvious Cam wasn't going to listen.

'Please leave.' His words had an air of finality to them as he handed her her bag and coat.

'I think if we all just calm down this can be sorted. Look outside, Cam. Where exactly will she go?' said Molly. 'The shelter is now too far to walk to and the buses aren't running.'

'It's okay, I don't want to stay where I'm not wanted,' replied Bree, taking her coat and slipping her feet into her boots. Taking her bag from his hand she opened her purse and took out her loose change, and placed it on the table.

'Money for three croissants and a cup of tea.' Then, with her bag slung over her shoulder, she walked towards the door. She looked back to say, 'For what it's worth, I didn't take your phone,' before stepping out into the cold, knowing that her hopes and dreams of a job in the bakery were well and truly shattered.

As soon as the door shut behind Bree, Molly could feel herself shaking and she hurried to the door after her.

'Molly, let her go.'

Molly grabbed the counter and closed her eyes. She exhaled loudly as the words 'Oh my God' passed her lips.

'What is it? Is it the baby?' asked Cam, noticing that Molly's face had paled.

'No, not the baby.' Molly took a deep breath as a memory that had been locked away for years suddenly became clear in her mind. She was clutching a teddy bear and being led away to her new family. Molly was suddenly engulfed with the fear of the unknown – the same fear Bree had described.

Where would Bree go?

Molly wasn't impressed by Cam's lack of compassion. She just didn't understand it. It wasn't like him. 'Cam, this isn't like you. What exactly is going on?' Molly was beginning to feel anxious. In all the time she'd known Cam she'd never known him to act irrationally, except for the very first time their paths had crossed in Primrose Park. At the time his personal life was in turmoil, and Molly had scared the life out of him by telling him she was pregnant with his baby after their one-night stand three months earlier. But since then, they'd always talked about everything.

Cam looked like he was going to say something but didn't.

'If you don't talk to me, how can I help?'

Cam held her gaze. He could feel himself shaking but he still couldn't bring himself to say anything.

'You know what? Have it on your conscience that a poor girl is out there in those freezing conditions and no doubt will die of hypothermia.' Molly threw her arms up in the air, exasperated. 'There's something you are not telling me, because this isn't like you. It isn't good for my blood pressure so please just tell me what's going on!'

For a second, Cam's eyes veered to the floor as he grappled with what to do. Telling Molly could cause her even more anxiety and that's what he was trying to save her from, but clearly he was failing miserably in that endeavour.

Molly shook her head, her feelings crystal clear. 'I'm going to ring Sam and ask for advice because no matter what's gone on, it's still too cold for any child to be walking the streets in this weather.'

'Here, you can use my phone now I have it back,' Cam offered.

'URGHH! I've got my own phone.' Needing space, Molly walked out of the bakery and up the hallway without as much as a fleeting glance behind her.

Chapter Seven

Looking out of the bedroom window of The Old Bakehouse, Molly tried to calm her beating heart. She'd left Sam a voicemail and was praying she got back to her soon.

Opposite, the green was deserted and still covered in a blanket of largely untouched snow, which surprised Molly, but no doubt it was just because the schoolkids had gathered at Primrose Park or were navigating their sledges down the snowy hills behind Foxglove Farm instead.

Still watching from the window, she heard voices and looked down to see George stomping across the lane to the green. He was pointing down to his wellington boots and squealing as the cold snow toppled inside them.

'Daddy, I'm stuck,' he shouted. 'I can't move my feet.' George couldn't control his giggles.

The snow was deep and Cam lifted him up clean out of his wellies and spun him around.

This was the side of Cam she fallen in love with – fun-loving, compassionate Cam. His bond with George was one of complete, unconditional love. It didn't matter how tired Cam was, spending time with George was always a must. Molly watched as Cam hugged George tight and held on to him for longer than usual. For a second, Molly thought his face had crumpled as he looked up towards the sky but she couldn't be sure. George was fighting to be released and Cam positioned his dangling legs right back inside his wellington boots. Then they chased each other, throwing snowballs, and it wasn't long before Cam patted a large snowball in his hand and the two of them began to roll it in the snow to make a bigger ball. Cam must have sensed he was being watched as he glanced towards the top window and caught Molly's eye, but she was still maddened by the fact that he hadn't let Bree explain about the phone and she moved away from the window to sit down on the edge of the bed.

What exactly was going on here? She was feeling a little bewildered by his unusual attitude. She turned the question over in her mind. Was Cam happy with his lot, or was she reading too much into everything? Her gut feeling was deepening, telling her something wasn't quite what it seemed. Yet he'd said everything was fine.

Molly tried to pinpoint exactly when the niggling between them had started, but she couldn't pin the timing down to anything specific. Standing up, she stared at the wardrobe. A fleeting thought crossed her mind. No, she couldn't … could she? Conscious that she had never felt the need to check up on him in any way before, Molly opened the wardrobe door. Without giving it another thought, she frantically began to search through his trouser and jacket pockets.

Her thoughts were chaotic. She had no clue what she was even looking for. After checking a handful of clothing, she turned and glimpsed through the window to check Cam was still outside and caught sight of herself in the mirror. What the hell was she doing? How'd it come to this? This was exactly what Cam had done – rifling through Bree's bag because he didn't trust her. Did that mean she didn't trust Cam? Stopping and closing the wardrobe doors, Molly took a breath and gave herself a long hard stare in the mirror. Disappointed in herself, she sat back down on the edge of the bed just as her phone rang.

Sam's name was flashing on the front of the screen and immediately Molly took the call.

'Sam, thank you for getting back to me.'

Molly's pulse began to race as she knew that she would have to come clean about Bree staying the night at The Old Bakehouse and she wasn't sure how Sam was going to react to that snippet of information. If Sam wasn't happy with her, Molly knew she'd take that on the chin. All she needed to know was that Bree would have a warm, safe place to sleep tonight.

She explained the situation to Sam, who fell silent for a moment. Molly listened to the silence on the other end of the phone and bit her lip.

'Even though I don't recommend you get personally

involved, as emotions can run very high in certain situations, I can see your intentions were good. Bree knows of all the places she can go for shelter and that includes the daytime too.'

'I know, I just—'

'You just wanted to help. Bree is young and it's human nature to be kind and I would never have turned her away from the shelter, you know that. You should have carried on knocking at the door or ringing my phone. Sometimes you have to gauge the level of involvement. Vulnerable people can get attached to you then depend on you more and more. Molly, you need to consider this because if Bree does begin to depend on you, what level of commitment can you really give to that? You have your own family, a baby on the way, businesses to put first. Sometimes being cruel to be kind is the best thing to do.'

Sam was saying exactly the same thing as Cam. 'But she's so young.'

'I know and because of Bree's age it's difficult to put it all in perspective.'

Molly closed her eyes. Sam was still talking but Molly was lost in her thoughts. She just couldn't get Bree out of her mind.

'Molly, are you still there?'

'Yes, sorry, I'm still here.'

'In Bree's case, for what it's worth, though I can't say I'm one hundred per cent certain … I don't think she would steal a phone and I wouldn't have any qualms about Bree babysitting. She is a very caring girl who has been dealt a tragic hand but she's strong and determined and she will go places. Giving her a little responsibility will certainly boost her confidence.'

Molly blew out a breath. Feeling relieved, she thanked Sam. However, she knew Bree's confidence would be at an all-time low after today. 'I'm worried she won't have a roof over her head tonight, especially with the temporary shelter a couple of villages away. Will you let me know if she arrives?'

Sam reassured her that Bree knew her number and there were designated phones around Glensheil that she could use to get in touch with her.

After hanging up, Molly felt a little better but she was still feeling perplexed by Cam's actions. Since Dixie was a little under the weather, Molly decided to grab some breathing space and check in on her. Slipping on her boots and grabbing her coat from the hallway, she walked into the bakery. She switched off the ovens as there was nothing else that needed baking today and as she turned to leave, she noticed there was a single loaf cooling on the rack. She took in the aroma. The loaf wasn't Cam's usual creation, but it looked and smelled divine. Feeling ravenous, Molly grabbed the bread knife and sliced off a huge doorstep. There were only so many weeks left when she could get away with eating what she wanted and blaming it on baby blubber.

'Wow,' Molly murmured as she took a bite. 'Just wow!' The loaf was a work of art, plaited in a round shape and risen perfectly and inside the bread was baked with chocolate but actually had another layer of chocolate running through the middle that was gooey and still warm. Taking another bite, Molly oohed and ahhed; it tasted like heaven. She savoured every mouthful and actually thought about taking another slice before realising that this was chocolate bread and Cam must have been practising for the baker's competition.

'Oh my gosh!' Molly brought her hand up to her mouth, mortified at her mistake. She was still staring at the half-eaten bread but inside she was secretly chuffed. This meant Cam was actually thinking about taking part in the competition, because otherwise he wouldn't have put in the effort.

'Don't panic,' she told herself. She would just explain it was the baby's fault and they'd agree it was the best loaf he'd ever baked.

As soon as she stepped outside The Old Bakehouse, George shouted to her and proudly pointed to the three snowmen stood in a line. 'Look, this is you, Mummy.' George indicated a snowman that had the biggest tummy Molly had ever seen. 'You have a baby in your tummy.'

Molly burst out laughing. 'She looks … very much like me. Even though I'm not sure why my head is bigger than my body.' Molly blew out her cheeks, making George burst into a fit of giggles.

Cam was looking more relaxed, the chilling temperature causing his cheeks to redden. He was still patting away at the snowman.

He looked up. 'You okay?' he asked.

'I'm just going to check up on Dixie, see if she's well enough for tonight's psychic antics up at the farm. These are looking good! But I want to know ... who is this cheeky one on the end?'

George began jumping up and down, pointing both hands to his chest.

'I think we've done a good job.' Cam high-fived George, who then ran off towards the trees, stomping in the untouched snow blanket.

'I gave Sam a call,' shared Molly once George was out of earshot.

Cam carried on patting the snowman.

'In her opinion, Bree is trustworthy for babysitting and she doesn't think she would have stolen the phone.'

Cam stopped what he was doing. 'Molly, I don't want to go over this again.'

'She did say Bree has her number, so she won't be left out in the cold, which has made me feel a little better.'

'That's good to hear, on both accounts,' replied Cam.

Molly turned to walk off.

'Mol, I don't feel good about anyone not having anywhere to live and I do my best by baking extra bread that comes out of our own pocket for the shelter.'

Molly stopped and turned back around, 'I just feel...' She cradled her stomach. 'If any of our children were ever in that position, with no parents, I just would hope someone would look out for them.'

For a second, Cam remained silent as Molly's words turned over in his head. This was exactly one of the fears that he'd thought about – his children possibly living a life without him in it. He briefly closed his eyes. It was a thought he prayed wouldn't become reality.

'Are you okay?' asked Molly.

He swallowed and glanced back towards her. 'Any child losing a parent is devastating and vice versa. I'm sure nothing can ever prepare you for it.'

'Oh, Cam, I didn't mean to dredge up painful memories.' Now it was Molly's turn to feel awful. Cam and his previous wife had suffered so many miscarriages and he'd been through so much before he'd met her.

'I am so happy. We have our family, and another baby on the way … and it's a terrible situation for Bree to be left with no one at such an early age, we can agree on that,' replied Cam.

She nodded. 'Bringing a new life into the world makes you think about a lot of things. How will this place manage to stay afloat if the weather is bad? How will we get the wheat from the mill?'

'By thinking positive … just think positive. We have got through the past few winters; this one is no different.'

Thud!

Cam spun round. 'Hey, you little monkey!' he called to a grinning George, who looked chuffed at having hit his dad with the snowball. Turning back to Molly, he continued, 'And with the good reputation of this place, it'll be going for years, long enough for this one to fit into Great-Uncle Ted's baking hat.' Cam swept George up and pulled his bobble hat off his head, twizzling it around in the air.

'Daddy! Give it back.' George was jumping up and down with his arm stretched high, trying to grab the hat.

Placing it back on his head, Cam grinned at him. 'I think it's time for a warm drink.'

'And some of the chocolate bread,' added George, putting his hands together in a prayer-like stance.

'I have no clue what you are talking about...'

But Cam's words petered out as George had taken off over the road. With the door to The Old Bakehouse wide open, he was sitting on the floor tugging at his wellington boots. The second they were off he ran away inside.

'I wonder what he's going to think of the new baby?' asked Cam.

'He'll make a brilliant older brother, I'm sure. I'd always wished for a sibling. At least they'll have each other.'

'And he keeps going on about chocolate bread and I keep saying I've no—'

'Come on, Daddy!' George was standing in the doorway dressed in a neon-green dinosaur onesie with bright pink polka dots. His hands were cupped around his mouth. 'Come on,' he shouted again.

'And for your information the bread tastes absolutely delicious. If I didn't know better, I'd think your reluctance to enter the star baker competition was all a ploy, and you've been perfecting that loaf for days.'

'I really have no clue what either of you are talking about.'

'And that's your story and you are sticking to it but I don't mind because my guess is you're your own worst critic. It's fine, I get it... You didn't want to share your creation until you had it perfect, but if I was the judge, it would be a clear winner, even if I am a little biased as your biggest flag-waver.'

With that, Cam was left standing perplexed as Molly crossed over the road and opened the gate to Bumblebee Cottage.

'I really do not have a clue what you are talking about,' he shouted after her but Molly had knocked on the door of the cottage and was disappearing inside.

Chapter Eight

'**D**ixie, it's only me,' called out Molly.

Hearing a clatter of paws on the red flagstone floor, Molly was greeted by Darling who was running down the hallway at great speed. Scooping the dog up in her arms, Molly plopped a kiss on top of Darling's head. They'd come so far in the last few years and Molly could still remember the very day that she met the Jack Russell. Even as a vet Molly hadn't fancied her chances, as Darling's barking and growling had been far from welcoming. There had been nothing darling about Darling.

'I'm in here,' Dixie's voice echoed down the hallway.

Kicking off her boots, Molly opened the living-room door. 'I'm just checking to see how you're feeling.' She stopped dead in her tracks and looked around the room. 'Dixie, have you been burgled?' She couldn't believe her eyes.

'Don't be daft.'

The room was full of boxes, piles and piles of stuff just everywhere.

'Are you moving house but you've forgotten to mention it?' asked Molly, placing Darling down on the only clutter-free bit of floor she could see. But Darling immediately jumped onto the arm of a chair and in a final leap made it to the window where she sat down and watched.

'The only way I'm leaving this place is in—'

'Don't say that, you are going to live for ever. Let me make us a nice cuppa and you can tell me all about what exactly is going on here.'

Following the hallway, Molly walked through the archway that led into the kitchen, which was a scene of domestic bliss. The log fire was burning, washing draped over the racing green Aga that stood proudly, spreading a lovely warmth into the room. Sitting on the worktop was a humongous home-made Victoria sponge, and numerous pans hung from the ceiling on a wooden rack, alongside bunches of dried lavender. Shelves lined one wall and were crammed with plates and Flora china cups. An old farmhouse table was in the centre of the room and the Belfast sink, positioned under the window, looked out over the magnificent garden.

Dixie's favourite mug was in the sink so Molly quickly rinsed it out.

'Can I have honey in my tea, please … it's good for my health,' Dixie shouted from the living room.

Molly smiled as she opened the pantry door. There were four shelves dedicated to honey alone. 'It's not called Bumblebee Cottage for nothing,' she murmured, taking a jar from the shelf.

A tray in her hands, laden with two mugs of tea and a plate of Dixie's favourite biscuits, Molly returned to the living room. 'And how are you feeling? I thought you would be resting, instead of … exactly what are you doing, Dixie?'

'It's just a cold, an annoying cold, but I'm not letting it get me down.' She was fiddling with some sort of black contraption at the back of the room.

'I can see that,' murmured Molly, dunking a chocolate biscuit in the hot tea and taking a bite.

'I am putting my affairs in order,' said Dixie.

'And those affairs being?' queried Molly, leaning across the coffee table and picking up a box of old photographs.

'Life.'

Molly raised an eyebrow.

'This is my life.' Dixie swooped her arm around the room. 'These are my memories and I thought I'd have one last look through them all. I tell you something, Molly dear, I have had the best life, the best husband, the bestest of best friends and family … though obviously we won't be including those who tried to swindle my cottage from me in the "best family" statement. The less said about those two, the better.'

Molly smiled sadly as she remembered a few years back

when Dixie's own daughter and grandson had forged medical papers declaring Dixie needed full-time care, claiming she was a danger to herself, then they tried to sell the cottage from underneath her. But thanks to Molly, their little plan had been busted.

'And I can't leave this lot to you.'

It dawned on Molly exactly what Dixie was up to. Immediately she swallowed a lump and tears sprang to her eyes.

'Oh, Dixie.'

'Now don't you go all weepy on me. We all know there's only one thing that is certain in life and that is death. It's not morbid, it's fact. I can't have you lot sorting through all this when I'm gone and I've had so much joy looking back through all these.' Dixie searched through an old suitcase of labelled film reels. 'Here it is! Now, if this doesn't bring a smile to your face, nothing will.' She had a glint in her eye. 'Shut those curtains to keep out the light.' Dixie flapped her hand.

As soon as Molly shut the curtains, she sat back and watched as Dixie attached the reel to the black box then wound the film. She pulled down on the handle and there was a whirling sound followed by a burst of light. Molly stared at the wall.

'Oh my, is that...' Molly sat up straight in the chair. 'He just looks like George.' The old film reel played out and there was Cam, approximately age five, stomping around the orchard of Bumblebee Cottage in his bright red wellington boots. 'Very cute,' admitted Molly, smiling at the footage. She watched as his grandfather appeared pushing a wheelbarrow and Cam climbed inside on top of a pile of apples and his grandfather began pushing him through the orchard with Cam singing at the top of his voice.

'Cam would spend all his school holidays here. I loved it,' admitted Dixie. 'Such fond memories, though he wasn't too fond of the beehives!' she said, smiling. 'And that's one of the reasons I have Gabe looking after the hives, instead of Cam.' Dixie pointed to the box of reels. 'There's so many memories in there. My George filmed everything and there's even tapes in there of The Old Bakehouse opening up. George took the film and Ted was so proud.' Dixie's voice faltered. 'So many lovely memories.'

'And there's plenty more to make when this little one comes along.' Molly patted her stomach. 'We haven't found out the sex of the baby – we thought we'd keep it a surprise – but I was going to ask Martha if she could see it in her crystal ball.'

Dixie was chuckling as she drank her honey tea. 'She has got a fifty-fifty chance of getting it right.'

'That's exactly what Cam said. He doesn't believe in any of it, whereas I see it as a little harmless fun and a night out with the girls.'

'I do believe Martha has the gift. Tonight should be interesting. She's got a bee in her bonnet about something so I'm not going to miss it for the world.' Dixie raised an eyebrow.

The old film was still playing and Cam was now collecting eggs from a chicken coop. He was merrily stomping around and seemed so happy. 'And look at his spindly legs,' Molly said, pointing.

'Always in short pants; it didn't matter what the weather was,' said Dixie, taking a chocolate biscuit off the plate on the coffee table. She was just about to bite into it when she stopped and looked over at Molly. 'The girl in your shop, I got the feeling I've seen her before.'

'That's Bree, the girl I was telling you about from the shelter.'

'She had a good aura about her but I have to say I felt a little spooked when I saw her standing behind that counter.'

'Spooked? In what way?'

'I got a feeling of déjà vu and I can't shake it off. She seemed so familiar and I've tried to wrack my brains as to how our paths may have crossed before but I can't quite put my finger on it. It's probably impossible that we have as she's so young,'

'Sixteen and pounding the streets with nowhere to go.'

Molly explained the situation about the phone and Cam's reaction.

'Oh dear. For what it's worth I can see both sides. You want to help someone who is vulnerable and no doubt thought, What if my own children were put in that position? – that's the motherly instinct in us. Men don't think like that. Cam works hard and he just wants to be surrounded by his own family in his own home. This girl has come from nowhere and maybe he feels uneasy about it all, even threatened.'

'But that's daft. She's just a young girl.'

'And where has she come from?'

'All I know is that she lived on the outskirts of Glensheil and her mum passed away. It's so sad.' Molly brought her hand up to her chest. 'I get emotional just thinking about it. Could you imagine being alone in the world at that age?'

Dixie was shaking her head. 'It's not a nice thought at all. But there's definitely something about that girl. She's been on and off my mind since meeting her this morning. So familiar.'

Molly could see that Dixie was still trying to place her, but with no luck.

She took a glance towards the window. 'Stormy weather warnings again. We are in for another bitter night.'

The reel of film stopped whirling and Dixie pulled back the curtains.

Molly's mind was elsewhere; she was thinking about what Dixie had just said and she felt exactly the same. 'Dixie, you know what you've said about Bree?' Molly paused. 'I've been having flashbacks, … and it all started the second I laid eyes on her outside the homeless shelter. Now, the flashbacks are becoming more frequent.'

'Flashbacks? What sort of flashbacks?' questioned Dixie, sitting herself back down on the chair.

'Back to my past, back to the time I was a little girl. It's triggered something in me but I'm not sure what.'

'Good or bad flashbacks?'

'A little bit of both. It's strange. I get a feeling of anxiety but wrapped up with hope. It all sounds so mad. I don't understand it myself.'

Dixie cupped her hands around her mug, listening without interrupting Molly.

'And I do know my emotions are all over the place with this pregnancy. I can burst into tears at a drop of a hat. I keep thinking about Di and Doug. They were just the best adoptive parents – beautiful people inside and out – and they would have loved George so much and the new baby. So that makes me feel sad as I think about them all the time, but these flashbacks take me way, way back.'

'To when?'

'To when I was a very small child – specifically the day the woman came and took me away to my new home. The flashbacks feature my biological mother, which is strange because I really can't remember her. Her face is quite blurry but it's the eyes. There's something about her eyes.'

Molly shut her own eyes. 'On and off over the years I've tried to picture her – you know when you try to force an image in your mind or think of someone's voice? – but there's been nothing for years. But seeing Bree something happened. There was something just familiar about her.' Molly paused and took a sip of her tea. 'In the memory I'm standing in a dingy flat with barely any sunlight filtering through the grimy window. A woman takes my hand, she smiles down at me and as we walk out of the door I look back over my shoulder at my birth mother. It all feels so real. I think it is real.'

'And you never had these memories before you met Bree?' asked Dixie, tentatively.

Molly shook her head. 'I've never had any real

memories of my mother.' She rubbed her stomach distractedly.

'You said you looked back over your shoulder. What happens when you look over your shoulder?' asked Dixie.

Molly swallowed. 'There's a look in my mother's eyes, one of sheer devastation, vulnerability, yet a small smile of hope.' Molly gave herself a little shake. 'It's really hard to explain, but that look in her eyes was the same look I saw in Bree's eyes. For a split second it felt like I was looking at the past, which I know is daft, but there was just something that triggered something in me. I'm really not making any sense now, am I?'

'Have you ever had any contact with your birth mother?' asked Dixie, offering Molly another chocolate biscuit.

Molly shook her head. 'No, and I'm confused how I actually feel about any of it.'

'How do you mean?'

'I'm really not sure what being adopted means to me. This is going to sound so heartless...' Molly could feel the tears welling up her eyes. 'Di and Doug were my world, they were my parents – I've never felt the need to know more about my birth parents even though they gave me life. That sounds so awful, doesn't it?'

'Not at all, it just shows how happy and loved you were.'

'But since giving birth to George and with another baby on the way I suppose I'm beginning to think more about my birth mother. Who exactly was she and why suddenly are these thoughts becoming more frequent? From what I understand, the reason I was taken away from her in the first place was addiction. It's a difficult one really.'

Darling jumped onto Molly's lap and gently nudged her arm. She softly stroked her. 'This one can sense I'm feeling emotional.' She smiled at Darling, who curled up on the arm of the chair. 'I think the pregnancy has generated feelings I've maybe buried. There's Cam's mum in New Zealand, and I know we have you, our fairy godmother and great-grandmother rolled into one, but I sometimes think that George is missing out by not knowing my side of the family. But then, I remember the reasons I was adopted. For all I know, my mother may still be an addict or could have ended up on the streets. If I wasn't adopted that could have been my destiny.'

'But it wasn't. You were adopted by two people who loved you wholeheartedly, and look at you now, such a wonderful woman with a strong family and a successful business, even though I may be a teeny bit biased.' Dixie gave her a warm smile.

'I don't want to see young girls on the streets like Bree, it actually makes me upset just thinking about it.'

'It sounds like these flashbacks have uncovered some things that maybe you have buried within yourself, and now that they are resurfacing, they might need addressing. Have you talked to Cam about it?'

Molly shook her head. 'I don't feel I can at the minute. He's not a fan of Bree and I've got this little niggle in my gut that something is bothering him and he's not talking about it … but maybe I'm wrong.'

'Can I give you a little word of advice?'

Molly nodded as she held Dixie's gaze.

'Talk to him. Don't ever feel like you're walking on eggshells. The second you start keeping things from each other, you are heading down a very slippery slope. It doesn't matter how tired you are, or whether you think he won't understand, what is important to you will be important to him. It's all about compromise and balancing each other's happiness. Over the years, George and I had some right humdingers. Believe it or not, I could be very stubborn at times.' Dixie had a glint in her eye. 'He used to call me feisty but I was just saying it how it was and that's better than dilly-dallying. There were things that we didn't see eye to eye on but we were united against the world and we never kept anything from each other, no matter how big or small. Talking and understanding each other's views is the recipe for a long-standing marriage and we are proof of the pudding.'

Everything Dixie was saying, Molly wholeheartedly agreed with.

'And there's always Ben and Katie at Peony Practice to chat to about these flashbacks. Talking always helps. We don't do enough of that – talking.'

'You're right, I need to explain to Cam what I felt when I first saw Bree and that it's triggered something.'

'You do, and as far as Bree is concerned, listen to what Cam is saying too. He works hard, you're pregnant. And he is right, there are organisations to support Bree. You can support her from afar without bringing the extra pressures into your home. You can't go taking on someone else full-time.'

'I know and I hear you,' Molly agreed.

Dixie leant forward and grabbed the old biscuit tin from the table. Prising back the lid, she gave a smile. 'Have a look at these.' She handed over a pile of photographs.

'Great-Uncle Ted! He looks so young.'

'He was young.'

Molly shuffled through the photographs.

'That one was the very first time he won the baking championship. I can remember it was the first because my George was on tenterhooks about the whole competition, whereas Ted was taking it all in his stride. We all travelled to Edinburgh and I'd sipped a couple of cocktails at the bar before we took our seats. Little did I know George had sneaked in his hipflask … full of whisky, it was.' Dixie gave a chuckle. 'By the time Ted had baked his bread my George was a little worse for wear. I know because he cut Ted's head off the photograph. That was the only one they took. Ted was not pleased.'

Molly laughed as she found the photo showing Ted standing proudly, his trophy held in one hand, in the other his baked loaf. On the front of his apron was a pinned rosette and the beam on his face said it all and like Dixie had just said, the rest of his head was cut off.

'It's that time of year. The invitations to take part in the competition will soon be posted out. Maybe Cam's waiting and wondering whether he will be one of the contestants. Every year Ted got a little on edge waiting to see if he'd been selected.'

'Cam's been invited to bake,' shared Molly.

Dixie gave a shriek, causing Darling to look over and give a tiny woof. 'That is bloody brilliant! And it couldn't happen to a more well-deserving person, even though I may be a tiny bit biased.' Dixie pinched her thumb and forefinger together. 'I can't believe he didn't tell me. How long have you known?'

Instantly, Molly felt guilty. Cam had told her not to tell Dixie and here she was blurting it out when it wasn't even her news to share. The second the words had left her mouth she wished she could take them back but it was too late now. 'A few days, but Dixie, you can't tell him you know.'

But Dixie wasn't listening. 'I just knew it. I knew he was good enough to be selected. You know what this means don't you? It means Cam's already considered one of the top elite bakers in Scotland. He must be overjoyed.' Dixie brought her hands to her chest. 'I'm bursting with pride. I wonder who they sent to the shop to taste the goods. Have there been any strangers in recently?'

'Dixie, the shop is full of tourists most days.'

'Oh yes, silly me, I just wondered if anyone stood out more than normal.'

'Come to think about it...'

Molly remembered a day in late September when she had been updating the blackboard outside the shop. A woman had stepped out of a small convertible sports car while looking at a piece of paper, which she promptly slid inside her bag as she walked into the shop. Her auburn hair fell below her shoulders, her chiselled cheekbones were streaked with blusher and Molly couldn't help but think she didn't look like your typical tourist. She was very businesslike in her in her pinstriped suit and heels. She oozed Baker of the Year judge all over but she wasn't very friendly.

Molly also remembered an elderly gentleman who came into the shop at the same time. He was looking over all the jams and chutneys and sampled the freshly baked produce that was cut up for tasting on the top of the counter. He was in his mid-sixties, dressed in a flat cap, waterproof trousers and green wellington boots. It may have been either of them. 'I'm just not sure,' said Molly, reminiscing aloud to Dixie.

Dixie was still smiling and Molly could see how chuffed to bits she was. She knew that at any second she was going to have to burst Dixie's bubble and tell her that Cam wasn't sharing her enthusiasm. But she couldn't get a word in edgeways as Dixie carried on chattering away. 'In all the time Ted was a baker, we never worked out who they sent into the shop because it wasn't any of the three judges that took part on the day; Ted would have recognised them. But it doesn't matter, because whoever it was thinks Cam's baking is top-notch.' Dixie clapped her hands together. 'You know what this means, don't you? A day out to Edinburgh. Is the competition still held at Crossley Hall Manor? Oh my, the set-up was spectacular, free drinks and a buffet for the family. What is the special element this year?'

'Chocolate,' answered Molly as Dixie continued.

'The studio is transformed into mini kitchens and the families are seated in the VIP area at the front. We were greeted with a glass of champagne, a choir singing Christmas carols and the most humongous Christmas tree that I'd ever set eyes on. What's the date? We need to plan, organise travel—' Dixie stopped mid-sentence noticing that Molly wasn't mirroring her enthusiasm.

Molly had to admit she hadn't thought that far in advance. That was down to Cam's current mood, because at the moment he had no intention of taking part. She was going to have to break this news to Dixie.

'I'm not trying to put a dampener on it all but, Dixie, I mean it when I say you can't say anything to Cam about this because...' She sighed. 'I shouldn't have told you.'

'Why not?' Dixie was looking perplexed.

'I don't want to burst your bubble but Cam has decided not to take part.'

For a second, the smile slid from Dixie's face, then she chuckled. 'You daft thing,' she said, leaning across and swiping her arm. 'You had me there for a moment.'

Molly bit her lip. 'Honestly, Dixie, the invite is on the pinboard in the kitchen. Lately he's been in a funny mood and I can't put my finger on why. I'm not sure whether he thinks he's not good enough. Cam has big shoes to fill and maybe he's worried he won't do Ted proud. Or maybe it's the fact he's so busy with the shop . . . or the fact that I'm pregnant.'

'Poppycock! I don't believe any of that. When Cam took over The Old Bakehouse his enthusiasm was soaring. His ambition was to be as good as his Great-Uncle Ted. He was looking forward to the day that envelope finally dropped through the door.' Dixie was looking despondent.

'Well, something has changed,' said Molly. 'However, today he baked chocolate bread, so maybe he's actually warming to the idea.'

'And with a little encouragement from his friends.' Dixie tipped Molly a wink then gave a fleeting glance towards the door. 'There's two things that are needed in times such as these … sherry and a slice of Victoria sponge.'

Molly laughed. 'I can join you on the Victoria sponge.'

'That's okay, I'll take one for the team and drink your sherry.'

'I thought you were feeling a little under the weather.'

'A couple of sherries will do me good. I'll pour, you go and slice up the cake.'

Molly was up and out of her chair heading towards the kitchen. She heard the clink of the decanter as Dixie poured her sherry. By the time she returned with two plates housing two giant slices of cake, Dixie had cleared all items off the coffee table except for a small shoebox. She tapped the box. 'This might just jolly Cam around.'

'What's in there?' asked Molly, slicing into the cake with a fork. 'This cake tastes delicious, by the way. I really do need to stop shovelling sweet things into my mouth otherwise I'll be giving birth to a sugar lump.'

'How long until the competition?' asked Dixie, sliding the elastic band from around the shoebox.

'A couple of weeks,' replied Molly.

Dixie took a black book out of the box and lay it on the table.

'And what is that?' asked Molly, shuffling to the edge of her chair, looking intrigued.

Dixie tapped the closed book. 'Ted's diary. A written account of the lead-up to his very first competition. From receiving the invite to competing for the title, with all the details of how he went about perfecting his recipe with constant attempts to bake his creation.'

'Oh my, that's amazing.'

'And I think this is just what Cam needs to urge him on. If he has any doubts that he's not good enough, that's exactly how Ted felt, and it's all documented in here.'

'Good idea,' admitted Molly. 'With the weather like it is, the bakery will be quiet and Cam will have lots of time to perfect his recipe.'

Dixie looked out towards the grey sky. 'The worst of the snowstorm is to hit us around three a.m., according to the news. I need Drew to drop off more logs for me before that happens.'

'Cam is hoping the lorry can get through from the mill.'

'It's come early.' Dixie nodded towards the window. 'It's there now. The snow plough has been attempting to clear the roads but by my reckoning the track leading to the bridge will become treacherous.'

Taking the last bite of her cake, Molly tapped the box. 'What else is in there?'

'Photographs that Ted kept from the competitions, The Old Bakehouse, members of staff that have worked there over the years … that sort of thing.'

'And that's exactly what Cam needs. A trusted assistant, an apprentice that he can train and rely on. In fact, that's what I'll do before we go to Isla's tonight. I'll get the advert posted, then at least if there are any suitable candidates, it might ease the pressure on Cam a little.'

'Ted never married, but he had a trusted assistant for over ten years, a slip of a girl who was in her early twenties when she started. Hours they spent in the kitchen at The Old Bakehouse. At first, he had the poor girl constantly baking bread, perfecting her craft. He trained her up so well there was a point when we couldn't tell who'd baked the bread that day.'

'This is exactly what Cam needs. As soon as I get back, I'm posting the advert for an apprentice assistant.'

'Cam will find someone. There's loads of young people out there willing and wanting to learn a craft, and a good baker will always have a job.'

'And there's nothing like waking up to the gorgeous aroma of freshly baked bread. Right, I best get back,' said Molly, standing up and returning the empty plates to the kitchen whilst Dixie sat back in her chair and sipped her sherry. After

Molly loaded up the dishwasher, she walked back into the living room to discover that Dixie had put together a bundle of stuff. She handed over the shoebox to Molly.

'This is Ted's diary, a few private letters, the photographs and some of the footage from the opening of The Old Bakehouse and the baking competitions. We could watch them together, maybe make a night of it. This might spur Cam on to take part.'

'But Cam didn't want me to mention the competition. If I go back with this stuff…'

'You just say I was having a sort-out – that's not a lie – and I felt this should be kept where it belongs at The Old Bakehouse. I know my grandson; he'll get curious and take a look. Ted was once in his shoes as a new baker.'

Molly nodded. 'Shall we go up to the farm together tonight?'

'I've already sorted it. Drew is coming out in the Land Rover; he's going to grab us both and drop us home later.'

'Perfect.'

Dixie walked Molly to the door with Darling hot on their heels. Whilst Molly was pulling on her boots, Dixie looked through the tiny window next to the door. 'Here it comes; the storm is starting.' The sky was dark, the snow beginning to swirl all around.

'Do you want to come and stay with us? It will save you loading up the fire with logs,' asked Molly, slipping her arms inside her coat.

'I'll stay this afternoon, but maybe I could drop Darling

off with Cam whilst we go out tonight? I don't want her to fret on her own.'

'I'm sure he won't mind. Thanks for the chat and the cake. Hopefully I can participate in the sherry very soon. I do love this cottage. There's a certain sense of calm about the place.'

'You try telling that to the new postman. Darling has nearly taken his hand off the last two times he's put the letters through the box.'

'God love her.' Molly looked adoringly towards Darling who was sitting on the hallway rug looking like butter wouldn't melt.

'Molly, can I just say – and I don't want to interfere as I love the bones of you both – but make sure you do talk to each other and listen to each other. There's always a compromise. This young girl, Bree, you can help her if that's what your heart desires – but in a way that is agreeable to you both. Family is everything.'

Molly nodded. 'You are a wise woman,' she replied, winding her scarf around her neck and grabbing the shoebox and bag of videos that Dixie had given her.

'Thank God you left out the "old".' Dixie was chuckling away as she opened the front door and was greeted by a blast of icy wind.

'Don't stand here getting cold,' continued Molly, giving Dixie a kiss on both cheeks. 'I'll see you in a little while.'

Even though it was a short walk to next door, Molly pulled her hat right down over her ears and dipped her chin under the warmth of her scarf.

'Family is everything,' murmured Molly to herself as she hurried down the path and shut the gate behind her, smiling across at the snowmen who were standing tall. After talking to Dixie, she was feeling better. Dixie was right, she needed to talk to Cam about how she was feeling and about the flashbacks. Of course, she wished the incident with Bree hadn't happened this morning, but hopefully Sam would ring her with the news that she'd made it to the shelter and that would put her mind at rest, knowing she wasn't out in the bitter cold all night.

Opening the shop door, she smiled at Cam, who was standing behind the counter looking happy. 'George is bathed, warm and watching a film, his clothes are drying on the Aga, his boots by the fire, and the mill have delivered the wheat early because of the storm.'

'It's definitely on its way; look at the sky,' she replied, taking off her coat and walking over to Cam. 'I don't want us to fight,' she said, hoping that things would get back to normal. She placed the shoebox on the counter along with the bag and looked at Cam.

Even after all this time, she still felt that tingle as he wrapped his arms around her.

'How's Grandmother? And what do you have there?'

'Stuff from Great-Uncle Ted.'

Cam's eyes widened. 'Have you been to the psychic night already? Martha is bloody good if she's passed you items from the dead as well as messages.'

'You daft bugger,' said Molly, swiping his arm. 'Dixie is having a clear-out. These are things that she said belong to

The Old Bakehouse. Great-Uncle Ted's diary, apparently, from when he won his very first competition, along with photographs of this place and former bakery staff. And I'm on a mission to find you the best assistant. I'll load up that job advert now and no arguing.' Molly was going to strike while the iron was hot. Taking a look around the shop, she noticed that most of the bread had miraculously disappeared from the shelves. 'Where is everything?' she asked. 'Have you had a massive surge of customers?' She looked towards the window but there was no one in sight apart from the three snowmen, which were slowly being camouflaged by the falling flakes.

'Drew came over in his four-wheel-drive with Fergus. They've loaded up the boot and are dropping deliveries in the village, so they offered to take the bread and pastries too. Anything that is left they are going to take over to Sam at the shelter. It's easier in their car then attempting to take the van. The track is icy as hell leading to the bridge and I don't fancy either of us skidding into the River Heart.'

'That's one job less to do. He's going to the shelter, you say?'

'Yes, his car will cope with those treacherous conditions. He said he's coming back to pick up you and Dixie later on too.'

'Shall we upload that job vacancy now? I can go and get my laptop.'

Cam nodded. 'Okay, but I'm only giving someone a job if I'm hundred per cent certain they aren't a time-waster.'

'You'll just know when it's the right person, and I'll help

you sift through the application forms. Also, Dixie has suggested a film night so we can watch these old videos together.' Molly pointed to the last slice of chocolate bread. 'I thought George was after that but I'm hoping that slice is saved for me. You are a baking genius; how did you make the swirls and have that thick, gorgeous layer running through the middle? It was pure genius. Definitely the best loaf you've ever baked,' complimented Molly, singing Cam's praises loud and proud. She might be a teeny bit biased but Cam was definitely the best baker in her eyes.

'Film night sounds good, but I have to tell you, I didn't bake that bread.' He was staring straight at her.

Molly laughed. 'You just need to learn to take a compliment.' She nudged him with her elbow and turned to walk away.

'Honestly, Molly. This has nothing to do with me, ask George.'

She hovered in the doorway. She could tell by Cam's face he was telling the truth. 'I know you're willing George to follow in your footsteps but he's a little too young to be baking bread to that standard at the moment.'

'Oh, I agree.'

'What are you trying to tell me? Who baked it then?'

'According to George, it was Bree.'

They stared at each other then back at the slice of loaf that was left. Cam reached up to Great-Uncle's Ted recipe bible and opened it up carefully. 'Great-Uncle Ted baked something similar when he won the competition. Look…' Cam slid the book over towards Molly. 'The round plaited loaf with an element of chocolate, but this…' He pointed to the even layer of chocolate that ran through the middle of the loaf. 'You're right, it is pure genius. The consistency, the plaiting of the bread, the shape, the swirls and the chocolate layer. That layer could actually be flavoured so many different ways. Orange chocolate, milk, white chocolate, you could have a Milky Way layer … absolutely anything.'

Molly walked back over to the counter and stared at the bread. 'Bree baked this? Are you sure?'

Cam was nodding.

'But this looks damn-near perfect. How the hell has she learned to bake like this?'

Cam shrugged. 'I've no idea.'

He still couldn't believe the taste and perfection of the loaf. It had taken him umpteen attempts with the help of celebrity chef and baker Andrew Glossop to even get the consistency right, never mind looking like a loaf. How had Bree done it? 'She's even managed to get the plaiting perfectly symmetrical. That's a skill in itself.'

'I don't want to state the obvious but isn't this exactly what you need for the competition?' Molly could feel the excitement rising in her voice.

Cam was quiet, still looking down at the loaf. 'It is but I'm looking for something a little different. But she's had me thinking, with this layer running through the middle.'

'You've been thinking about an entry?'

'Yes, but Molly, I've made a decision. I've decided not to enter this year.' Cam was not meeting her eye. 'And I know that's not what you want to hear.'

'But—'

Cam put up his hand like an over-zealous traffic warden. Molly knew he didn't want to get into this conversation but she didn't understand why he was so adamant about not entering.

'I don't understand. According to Dixie, you've been hungry for this moment, hoping one day that invite would land on the mat.'

Hearing those words, Cam's eyebrows shot up and Molly knew she'd said the wrong thing.

'You've been talking about me, haven't you? You've told my grandmother I've been invited to compete after I asked you to keep it to ourselves.'

Molly exhaled. 'Sorry, it just slipped out, but she is over the moon. You should have seen her face, Cam. You've done her so proud by even being asked to compete. She was bursting with pride.'

'You had no right to tell her. This is my decision.'

'Why?' Molly threw up her hands. 'Give me a good reason why you don't want to compete and I'll shut up about it. It could open so many new opportunities for you – for us – and the prize money would come in extremely handy. Think of the future.'

'I am thinking of the future.'

Molly was just not understanding. 'How? Please talk to me, help me understand. Bree could help you; she could share this recipe with you.'

'Now you are making it sound like I'm incapable of baking and need a child's help.' Cam's voice rose slightly.

'You know that's not what I'm saying.'

'It doesn't matter. This year's competition has just come at the wrong time.'

'You're making excuses and I don't understand why. This will be brilliant. We can all have a day trip to Edinburgh – I can picture how grand it will look this time of year, surrounded by Christmas trees, at Crossley Hall Manor. We could take George, I'm sure he'd love a day off school, and Dixie would come too—'

'No, Molly,' interrupted Cam. 'The answer is no.'

Cam was not budging an inch. She remembered what Dixie had said to her a little earlier. *Talk to each other.*

'Why exactly not? With the storm coming, we could be holed up in here for days with barely any customers. This would be the ideal time to perfect your recipe. The mill has delivered the wheat. Put it to good use.' Molly had no clue what would stop Cam entering the competition, now that Dixie had convinced her this was what Cam had always wanted. 'We should be getting excited about this, sitting down together, plotting your first recipe just like Great-Uncle Ted!' She pointed to the recipe bible in the shelf. 'Don't you want your own book up on the shelf next to Ted's in years to come and for George to be standing here, looking up at them proudly?'

But Cam still wasn't showing any sort of enthusiasm and Molly noticed his mood had shifted considerably. She didn't say any more and waited for Cam to share the real reason why he wasn't going to enter. His mouth opened then closed.

'Talk to me, please.' Molly didn't know what to think.

'I'm not entering because . . . you don't know what's going to happen in life.'

Molly was puzzled. What an absolutely bizarre thing to say. She was a little lost for words and didn't know what to think or say next.

Luckily, Cam was saved by the bell and they both looked towards the shop door as it opened. Dr Sanders walked in looking like he'd just returned from a hiking exhibition in the artic, wrapped up in numerous layers. He unravelled his scarf and beamed. Molly had no choice but to paint a smile on her face.

'Good afternoon, Ben. Dressed for the occasion, I see,' Cam said with a smile.

'It's chuffing cold out there.' Ben took off his gloves and laid then on the counter as he blew into his hands then rubbed them together. 'The temperature is already in the minus. Thank God, I'm going home to a very warm flat. Any pastries or bread left?' He cast a glance over the counter and pointed to the glass dome. 'Can I take one of those, and those ... oh and put me one of those in.' He looked towards the shelves. 'Bread and jam too. Got to love a good doorstop smothered in jam.'

Molly rang up the total on the till whilst Cam placed everything inside a bag.

As Ben paid and put the items in his rucksack, he turned towards Cam. 'Everything okay?'

The look between them didn't go unnoticed by Molly as the bell above the shop tinkled again. Molly's heart was racing. There had barely been any customers all day, and now, just when she wanted to talk to Cam, The Old Bakehouse was suddenly as busy as Glasgow Central. She watched as Cam touched Ben's arm and nodded towards the door.

'You're okay to serve Ash, aren't you?' asked Cam.

'Of course,' she replied, smiling up at Ash, but keeping one eye on Cam and Ben, who were now in a hushed conversation on the pavement outside the bakery, which Molly found a little odd, since snow was falling heavily. She couldn't hear what they were saying but, by the look of both their faces, it was a conversation she wanted to be privy to. They looked so serious. What was with all the secrecy? Why did they need to step outside? She watched as Ben patted Cam on the back then took off up the road as a nodding Cam stepped back into the shop.

He still looked serious but he seemed to rally himself when he saw Ash and patted him on the back before joining Molly behind the counter.

'Where's my favourite shop assistant?' Ash asked with a grin, placing his heavy bag on the floor. 'Today's round is taking forever by foot. Thankfully, the kind residents of Heartcross keep passing me coffee on the way and I got a lovely hot sausage roll from Bonnie's teashop.'

'I think Ash is hinting at a warm drink,' said Molly, looking towards Cam with a smile. 'And favourite shop assistant...' Molly pointed. 'Do you mean me or him?'

Ash laughed. 'A cup of tea would be brilliant, and neither. I meant Bree, your new shop assistant. I'm assuming she just works mornings? Has she left already today?' Ash was looking a little disappointed.

'Bree? Bree doesn't work here,' replied Cam, his words taking Ash by surprise.

'But I'm sure that's what the girl said her name was. She was standing right there, behind the counter...' Ash was sensing he had put his foot in something, but he wasn't quite sure what. 'I hope I haven't said something wrong; she was really kind to me this morning. A warm drink and a croissant were just what I needed in this weather.'

They all looked towards the window. The snow was heavy outside and didn't look like it was going to let up any time soon.

Ash swallowed, and Molly noticed a tiny blush on his cheeks. 'I popped back in because ... umm... Would you possibly have a number for Bree?' he asked nervously.

Molly smiled. Ash obviously wanted to ask her out on a date. 'She's already left today, but we could possibly pass a message on, if you want to write down your number.' Molly was playing Cupid.

'Would you? That would be brilliant!' Ash sounded excited and Molly pushed a white paper bag and a pen over the counter. 'So, you do know her then? I wasn't sure if she was from here. I hadn't seen her around before.'

'I'm sure we'll see her in the next couple of days,' replied Molly, hoping once again that Sam would ring to say that Bree had made it to the shelter.

'Usually girls my age have attitude but there was something about her,' said Ash, now wearing a lopsided grin as he handed the paper bag back to Molly with his number written on it.

'We'll make sure she gets it,' said Molly, folding up the bag and popping it into her pocket. 'And here, let me get you a hot chocolate. It'll keep you warm on the way home.'

Within a couple of minutes, with a hot chocolate in hand, Ash thanked them both and picked up his bag. 'Oh, and I am sorry about the mix-up with your phone.'

The words hung in the air as both Cam and Molly stared at Ash then at each other.

Molly was the first to speak. 'Mix-up?' she queried. Her heart was beating nineteen to the dozen as she waited for Ash to answer.

'Yesterday morning, I dropped your post off early but realised later on in my round there were still a couple of letters belonging to you, mainly junk. So I popped back. I was texting on the way in, slipped my phone into my bag, and then somehow thought yours was mine when I saw it on the counter. I picked it up and... Anyway, sorry.'

'You took Cam's phone?' said Molly, wanting to hear exactly what Ash had just said again.

'Yes, picked it up by mistake, thinking it was mine. I left you a message on your landline and gave it back to Bree this morning, to give to you. You've got it, haven't you?'

Molly gulped down a breath to stay quiet. Cam had suddenly gone puce and though Molly gave him a sideward glance there was clearly no way he was going to look in her direction.

'You took my phone?'

'Yes, sorry, mate.'

They both watched in silence as Ash left the bakery, his snow boots trudging through the fresh onslaught. Before Cam could say a word, Molly hot-footed it towards the landline, dialled in to the answerphone and there it was, Ash's voicemail. She held the receiver up in the air even though Cam couldn't hear the message. 'Ash is telling the truth,' she said, stating the obvious.

'How was I supposed to know? It was you who said that no one had been into the shop. You didn't even hear Ash come in. Anything could have been taken,' Cam said defensively.

Molly knew the best form of defence was attack and Cam's accusing tone was causing her annoyance to grow tenfold.

She threw her arms up into the air. 'So it's all my fault now, is it?'

'If you had heard Ash come into the shop then none of this would have happened.'

'You didn't even give the poor girl a chance to explain. If you did, we would have known it was Ash who took your phone.' Molly flashed him a dark look, annoyed. More than annoyed, actually. She picked up the phone and began to dial another number.

'Who are you phoning now?'

'Sam. There's a young girl out there in the freezing cold, no doubt upset about being accused of something she didn't do.' Molly was shaking her head in despair. 'I'm just hoping she's somehow made it to the shelter.'

After three rings Sam picked up the phone. Molly was straight to the point. 'Sam, it's Molly. Has Bree by any chance made it in yet?' She closed her eyes briefly, hoping the next word she was going to hear was 'yes'.

'No, I'm sorry, she hasn't,' replied Sam.

'She didn't take the phone, Sam. It was a misunderstanding. Ash – the new postman – had picked it up by mistake thinking it was his.'

Disheartened, Molly hung up the phone and walked over to the window. The last time she'd seen a snowstorm like this was more than a few years ago. No one in their right mind would brave these conditions. She turned back around to Cam. 'What have you done?'

'What do you mean, what have I done?' As soon as the question left his mouth, Cam knew he was about to get it from both barrels.

Molly's voice rose and she could feel her pulse thumping in the side of her head. She'd had every intention of returning from Dixie's and talking to Cam about everything in a calm manner but now all she could see was red mist. 'You didn't give her a chance to explain. You were adamant she took that phone and if you'd given her a chance to speak, she would have explained everything and we could have got her over to the new shelter.'

'There was no way we would have got her to the new shelter. You would have come up with another reason why she should stay the night.'

Still staring at Cam, Molly exhaled. 'You haven't even said sorry.'

'This is getting us nowhere. Ever since you've come across this girl, we've done nothing but argue.'

'Is that all you can say?'

'Okay, I'm sorry. It just didn't feel right to me, suddenly this girl turns up—'

'She has a name,' interrupted Molly.

'Suddenly Bree turns up and my phone goes missing. That phone is my life, it has all my contacts and appointments.'

'And it will all be backed up to the cloud,' Molly pointed out. 'It's not a huge deal, but what is a huge deal is there's a vulnerable girl out there in need of warmth and food.'

'Okay, I'm sorry, I should have listened, there's no point standing here screaming at each other, so what do you want me to do?'

'Go and find her, and tell her you are sorry,' blurted Molly.

Cam looked towards the window.

'And don't let the weather put you off, some people have to sleep in shop doorways in this.'

Without another word, Cam untied his apron and handed it to Molly before pulling on his coat. Picking up his van keys, he walked towards the door then looked over his shoulder. 'What do I do if I do find her?'

'Either take her to the shelter or bring her back here. I'll leave that one with you. As long as she's safe.'

As the door shut behind him, George ran into the bakery and wrapped his arms around Molly's legs. 'Where's Daddy going?' he asked.

'He's just got to nip out for a while.' Molly didn't elaborate further.

She watched as Cam started the engine before scraping the snow and ice off the windows. A moment later he was sat behind the wheel but the van was going nowhere fast. The engine cut, and the door slammed as Cam started out on foot, striding across the green, his boots sinking deep in the snow as he walked. He started waving his arms in the air, fighting the snowflakes as the blustery winds carried him across the blanket of snow.

Molly squinted. Drew's four-wheel-drive was at the side of the road with the engine running. The swirling snow obscured Molly's view but she watched as Cam climbed in the passenger side and the four-wheel-drive pulled off and slowly drove away.

Her heart was racing. It was going to start to get dark very soon and the temperature was already dropping. She hoped they could find Bree and get her into the warmth but she knew it would be like trying to find a needle in a haystack. If Bree couldn't get to a shelter Molly couldn't stand the thought of her huddled in a doorway trying to fend off the perishing weather. She knew Bree would be in for a very bleak night.

'Mummy, I'm hungry, is there any more of that chocolate bread?' George was staring at the last slice.

'You go into the living room and I'll bring it in to you.'

George zoomed towards the living room like a fighter jet with his arms stretched out wide. Molly draped Cam's apron on the counter and switched the sign to CLOSED before placing the last of the chocolate bread on the plate. George was lying in front of the warm fire, his legs waggling in the air as he pushed his cars around the rug. She placed the plate on the table, sank into her favourite armchair and picked up her laptop.

Whilst waiting for any news, Molly propped her feet up on to the coffee table and balanced her laptop on her knees. She'd had great intentions of talking with Cam when she returned from Dixie's but that hadn't quite gone to plan. George was chattering away but Molly was lost in her own thoughts. She knew that there was more to Bree than met the eye. That talent she had had gotten Molly's thoughts tumbling all over each other as she stared at the job application note Cam had come up with for her to type. Why couldn't Bree apply for this job? Surely Cam couldn't object now that he knew Bree hadn't stolen the phone. This would be perfect for her – a chance, a new beginning. Molly knew an apprentice wage wasn't going to fund a house on Millionaires' Row but Bree could start to save for a deposit on a flat. A little excited by the prospect, Molly placed the notepaper with the job description back on the table alongside her laptop.

Resting her head back on the chair she closed her eyes for a moment. Talking to Dixie about the flashbacks had lifted a weight off her shoulders, but her thoughts were turning more towards her biological mother. Molly knew she must be around forty-five years of age, but where did she end up? Was she still with Molly's father? The funny thing was, no matter how hard she tried, Molly couldn't picture his face at all, yet she could see a darkened figure with his fist raised in the air and her mother crouching down. She hoped her mother had escaped his clutches but her memories were distorted. Being so young, Molly couldn't know for sure then what was real and what wasn't. She thought for a second about what it would mean to search for her mother. What could that bring to her life? Molly knew her romantic notion of them falling into each other's arms and living happily ever after was probably far from reality, and not knowing was probably easier to live with than knowing.

It only seemed like minutes since she'd closed her eyes when, hearing a door slam, Molly sat up straight and glanced at the clock. She'd been asleep for nearly two hours. She couldn't believe it. George was no longer on the rug but snuggled up on the settee, with his teddy-bear and a family picture that he'd drawn. Molly had to smile; he'd drawn her as a stick person with a round circle for her tummy and inside the circle was another face with a smile. That picture was going to have pride of place on the front of the fridge. Just at that second, a gust of wind rushed down the chimney. The log flames were no longer dancing. Damn, the fire had nearly been extinguished. And, judging by the rattling of the old timber-framed window, the TV reports had been correct: they were indeed in for a night of more snowstorms.

The news was blaring out from the TV and Molly watched for a second as it showed a coach that had been turned over by the blizzard and had fallen a distance from the road, down the side of a mountain, with the passengers trapped inside. Molly shivered; it must have been terrifying. She was grateful to be sitting in the comfort of her own home and had no intention of venturing anywhere. Then she thought of Bree. Hearing the thud of his boots, she realised Cam was back. Quickly pushing herself up and off the chair, she hurried into the bakery to find Cam peeling the sodden coat from his back. She stood in the doorway waiting for him to speak as he pulled the hat from his head, his hair springing in every direction.

Cam turned around. His cheeks were crimson from the biting cold and he looked frozen to the core. 'There's not much point baking too much tomorrow, with the weather like this. It's unlikely anyone is going to venture out.' He pulled his phone out of his pocket and hung up his coat up. 'It's already minus four out there.'

Molly knew how bad it was out there. She'd just seen it on the news.

'And…' She didn't want to know about tomorrow, she was desperate to hear about the here and now. 'Did you find Bree?'

Cam looked down and regretfully shook his head.

'How hard did you try?' There was an urgency to Molly's voice.

Cam stared straight at her. 'Bloody hard. I can't even feel my feet, and my body is numb to the core.'

'It's not good enough. You have to go back out and find her.' Molly pointed to the window, the light from the lamppost outside The Old Bakehouse revealing how brutal it was outside.

'I've looked for hours, it's dark and I'm lucky to even have got home in one piece as they've temporarily shut the bridge.'

'They've shut the bridge?' Molly repeated.

'Unfortunately, yes, and I had to abandon the van before I'd even set off. Drew was over the road and helped me search.'

'Did you check whether Bree had made it to the shelter?'

'Yes. She hasn't.'

Molly fell silent and walked to the window, where there was no majestic scenery, no mountainous terrain or the woodlands of Primrose Park to be seen. It was just dark, foggy, eerie, with a blizzard swirling all around. She continued to stare out of the window and exhaled. She could feel the worry and anger once again rising inside her. With tears of frustration now blinding her eyes Molly knew she was spoiling for a fight but she couldn't help it.

'Well? Have you got any other suggestions of what we can do to find her?'

'I've done all I can. Hopefully, she's safe somewhere. I'm sure she would have located a place to stay as soon as she left here.'

But Molly wasn't convinced. All she could do was visualise a small frightened teenager huddled in a shop doorway, shivering with the cold, and once more she was transported back in time, huddled in the corner of a dingy flat whist her parents argued, her hands clamped over her ears trying to block out the row. She inhaled deeply as she noticed Cam walking towards the door.

'Where are you going? We need to know she's safe.'

'Molly, there is nothing more I can do. We have searched every inch of the village and now the bridge is shut.'

'We can't just do nothing.' Molly could feel the panic rising inside her.

'Look, we can't get back across the bridge until it's deemed safe, but...' He pulled out his phone from his pocket. 'We have a lot of customers and businesses both sides of the bridge. I could message the different WhatsApp groups I'm in and ask them to check their properties and outbuildings?'

Molly felt her fast-beating heart calm a little. 'Thank you, that would make me feel a little better.'

Instinctively she extended her arms for a hug she but she noticed Cam hesitate.

'I don't like it when we argue but I am worried sick.'

'I know and I am sorry,' he replied, finally pulling her in close.

'Did you just hesitate to hug me?' she asked, a feeling of uncertainty hitting her.

Cam didn't answer.

'You did, didn't you? We need to talk about this. What is going on with you?'

'I'm sorry, not now,' he replied, his voice barely a whisper.

He kissed the top of her head and let go of her. Molly

could have sworn he had tears in his eyes as he headed towards the hallway.

Standing there, Molly felt rejected. He'd actually hesitated to hug her. Feeling her heart beat faster, her anxiety increased. They used to grab any moment to be wrapped up in each other's arms.

'You don't find me attractive anymore, do you?' Molly heard her voice crack. 'It's because I'm pregnant, isn't it, and put on all this weight?' she blurted before she could stop herself.

Cam stopped and turned back around. 'Don't be silly, I love the fact you're pregnant. I'm just exhausted, cold and in need of a warm drink.' He turned back towards her and enveloped her in his arms. 'I love you and don't you ever forget that.' He held on for longer than normal and Molly was sure she felt him shaking.

'I won't,' she replied. 'How about you wait up for me tonight, if the bakery isn't going to be such an early morning tomorrow?'

'We'll see,' he replied, popping a kiss on the top of her head.

His words preyed on her mind. They were the same words she would say to George when she knew the answer was no.

'Are you still going to Isla's? You can't walk in this weather and the van won't get you there.'

'Drew is picking us up in the four-wheel drive.'

'Okay, try and enjoy yourself. If there's any news of Bree, I will let you know.'

Bewildered, she watched Cam walk away down the hallway. He kicked off his boots and slipped his feet inside his slippers, and she heard George's excited voice filter out from the living room as Cam pushed the door open.

There was something different about the way he'd just hugged her but Molly couldn't put her finger on it, and she couldn't work out whether it was because of guilt … or fear.

Chapter Nine

All the way to Foxglove Farm, Molly had mulled over the way Cam had hugged her. She couldn't get it out of her mind and had an uneasy feeling in the pit of her stomach, but as soon as Isla swung open the front door to the farmhouse with her usual welcoming smile Molly tried to push that feeling to the back of her mind.

'Look at you, every time I see you that baby gets bigger,' exclaimed Isla, taking a step forward and admiring Molly's round stomach.

'Believe me, it has,' Molly replied, hanging her coat on one of the hooks in the hallway.

Hearing Aggie and Rona's laughter filtering from the living room, Dixie was determined not to miss out on the fun and soon joined them, leaving Molly and Isla standing in the hallway.

'I'm not sure it's all baby. Honestly, I'm expanding by

the hour. I can't stop eating, I'm like a human hoover,' said Molly, patting her stomach and smiling.

'Make the most of it whilst you can. But I have to say, you look like you have the weight of the world on your shoulders.'

'Nothing gets past you, does it?'

Surprised, Isla narrowed her eyes. 'What's up?'

Molly didn't want to go into the ins and outs of the phone saga, Bree, and the fact she was worried something was bothering Cam. She just wanted a change of scenery and to try enjoy the night so she shrugged. 'Ignore me, I think my baby blues have arrived before the baby.'

Isla enveloped Molly in a hug. 'I can remember it was the same with my pregnancies; I was an emotional wreck. I cried at absolutely everything and still do.' She squeezed Molly's arm. 'Us women have to put up with so much, so it's a good job we all look out for each other. Come on, let's get you a drink. I've got some of that flavoured water you like, or there's a pot of tea on the go. Not long until you can drink again.'

Molly followed Isla into the living room. Despite the weather, everyone seemed in good spirits. Allie was sitting next to Felicity and enjoying a glass of wine, whilst Dixie had squeezed onto the sofa next to Aggie and Rona and the three of them were chatting about Martha, who appeared dramatically in the doorway, causing Molly to chuckle as she slipped into the spare chair next to Allie.

Martha was barely recognisable as Isla's grandmother and Molly was taken in by her appearance. Her hands were wrapped in fingerless gloves, her wrists laced with bangles and her bony fingers stacked with silver rings. Draped around her shoulders was a black shawl and from her tiny waist hung a black skirt covered in gold crescent moons. There was no denying she played the part well.

'She really does take this seriously,' whispered Molly to Allie.

'You better believe it,' replied Allie.

'Remember that whatever I tell you tonight, you are in charge of your own destiny and the future *can* be changed,' spouted Martha, casting an eye around the room.

'Doesn't that mean you can just make up what you want?' Drew shouted from the kitchen, causing everyone to laugh. 'What's going to happen is Martha will set the cat amongst the pigeons by planting a seed in your head and all hell will break loose,' he continued.

Martha's eyebrows shot up and she waggled her finger towards the kitchen. 'Don't listen to him. There is something brewing in this village, I can feel it in my water.'

'That's just our age,' chipped in Aggie with a chuckle. 'I've had to cut down on my cups of tea. Honestly, I could spend all day going to the toilet.'

'Decide amongst yourselves who is first up and I'll be in there waiting.' Martha gestured towards the snug then promptly disappeared into the other room.

Drew was now standing in the doorway. 'Absolutely not me,' he chipped in again. 'It's all a load of nonsense. '

'Don't let Gran hear you say that; she takes her psychic powers very seriously and she's made good money out of this over the years. She's travelled with the circus, at one time had her own hut in some seaside town, and now she's even thinking of making it a permanent thing, setting up in one of the vintage vans. There's no denying that more often than not her predictions have come true.'

Drew looked horrified at the idea of Martha setting up shop in one of the vans. 'That is not happening. But she would already know that as she can predict the future.'

Everyone laughed. Then Martha's voice could be heard bellowing out from the snug, 'You non-believers get on your way.'

Drew was grinning as he held his hands up. 'You ladies have a lovely evening.' He turned and kissed Isla on the cheek. 'The kids are in bed and I'm going to watch the TV upstairs. Let me know when you need me to take your friends home,' he said, before disappearing upstairs.

Dixie stood up. 'I'll go first.'

Molly watched as Dixie disappeared towards the snug.

'So, what has Martha predicted that has come true?' Molly asked curiously.

'What *hasn't* she predicted is the better question,' replied Isla, pouring a glass of wine and taking a handful of peanuts from the bowl on the table. 'Honestly, everything and anything. I swear it's not an act. Whether she is actually a psychic or her hunches are just spot-on, there's never a dull moment. It was only this morning she mentioned over breakfast that Sam was going to be faced with some sort of trouble and look what happened to the shelter.' Isla raised her eyebrow. 'She knows stuff and I've no idea how.'

'You're winding me up, aren't you?' Molly looked around the room to see Aggie and Rona nodding.

'I'm absolutely not,' added Isla. 'And half an hour later the phone rings out – it's Sam, asking for help.'

'Wow,' replied Molly, listening as each of the women sitting in the room told a different story about Martha and her powers. Though she had walked past places on seafronts enticing you inside, Molly had never had her fortune told because it had never been high on her to-do list.

'I remember a time – I must have been in my early twenties – Martha predicted my boyfriend at the time was not to be trusted.' Aggie was looking towards Molly. 'And she was right, he couldn't be trusted. One Friday night, he told me he had family plans and so we had a girls' night in the Grouse and Haggis. The landlady at the time had organised a card reader to turn up but she failed to show, leaving a lot of disgruntled people without a fortune teller, and that's when Martha stepped in. We couldn't believe it – we thought it was joke – but she was incredible, a huge hit. And that's when, during my reading, she told me my boyfriend wasn't at a family party. I had a bee in my bonnet all evening and rounded up the girls and headed over to a dance in the town ... and there he was ... kissing Elaine Jones, who'd been round the block more times than the ice-cream van!'

Allie and Molly burst into laughter.

'Oh gosh, I'm not sure I want to go in there now. What if

Martha tells me something I don't want to hear?' exclaimed Molly.

'You are in charge of your own destiny and your future can be changed,' the room chorused, leaving Molly chuckling.

'Martha also predicted I was going to have a son when I was under the impression that I couldn't have children and she even predicted his name would begin with F and that's exactly what happened. Against the odds, Fergus was born.' Aggie gave Molly a knowing look.

'Who is next up?' asked Isla, looking around the room.

'Go on, I'll go next. Let me get it over and done with,' volunteered Molly, looking towards the door as Dixie walked back into the room.

Molly stood up and placed her drink on the table then smiled at Dixie.

'And how did that go?' asked Aggie before Molly had the chance.

Molly hovered in the doorway and watched Dixie as she sat down on the settee and took a huge swig of her drink.

'That was a strange one,' admitted Dixie, looking around the room and holding Molly's gaze.

'Don't leave us in suspense,' urged Rona, giving her friend a nudge. 'Let me guess, Martha has found out the winning lottery numbers and you're going to share the winnings?'

'Apparently, a scandal from the past is going to change my family's life.' Once more Dixie looked towards Molly and gave a little shrug. 'I know I've enjoyed life to the max but I've never been involved in any sort of scandal. Always kept my nose clean... It's certainly intriguing ... Let's see what unfolds.'

'Yikes,' replied Molly. 'I'm worried about going in there now.'

'It's not set in stone, just take anything she says with a pinch of salt,' reassured Isla, giving Molly a look of encouragement. 'It's just a bit of fun, not a game-changer.'

As Molly turned and pushed the door open to the snug she felt apprehensive about what Martha would say. But there was only one way to find out her fortune.

As she stepped inside, she parted a curtain to reveal Mystic Martha sitting in dimmed lighting behind a small oak table, running her hands over a crystal ball. Martha was taking this absolutely seriously and didn't look up but gestured towards a bowl which had one five-pound note. Molly quickly rummaged in her pocket and added to the pile before sitting down in front of Martha. She could feel her heart racing and her throat was dry as she swallowed. She sat in silence as Martha rolled her hands over the crystal ball, looking up briefly before gazing down at the ball again with deep concentration.

'Don't tell me, there's a new arrival on the cards,' joked Molly, trying to lighten the mood a little.

Martha looked up and arched an eyebrow. 'Oh there's definitely that all right,' she replied. Her voice was low and eerie, making the hairs stand up on the back of Molly's neck.

'Just remember you are in charge of your own destiny and your future is not set in stone.'

Molly was mesmerised, her gaze not leaving Martha, and for a split second she could have sworn she noticed a fleeting look of worry flicker across the older woman's face. 'What is it? What can you see?'

'Health issues,' replied Martha. Molly immediately cradled her stomach.

'Huge changes ahead. I can see a death, a letter and new beginnings.'

Molly was puzzled. 'A death? And new beginnings in what way, the baby?' Her voice was jittery.

Martha's eyes were drifting in and out of focus. 'I see a small girl standing in a dark room.'

Molly swallowed, her thoughts immediately taking her back to her childhood.

'She's being led away. There are bright colours, happier times. Does this sound familiar to you?'

'That was me, Martha, that was me.' The words left Molly's mouth before she could stop them.

Martha looked up and met Molly's eyes. 'I can see a ring of secrets.'

'What secrets? Who has secrets?'

'That, dear, I cannot see. However, I can see a scandal, arguments, upset, a niggle that you can't let go of. My advice is don't give up on that niggle. It's going to make the future brighter for another child and your life a whole load easier. Family is everything.'

Feeling confused, Molly stroked her stomach. Martha was talking in riddles. What the hell did any of it mean?

'Don't go to bed on an argument. Talking is the key. You will get through this.'

All Molly could think was, get through what? 'But you said health issues. Is there something wrong with my baby?'

Martha looked up and smiled. 'Your baby girl is just fine.'

'A girl, you're predicting a girl?' Molly had brought her hands up to her chest and gave a tiny gasp.

Martha gave Molly a knowing smile. 'It's a girl and…' Martha concentrated on the crystal ball. 'Her name will begin with L … and that's all I have for you,' she said, standing up and disappearing out of another door behind her, leaving Molly sitting there, perplexed.

She wasn't sure what to think or whether she should take any of it seriously. Leaving the room, she parted the beaded curtain that hung in the doorway and blinked. She hadn't realised how dim the lights had been in the snug until she stepped back into the living room. All eyes were on her.

'Anything to report?' asked Allie, patting the empty chair next to her.

'No, just the usual – there's going to be a new arrival, etcetera.' Molly looked around the room and smiled. She knew Martha's words were worrying her a little but was that daft? 'However…' She looked down at her stomach. 'Martha has predicted a girl.'

There was a loud whoop around the living room and Dixie clapped her hands.

'A girl, we are having a girl.'

'Martha has a fifty-fifty chance of getting this right,' said Rona.

'We need to think of names,' Dixie added excitedly.

'Let's not get carried away,' said Molly, smiling at Dixie's enthusiasm. Martha's words were turning over in her mind. The baby's name begins with "L". She picked her drink up from the table and took a sip as Felicity stood up. It was her turn next.

'There's absolutely nothing going on in my life whatsoever, so this should be quick,' shared Felicity, as she walked through the door.

Molly watched Dixie brimming with excitement while she chatted with Rona and Aggie. 'A girl, I can't believe it. It's always been boys in our family. My George would be so chuffed.'

But Dixie's words were washing over her because there was one thing that Molly couldn't get out of her mind. Secrets and scandals. She thought about the flashbacks of her mum. What did all that mean? Then she thought of Cam. From the outset of their relationship, she knew she'd had a confidence-boosting effect on Cam, encouraging him to believe in himself and reopen The Old Bakehouse when he thought he wasn't good enough to step into his great-uncle's shoes. Cam described her as his rock and Molly was always praising his work ethic, his dedication to learning how to bake bread perfectly. Yet she could sense there was something wrong and for a split second it had crossed her mind to question whether Cam was truly happy. She gave herself a shake. Of course he was happy, they were about to have another baby! It was his suggestion they expand their family and the excitement on his face when the pregnancy test confirmed she was indeed carrying their second child was infectious. He'd literally picked her up and spun her around. So why was she feeling like he was holding something back?

Feeling a wrench in her stomach, Molly looked at her watch. There was no way she could make a move to go home just yet as they'd been there less than an hour.

'Penny for them?' Isla slid in the chair next to her. 'You don't seem your usual self.'

'I'm okay,' replied Molly, not wanting to bring any attention to herself.

'I'm not convinced. Was it something that my grandmother said? Honestly, you have to take what she says with a pinch of salt.'

Molly looked towards the window. 'It's just been one of those days and I'm shattered.'

'As long as that's all it is. Just remember that I'm always here with a shoulder or two to cry on. A problem shared and all that,' said Isla, gently bumping her shoulder against Molly's.

'I know, thank you.'

Hearing her phone beep, Molly quickly rummaged in her bag. She saw it was a message from Sam and her mood slumped a little further when she read the text. Bree had not made it to the shelter and she had not been in touch. All Molly could do was hope she was somewhere warm and dry.

As Felicity returned to the room with a grin on her face, Molly dropped her phone back into her bag. 'I have the winning lottery numbers but as I'm going to run off with a multi-millionaire and am moving to the Maldives, I need to go and pack my case and say farewell to you all.' She bounced back on to the chair looking pleased with herself.

Aggie looked horrified. 'Are you serious?'

'Of course not, Aggie! Your son doesn't get rid of me that easily. He's been trying for years and hasn't been successful so far.'

Everyone laughed.

'Me and Fergus are together for ever. In fact –' Felicity looked around the room '– I think us youngsters have all been lucky in love.'

'Unlike us oldies,' Martha said as she appeared in the doorway. 'Tinder at my age ... be careful what you swipe for, is all I can say!' She chuckled.

'Surely the crystal ball can predict whether you are going to find the love of your life,' mused Allie.

'I'm sure it can, but I'm all about the mystery. Now who's next?'

Allie disappeared into the snug after Martha, and seconds later Drew appeared in the doorway.

'Are you hoping for a turn? Allie's just gone in but we don't mind if you're up next,' said Isla.

'I think I'll give that a miss . . . though Mystic Martha's powers may be needed. It seems a body has been found.'

Drew had everyone's full attention.

'Where? Who?' questioned Isla as the room fell silent.

'The news just came in and it's splashed all across the TV. The body has been discovered up the mountain pass. Just a few hundred yards from the hut we used to knock about in when we were kids. The only information they've released is that they don't think it's suspicious, and it's possibly weather-related. However, Sam is helping the police with their enquiries.'

'Sam from the shelter?' asked Dixie, looking at Molly.

'Yes,' replied Drew. 'They had to reopen the bridge to let the police and ambulance vehicles through. They've cordoned off the top of Love Heart Lane, right by the teashop.' Drew looked at Rona.

'Do they think it's a homeless person then, if Sam is helping them with their enquiries?' asked Molly. Her heart was pounding. All she could think about was Bree alone in the cold.

'One can only assume. Ladies, I know you've been looking forward to tonight and I don't want to be a party pooper but this weather is beginning to worry me. There's power down in Glensheil, Andrew and Grace have already lost a couple of roofs on some of the old out buildings up at the castle and the temperature is going to be at an all-time low. I'd like to get you all home safely and then get back here to my own family.'

Isla switched on the TV. Aidy Redfern, the local reporter,

was standing outside Bonnie's teashop, fighting against the blizzard and gripping his microphone with both hands. They all watched in silence as the news report played out. Along the bottom of the screen flashed a red caption with the words 'BODY FOUND'.

'It could be someone we know,' said Felicity, to find she was hushed by the others as they listened to the report.

'Over a week ago, the first flurries of snow transformed the Scottish Highlands into a winter wonderland. But now, as the snow continues to fall, we are being told to stay indoors and not to travel unless absolutely necessary as we are in for several more days of blizzards and sub-zero temperatures. With many homes and businesses already buried under several feet of snow, we are urging you to check up on friends and family. Gritters are struggling to clear roads, which has led to an increase in accidents, and as schools continue to stay closed authorities are urging residents to please stay indoors.' Aidy was joined then by a police officer who confirmed that a body had been discovered and that there were no suspicious circumstances, just a strong possibility that the victim had been caught out by extreme weather conditions.

'Drew is right, we should never have come tonight,' continued Felicity. 'We should know by now that winter in the Scottish Highlands can be brutal at times.'

Molly was oblivious to the conversations happening all around her. Why the hell hadn't she gone after Bree the moment she left?

A feeling of nausea swept through her entire body. Was

that Bree lying on the side of the mountain? Was she heading to the hut because she had nowhere else to go, and had she found herself caught out by the strength of the blizzard?

Taking deep breaths, Molly stood up and excused herself as she hurried to the downstairs toilet. Quickly closing the door behind her, she leant against it, feeling dizzy and replaying in her mind the moment this morning when Bree had walked out of The Old Bakehouse. She was never going to forgive herself or Cam if that was her body found on the mountain track. Unable to stop herself, she vomited. Taking shaky breaths, she rinsed her face and then stood up and looked at her reflection in the mirror. She blinked back the tears and briefly shut her eyes as she continued to pray it wasn't Bree.

Hearing a knock on the door, Molly quickly patted her face with a towel and opened the door to find Isla standing on the other side. 'You okay? I'm not prying, I'm just getting everyone's coats and you sounded like…'

'I've just been sick. Morning sickness still gets me from time to time, even when it's not morning. I just need a good night's sleep.'

'You aren't worried about anything that Martha has said to you, are you?' asked Isla tentatively.

'Of course not,' replied Molly, telling a little white lie. 'After all, my destiny is in my own hands.' She smiled.

'Unlike that poor bugger they've just found on the mountain. We probably should have postponed tonight. Let's get you home safe. Drew and Dixie are already in the car.' Isla handed Molly her coat and gave her friend a hug. 'I'll message you in the morning.'

Fifteen minutes later, Dixie was safely back inside Bumblebee Cottage after grabbing Darling from The Old Bakehouse. Molly didn't shout out to Cam but instead slowly took off her coat and kicked off her boots before opening the living-room door. Cam was lying across the settee laughing at a comedy sketch on the TV. On the table beside him was a half-drunk beer.

He looked up and smiled. 'You're back early.' He stretched and swung his legs to the floor. 'Why are you back early? You look kind of green.'

'A body has been found,' Molly blurted out, sitting down on the chair opposite him.

'What do you mean?'

'Exactly that. Up on the mountain pass. It looks like a person was taking the track to the hillside hut to shield from this weather. Sam is helping the police with their enquiries as they think it was a homeless person looking for shelter. It's been all over the news.'

Cam paled. Molly had his full attention as he turned down the volume on the TV. 'Man or woman?'

'They haven't released that information...' Molly's voice quivered. 'What if it's Bree?' Tears slowly rolled down her cheek.

Cam stretched his arms towards her and attempted to pull Molly in for a hug but she resisted.

'This is because of you. That poor girl died on the hillside because you drove her out of here into those hideous weather conditions.' Molly pointed towards the window.

'Let's try and stay calm. We don't know that it's Bree. It could be anyone ... a hiker, maybe, who'd gotten into trouble.' Cam knew he was clutching at straws but he could see the anger in Molly's eyes and was trying his best to calm the situation.

'Stay calm. How can I stay calm when a body has been found? We need to do something. I can't just sit here and wait for news.'

'You have no choice; you can't go out in this. We've been advised to stay indoors.'

Molly was shaking her head as she reached for the remote control and flicked over to the news channel. 'We need to ring the police and tell them what happened.'

'And what is that going to achieve?' Cam gave her a long-suffering look. 'Try not to overthink it until we know more details. Molly, there isn't anything we can do right at this moment. I'll make some tea.'

'I don't want tea. Why would I want tea? Do you not feel guilty at all? Is there not a part of you thinking, if I had listened to that poor girl this morning none of this would be happening?' Molly barely paused for breath as she continued. 'There isn't a hiker mad enough to attempt conditions like those on the mountain in the dark. It must be someone who was desperate to find shelter, and if Sam is helping the police with their enquiries they must know who it is, but just haven't released the details yet.'

'We don't know that. Let's just wait until we have more information.' Cam was trying to be the voice of reason but Molly wasn't having any of it.

'This is your fault.'

There was an awkward pause as Molly tried to get her thoughts in order.

'Let me get you a cup of tea.'

'I don't want bloody tea.' Molly's voice rose an octave.

'Well, I bloody do.' Cam stood up and walked into the kitchen. He exhaled and looked out of the window into the pitch black night. He could see the flakes right in front of the window and hear the wind whistling. According to the news, this blizzard was the worst they'd seen in a few years. After making a pot of tea, he returned to the living room.

Before he had a chance to sit down, Molly continued. 'I want to turn back time to this morning when there was a sixteen-year-old girl here baking bread and looking after our son with a smile on her face.'

Cam didn't say anything as he watched the same news report play out on a loop. The report hadn't confirmed if the body was male or female, or the age of the deceased.

'We need to just sit and wait for news.' Cam offered his arms for a hug but again Molly rejected him and picked up a mug of tea, her hands visibly shaking.

'Please, Molly, come and sit next to me,' Cam said, trying to extend the olive branch again.

Molly didn't answer. She desperately needed to know who they'd found on the mountain and thought about ringing Sam. But it was getting late and Sam was helping the police with their enquires. It pained her to think that all she could do was sit and wait for news to filter through.

Cam sat back in the chair. He didn't know what to do or say. The tension in the room wasn't going to be easy to lift but Cam knew he had to try. 'Why don't you go and try and get some sleep and I'll wait up to see if there is any more news. There's no point us both sitting here.'

'I don't think I can sleep until I know...' Molly wiped a tear with the back of her hand.

'Please, Molly, don't get upset.'

She gave him an incredulous stare. 'How can you say that? That poor wee girl left The Old Bakehouse this morning and that might have been the last morning she ever saw.' She sipped her tea before staring back across at Cam. 'And the other revelations of the night took me by surprise too, if I'm truly honest.'

'Revelations, what revelations?' asked Cam.

'Martha had some very interesting things to say.'

'Come on, you can't really take anything Martha has said seriously? Surely? Unless she told you we are expecting a baby, because I think there's a little bit of a giveaway,' he said, pointing towards Molly's stomach and rolling his eyes, but all that did was add fuel to the fire.

'What are you keeping from me?' Molly asked sharply, her eyes never leaving him.

Cam was quiet. Yes, he was keeping something from

Molly, but there was no way on this earth Martha could know any of his business.

'Scandals, lies and health problems. Would you like to elaborate on anything?'

'Would you?' Cam threw the question back at her but Molly remained silent.

'You are winding me up, aren't you? This is just silly. Look, I am really sorry about tonight's news, and if I could turn back time then of course I would in a heartbeat, but please tell me you don't believe every word that Martha said.' He sat up straight, looking at Molly in disbelief.

'But there's something in my gut that is telling me something isn't quite right, that there's something going on with you. You won't even commit to the baking competition when this is the ideal time to be practising. You told Dixie it was your dream to be invited and we can't fathom why you wouldn't be shouting it from the rooftops. It just doesn't make any sense to me or her.'

Cam raised an eyebrow. 'It doesn't actually need to make any sense, though, does it? It's my choice, my decision, and the timing isn't right for me.'

'Why isn't the timing right for you?' Molly asked, pushing him further.

'This is getting blown up way out of proportion. I'm really not going to argue with you about something Martha has made up for entertainment value. It's just ridiculous and I'm not getting into this. There's no talking to you when you are like this.'

'Like what?' replied Molly, on the defensive.

'This conversation is getting us nowhere.'

Molly was shaking her head in despair. 'You are right, it isn't, but just for the record, I think Martha is right.'

Cam was still shaking his head as Molly placed her mug on the table.

Molly had never rowed with Cam on such a scale and she was hurt and upset by his unusual attitude. Determined not to cry in front of him, but feeling as though the tears were bubbling just underneath the surface, Molly stood up. 'I need some space.'

Taking one last glance at the blizzard outside, she pulled shut the living-room curtains before walking straight past Cam and up the stairs to the spare room.

Molly was angry, saddened, frustrated and confused.

Sitting on the bed, she tried to calm her beating heart. She propped herself up on the pillows and rested her hands on her stomach. Closing her eyes, she took in deep breaths. The last thing she needed was her blood pressure rising. It had been a very long time since Molly had prayed, but that's exactly what she did, quickly saying a prayer for Bree's safety. Opening her eyes, she caught her reflection in the dressing-table mirror. She stared at herself for a moment wondering if there was any truth in what Martha had said.

Hearing Cam walk up the stairs, Molly looked towards the closed door. Her heart was thumping as she heard his footsteps petering out towards their bedroom.

'Where are you?' he shouted.

For a moment, Molly stayed quiet, which was stupid because there weren't many places a pregnant woman could hide, but she just wanted to be on her own and have a little space to calm down.

She was beginning to wonder where all the fun had gone in their relationship; when had they last spent some real time together and talked about stuff other than children and routine? She remembered the first time she'd ever set eyes on Cam, in the car park of a posh hotel. Well, actually, she wasn't looking where she was going and knocked his unzipped holdall clean out of his hands leaving his pristine white Calvin Klein boxer shorts lying on the ground in front of them both. She smiled at the memory of how lovestruck she'd been, mesmerised by his handsome good looks. He'd had a glint in his eye and fitted into his tight white T-shirt with perfection and she'd acted like a schoolgirl with a crush. At that moment she'd believed in love at first sight. And now she was hiding away in the spare room after an argument. They'd always promised each other that they would never to go to bed angry but Molly knew she was about to break that promise, because she had every intention of spending the night in the spare room.

'Molly, are you in there?' Cam had sussed she was in the spare room and opened the door wide. 'What are you doing in here?'

'I just need some space.' Molly could barely look in his direction.

'Are you serious?' he asked.

'Deadly serious.'

They stared at each other for a second until Cam broke the silence.

'Can I get you anything?'

Molly shook her head, not trusting herself to speak, and felt her lip beginning to quiver.

Cam didn't say any more, he simply turned around and shut the door behind him.

Sitting on the bed, she felt the hot frustrated tears slip down her cheeks. He hadn't even put up a fight, he'd just turned and walked away. Not only was she down in the dumps, but she knew staying in the spare room would escalate things to another level. She couldn't help it though. Cam hadn't given her any sort of answers, except to say that Martha was not to be believed. So why had Molly got a niggling feeling that what Martha had said was just the beginning and something was about to unfold?

Taking off her clothes and slipping under the duvet, Molly turned on her side and cradled a pillow in her arms. She let her tears freely fall as she held on the pillow tighter, and as she closed her eyes she prayed that Bree would turn up safe and sound.

Against the odds and despite the anxious feeling swirling in the pit of her stomach, Molly fell asleep.

Chapter Ten

L ast night Molly had barely slept a wink, worrying
  about the state of her relationship with Cam, not to
mention her anxiety regarding the body on the
mountainside. When she finally drifted off to sleep it felt
like only five minutes had passed before she woke up. Her
eyelids were heavy, she felt exhausted and all sorts of
scenarios involving Cam were spinning around in her head.
When had they stopped being able to talk about anything
and everything? Maybe she had neglected him, maybe the
pregnancy and motherhood had taken over her life, but that
went both ways. When was the last time he'd suggested
they get a babysitter and go out for a meal or watch a film at
the cinema in town?

Molly knew his mood had changed and that there had
been a time when he would have listened to Bree and
gotten both sides of a story before jumping to conclusions.

She took a deep breath and looked at the clock on the bedside table. It was just after eight a.m. She was surprised to see a cup of tea next to the bed. Despite their argument, Cam had still made her a cuppa, just like he'd done every morning since they'd moved in together.

'It's still warm.'

'Jeez!' Molly nearly jumped out of her skin. 'How long have you been sitting there?'

Cam was in a chair next to the bed and looked like he hadn't had a wink of sleep either. He was leaning forward with a letter clasped in his hands. Molly knew something was wrong, terribly wrong. She pushed herself up. 'What is it? Is it Bree?'

Cam shook his head. 'I've watched the news all night and it was only a little while ago that they confirmed the body was that of an elderly homeless man ... Stan Edwards.'

Sadness engulfed Molly. 'No, not Stan.'

'Sam identified the body.'

'Such terrible news.' Molly was wracking her brains. Surely Stan had been on the truck when they transported the residents to the new shelter? She couldn't picture him. How had she not noticed? Her heart sank. 'How can someone's life end like that?' Molly closed her eyes and tried to recall her last images of Stan. 'I feel so sad, like the wind has been kicked out of me. Stan was so kind, so considerate, always took time out to have a conversation with me.' Molly placed her hands on her heart. 'I can't believe he's gone. He looked out for Bree ... Bree, is there any news of Bree?'

'I've heard nothing, but here's hoping she found somewhere safe to stay.'

Molly noticed that Cam's tone had changed; it was soft and caring.

'Why do I get the gut feeling you are preparing me for something else?' Her voice was shaky and her heart was beating nineteen to the dozen. 'You aren't happy, are you? All this is too much ... family life, another baby on the way. You're leaving, aren't you? You don't want any of this. Oh my gosh, you don't, do you?'

Molly knew she was putting words in his mouth but whatever he was going to say she wanted it over and done with quickly, as the agony of not knowing was twisting her stomach in anxious knots.

'We do need to talk.' Cam looked solemn and exhausted, his hair bedraggled as he looked at her in a way she'd never seen before.

With his words her chest tightened. The words 'we need to talk' were usually said when something was wrong. Everything flashed before Molly's eyes – George, her home, the business. She swallowed. 'What is it? You're really scaring me now.'

Cam shifted from the chair to the edge of the bed. 'In a roundabout sort of way, Martha was right.'

Molly's eyes widened. 'What have you done?'

'I'm not involved in any scandal – I've no idea what she

is going on about there – but I have been keeping something from you and…' He took a breath. 'I was trying to protect you as I didn't want to cause you any upset without knowing all the facts, but it seems things are escalating … you sleeping in here … me in there … and I suppose this is the real reason I can't commit to the baking competition because I just don't know what is going to happen. I've been trying to keep it all together, as that's what us men are supposed to do, but I'm not coping very well.' Cam barely paused for breath as he held out the folded letter in his hand towards Molly.

'What's this?'

'Just open it,' he replied.

Taking the letter, Molly unfolded it and with a thumping heart stared at the heading in bold red type: 'Glensheil Health Authority'. She blinked and read the words on the page carefully. According to the letter she was holding, Cam had an appointment at the hospital for a scan in a couple of days' time.

'I don't understand, why do you need a scan?'

'I found a lump.' He looked down towards his trousers. 'I find it difficult to talk about this sort of stuff. It's kind of embarrassing.'

This wasn't how Molly had expected the conversation to go and her thoughts ricocheted from confusion to complete dread. The first thought that crossed her mind was that everything was going to be okay, but that wasn't what Cam needed to hear right now. He was uncertain of the unknown and Molly knew that must be a terrifying head space to be in. Even though she felt a shakiness in her limbs and her heart thudding in her chest, she knew she needed to muster up some strength and quickly.

'Oh Cam,' said Molly, fraught with emotion. She felt helpless. Her voice shook before it steadied as she reached out to grab him. She slid her arms around his neck and they clung to each other. It was clear that Cam was terrified about what this meant for him and his family.

However hard Molly tried, she couldn't stop the tears from rolling down her cheeks, and though her mouth was completely dry and she was in complete shock, she hitched a smile on her face then took both of his hands in hers. Cam was visibly upset and was clearly finding it difficult to talk about this. 'There is absolutely nothing to be embarrassed about,' she soothed. 'Do you mean in your testicles?'

Cam nodded.

'When … when did all this happen?'

'A few weeks ago. I tried to pretend it wasn't there and it was just my imagination but it's still there all right. I went to the doctor's and Ben arranged for the scan.'

Molly picked up the letter again and reread it before placing it back down on the bed. 'And why didn't you share this with me at the time? It's kind of important.'

Cam was finding it difficult to look her in the eye. 'Because I couldn't. You're pregnant and all I think about is the worst-case scenario. Letting you down, leaving you with two young small children. It's been eating me upside. What if—'

'Woah! Stop right there. You aren't letting anyone down

or leaving me with two small children. We aren't thinking like that; we are thinking positive. Let's not second-guess anything. We take one step at a time … together,' she said, bolder than she felt, squeezing out a wobbly smile.

Cam nodded. 'I'm so sorry.'

'There is nothing to apologise for. We are in a little bit of shock but this will be okay because we will make it okay.'

Cam still couldn't look at her. 'I feel like I've let you down.'

'We aren't talking like that, do you hear me?'

Cam was crying as he pulled Molly in close again. They held each other like their lives depended on it.

'This is going to work out okay,' she reassured him, her body relaxing for a moment. Feeling guilt-ridden, she added, 'I'm sorry, I've put you through the mill. I understand now why you wouldn't want someone else in our home and I'm guessing this is the reason for your reluctance to enter the baking competition?'

Cam nodded. 'I'm sorry, I know I should have told you the truth but I just find it so hard to talk about this stuff.'

'I think men in general find it difficult to talk about personal stuff like this – but this is me.'

'I know.' Cam took a breath. 'I was going to talk to you last night when you arrived home. I was actually on edge all night wondering what the hell Martha would come up with.' He gave a small chuckle. 'And it seems possible that woman *has* got some sort of psychic power after all.'

'We just need to sit back and wait for this scandal to

unfold,' Molly said with a smile. 'She was adamant something is brewing and said the same to Dixie.'

'Interesting.' Cam raised his eyebrow. 'At least that might give us something else to think about until this appointment.' He looked at the letter.

'In other news, Martha predicted the baby is going to be a girl!' she said with a forced uplift to her voice. Molly knew it was best to try to steer the conversation away from the worry of the appointment.

'Really?' Cam placed his hand on Molly's stomach. 'I suppose Martha does have a—'

'Fifty-fifty chance,' they chorused, then laughed.

They were quiet for a second and Molly knew exactly what Cam was thinking.

'Don't slip into those thoughts. You will be here. We will be a family. We carry on as normal.'

'It's just hard.' He breathed in and smiled at Molly's stomach. 'A girl. . . We best get thinking of some names.'

'That shouldn't be too difficult because according to Martha the baby's name begins with "L".'

'"L"?' repeated Cam. 'We best get out the baby name book.'

'Let's do that tonight?'

Cam nodded. 'I am sorry about Stan, I know you liked him.'

'I did. It's so sad that anyone's life can end in such a tragedy, and it still leaves the question of where Bree stayed last night and when – and if – she will reappear.'

'I really am sorry for yesterday,' said Cam.

Molly nodded. 'I know.' She paused. 'We always talk about anything and everything. I can remember when we first moved in together, we'd still be chatting away, wrapped up in each other's arms, when the dawn chorus could be heard.' She smiled. 'This is important.' She pointed to the letter. 'And we are in this together. Look how far we've come in the past five years. We're no strangers to coping with pressure and life.'

George, their son, was conceived during what they'd both thought would be a one-night stand and Molly had prepared herself to be a single mother, until Cam crossed her path unexpectedly three months later walking his dog in Primrose Park. Cam was going through a divorce when Molly revealed she was carrying his child but they pulled together, creating a solid family unit.

'It was just difficult to wrap my head around. I've tried to put it to the back of my mind until I know exactly what I was dealing with.'

'You were trying to shield me from worrying, I do understand that, but knowing something is bothering you, I've had many things spiralling in my thoughts, the main one being that you weren't happy and were on the verge of leaving me.'

'Believe me, I am the happiest I have ever been, but that's exactly what I'm scared of – leaving you,'

Molly could see Cam's eyes filling with tears. 'And we won't let that happen. Positivity is the word of the day. We carry on as normal. Do you hear me?'

Cam nodded as they hugged each other once again before he held out his hand and helped Molly out of bed. 'I'll need to phone Sam to make sure she's okay,' Molly said. 'And what are we doing about the shop today?' She pulled back the curtain. 'Oh my lord. Is the van actually buried?' Her eyes were wide as she stared at Cam and then back at the road. 'And look.'

There were a couple of trees on the far side of the green that had fallen, and bins tossed on their sides on the pavement.

'How deep do you think that snow is?' asked Molly, still staring out over the icy white blanket.

'Blooming deep. I've literally only baked a handful of bread today, as who is going to venture out in this?' said Cam, slipping his arms around Molly's stomach and resting his head on her shoulder.

She glanced back at him and kissed him lightly on the lips. 'If it's going to be quiet today why don't you think about the baking competition?' she suggested, giving him a sideward glance. 'Like we've just said, carrying on as normal is the key here.' She closed her eyes briefly and waited for his answer. 'And just think how chuffed Dixie will be. She's waited for this moment…'

'There's nothing like emotional blackmail,' he replied, holding his hands up in protest. 'However, with the bakery being quiet today I will have a look over Great-Uncle Ted's recipe bible. Let's see if it gives me any inspiration.'

'Will you really?' There was hope in her voice and for

the first time she felt an inkling of excitement. This was the first real interest that Cam had shown in the competition.

'I will. Maybe we could take a look together.'

'I'd like that,' replied Molly. 'Look!'

Cam looked and laughed. There was Ash attempting to stomp through the snow, with his post bag slung over his shoulder. 'Now, that's a job I wouldn't want to do in this weather. I'll go and make him a warm drink. Goodness knows what time he started this morning.'

Molly pulled on a pair of trackie bottoms, slipped a sweatshirt over her head and followed Cam down the stairs. She noticed the welcoming warmth coming from the living room where the open fire was already crackling away. She stood behind the counter and watched as Cam opened the door and hitched a friendly smile on his face. 'Warm drink?' he asked Ash who nodded gratefully.

'Superstar, I can't actually feel my fingers, it's brutal out there. There are trees down over at Primrose Park, chimneys pots scattered in the street, and this morning I woke up to a random garden furniture set sitting on my patio. It's quite nice, to be fair.'

Cam was grinning. 'We could do with a nice new patio set. Maybe I need to check the garden. Is it really that brutal out there?'

Ash nodded. 'Brutal,' he repeated, looking down at his waterproof trousers and gesturing to his thigh. 'The snow has been up to here in places and it's minus seven out there at the moment. The high street looks like a mini tornado has hit the village as there are fences missing from gardens, and everywhere is under inches of snow. Even the pub sign has been battered with the blizzard. The bridge is open for pedestrians but I wouldn't recommend it and there are no vehicles getting through on the track until the snow has thawed. The River Heart is just a layer of ice.' Ash shivered. 'And the police have cordoned off the top of Love Heart Lane. It's so sad to hear about what happened to one of Sam's residents.'

'It is,' agreed Molly. 'Very sad.'

'It took me over an hour to walk from the town post office to here,' continued Ash.

'Sounds like not many people will be venturing out today,' remarked Molly.

'Not if they have any sense,' replied Ash, looking longingly at the few croissants that Cam had baked before waking Molly.

'Go on, help yourself,' said Cam with a grin, offering him the tray.

'Don't mind if I do.' Ash took a croissant and tore off the end. He waved it in the air as he spoke. 'Talking of no sense, I couldn't believe Bree was up and about at this time in the morning, especially when everyone has been advised to stay indoors. I shouted at her but she seemed to be in a world of her own.'

With a sharp intake of breath, Molly asked quickly, 'Bree, you've seen Bree this morning? It was actually her? Are you sure?'

'I'd recognise that smile anywhere, not that she was smiling though. In fact, she looked sad … but I might be mistaken as I was a distance away from her.'

There was a pause as Molly tried to get her thoughts in order. 'Was this just now?'

'Yes, just now, outside the church. She was sitting huddled up on a bench, which I thought was odd because I'm not sure I'd want a cold, wet backside.'

Cam met Molly's worried stare.

'Are you okay to keep an eye on George?' she asked.

'Of course,' replied Cam.

Molly hurried up the stairs, all fingers and thumbs as she got dressed as quickly as she could.

Ten minutes later she was pulling on her boots and Cam was handing her her coat.

'I'd offer to go, but I'm sure as soon as she saw me, she would bolt. But I will go if you want me to?'

Molly was shaking her head. 'It's best left to me.'

She couldn't stop wondering why Bree would choose to be sitting in the cemetery instead of a warm café or even the library. But then she realised that staff would find it difficult to travel today, so maybe nothing was open and there was nowhere to go.

'Gloves, hat,' said Cam and as soon as they were pulled on Molly was walking through the bakery door. As she glanced back at Cam and waved, he gave her an encouraging smile.

Thankfully it was only a short walk to the church and despite the storm and the freezing temperatures Heartcross Mountain looked majestic covered in glistening snow. The duckpond was completely frozen as Molly trudged over the wooden bridge and made her way up the crest of the hill towards the church. The weathered wrought-iron gates were laden with icicles, creating an impressive entrance to the graveyard, though the ornamental statue had been broken in the blizzard and was lying on its side. Usually, one could see the paved footpath between the graves and the well-maintained gardens, but with the inches of snow that had fallen overnight it was hard to make out the pathway.

Molly's eyes darted around the graveyard but it was deserted and Bree was nowhere to be seen. She glanced across to the bench to see that the snow had been swiped away and there were a couple of church pew cushions lying on top. Someone had definitely been sitting on it. As Molly continued to follow what she hoped was the path towards the entrance of the church, she passed her own parents' grave. Many tears had been shed standing in front of the snow-covered headstone, but being here always gave her some sort of comfort and every time she had a bit of family news, good or bad, she would find herself telling all to her parents. Brushing the snow from the headstone she read the inscription out loud.

In loving memory of Douglas McKendrick
and his beloved wife Diane
Reunited at last
Treasured parents of Molly McKendrick

She took a moment and murmured that she loved them. With the cold air stinging her cheeks and her hands growing numb, she hurried towards the door of the church, pulling her scarf tighter around her neck. Someone had definitely been here as she could see a pair of footprints embedded in the snow heading towards the church door. She read the note pinned up outside saying all sermons had been cancelled until further notice. The clock struck nine a.m. and an eerie silence echoed all around as Molly turned the wrought-iron knob and the creaky door opened.

The church was stone cold. Stepping into the nave, Molly shivered and was immediately hit by the aroma of polish as she slowly walked down the aisle between the wooden pews. The lights were dimmed and there were no candles lit as she cast her gaze up at Jesus on the cross before looking around the silent room once more.

'Bree,' Molly called out but there was no answer. She continued to walk towards the altar and glanced up to the wooden pulpit where the local vicar would deliver his sermon.

Her hopes faded as she concluded that there was no one here. She must have missed Bree by a matter of minutes. She wracked her brains as to where she would go next –

possibly the library, maybe the village hall? Molly sighed and turned to walk back down the aisle then stopped in her tracks. On the front pew was an empty can and a scrunched-up white paper bag with The Old Bakehouse logo. Her heart was thumping as she quickly walked up the aisle checking every pew. Bree had been here and no doubt had taken cover in the church overnight but where was she now? Hearing a cough, Molly spun round and quickly followed the sound through the chancel arch. That's when she noticed a figure cocooned tightly in a blanket and huddled up in a foetal position, trying to keep warm on a bed of pew cushions.

'Bree, is that you?'

Bree's startled eyes peered over the top of the blanket. Molly noticed that her lips were tinged with blue, her teeth chattering. The poor girl must be frozen to the absolute core.

With a sudden movement, Bree threw off the blanket. Clambering to her feet, she attempted to run, her eyes never leaving Molly's as she reached for her bag.

'No, Bree, wait. It's okay.' Molly's voice was desperate. She didn't want Bree running off, heading back out into the snow. 'I promise you it's okay. We know that Ash took the phone by mistake and we are so sorry.'

Her words echoed around the church and Bree stared at Molly through wide hazel eyes but didn't speak.

'Honestly, it's fine.' Molly had her arms stretched out in front of her with her hands wide open – the international sign of 'I come in peace'. 'Please. I just need to make sure you're okay.'

The uncertainty was clear in Bree's eyes; she didn't know whether to trust Molly.

'Have you slept here?' asked Molly, her voice soft.

Bree nodded.

'It's freezing in here.' Molly could see her own breath as she wrapped her arms around her body and dug her chin under her scarf for a moment. 'I'm sorry about yesterday, and that we didn't give you a chance to explain.'

All Molly wanted to do was get Bree out of there into a warm place. She watched as Bree's lips began to tremble. 'Please come with me ... please.'

Bree was still staring at her like a rabbit caught in the headlights and Molly wasn't sure whether she was going to attempt to make a run for it or not.

'I'm not here to cause any sort of trouble. You look frozen to the core and I just want to get you to somewhere warm. Would you like that?'

Bree nodded, a tear slipping down her face, leaving a streak in the dirt.

'Hungry?' asked Molly.

Bree hesitated, then nodded.

Molly cautiously bent down and picked up Bree's bag. 'Have you got everything you need in here?'

'Yes,' said Bree, watching Molly slowly take a few steps towards the altar.

'Come on, it's going to be okay,' encouraged Molly and she was relieved to see Bree taking small steps behind her.

Together they walked back towards the magnificent sturdy oak doors and Molly opened one for Bree.

'Last night, why didn't you call Sam at the shelter? Why stay in here?'

'I couldn't leave; I needed to be here.'

'Needed?' queried Molly, pulling the church door shut.

'It's Mum's birthday today. It's the only place I feel close to her.'

'Oh, Bree.' Molly's heart went out to her. A sixteen-year-old girl all alone in the world. Molly held out her arms and Bree hesitated for a moment then stepped into her warm embrace.

The hug reminded Molly of Cam. Bree was clinging on to her for dear life. There was vulnerability, and a smidgen of hope that someone was interested in helping her.

'Have you eaten this morning?'

Bree shook her head. 'Not this morning.'

'Okay, let's get you out of the freezing cold. If I remember rightly there's some sausages in the fridge and I'm sure we can find a loaf of bread. It's one of the joys of living with a baker.'

Bree smiled.

'Cam is sorry too and no doubt will apologise.' Molly pulled her scarf tight then pointed at the path. 'The snow is very deep in places,' she said. 'If I stomp it down and you step in my footprints it might make the walk a little easier. Have you got everything?'

'My life,' replied Bree, holding up her bag before staring over at an area of ground just left of the wooden bench.

'Is that where your mum is buried?' asked Molly tentatively.

'Yes.' Bree's voice wavered.

'Is there no headstone?'

Bree shook her head, 'I couldn't afford one but I made a promise to myself that as soon as I get my very first job and my very first pay packet, I'll put some money towards a stone. My mum deserves a lovely grave. I'll do it, I know I will.'

'I'm in no doubt and I'm sure we can have it looking lovely soon.'

'We?' queried Bree.

'I'm always here to help,' replied Molly, pushing open the wrought-iron gate. 'You ready?'

Bree took a moment to stand by her mother's grave and Molly watched in silence as Bree uttered the words, 'I miss you.' It was breaking Molly's heart just watching the tender moment. The love Bree had for her mother wasn't in doubt, they must have had a wonderful bond. When Bree was ready, they made the short walk back to The Old Bakehouse. Molly was relieved to see the smoke spiralling out of the chimney pot and thankful that Cam had kept the fire burning.

As they stepped into the empty bakery, Molly saw that Ash had left and the shop was unmanned. She could see the reluctance on Bree's face as the bell above the shop door tinkled, and she reassured her that everything was going to be fine.

'It's only me,' shouted Molly, unwinding the scarf from her neck.

Cam's voice sounded from the bakery kitchen. 'I can't master this bread; the chocolate is all lumpy. How Bree got that recipe so spot-on is beyond me.' Cam appeared in the doorway looking like the victim of a chocolate explosion. There was chocolate smeared on his face, in his hair, splattered on his hat, and his apron needed a damn good wash.

Molly burst out laughing. 'Very Paul Hollywood!' she teased. 'What the hell have you been doing? I thought it would be George's job to lick the bowl, not yours.'

Cam rolled his eyes whilst smiling. 'You found her.'

'I did.'

'Get your coats and boots off. The fire is lit and there's a possibility you will find a plate of cooked sausages and bacon in the bottom oven of the Aga.'

'You are a keeper is what you are.' Molly pressed a swift kiss to Cam's cheek. 'Thank you,' she said, impressed by the way Cam immediately put Bree at ease.

'And that bread you made, that's some seriously genius baking.'

Bree looked unsure what to say so Molly chipped in. 'You did very well, Bree. Maybe you could give us some tips on how to bake the chocolate layer to perfection?'

'Never mind the bread, you should taste my chocolate slabs – Layers Treats,' enthused Bree.

'Layers Treats?' repeated Cam.

'On my mum's birthday we always made our special

chocolate slab and that's what she called it – Layers Treats. Creamy Belgian milk chocolate layered with a gooey chocolate orange centre and then topped with Terry's chocolate orange segments was our favourite, but we baked it using many different ingredients like brownies, cookies, et cetera. It tastes amazing.'

'And you've baked this?'

'I have,' replied Bree. 'The chocolate loaf was the first loaf I'd baked since Mum passed away but we always baked the chocolate slabs on her birthday.'

Cam was impressed. 'Well, I have to say you should be proud of yourself. As you can see, I'm not having much luck with my attempt at baking anything chocolatey.' Cam looked down at his apron, then back up at Bree.

'It's Bree's mum's birthday today,' added Molly softly.

Cam looked between the two of them. 'How about you get yourself cleaned up, eat some breakfast and then, if you would like, show Molly and myself how you make your wonderful chocolate slabs … Layers Treats, you say?'

'I think I'd like that,' replied Bree, with a smile on her face. 'Thank you.'

'Bree, I am sorry about yesterday.' Cam's apology was heartfelt.

Bree nodded. 'Thank you.'

'And I'm sorry to hear about Stan,' he added, then noticed Molly opening her eyes wide whilst discreetly shaking her head.

Damn, knowing he'd just put his foot in it, Cam prayed that Molly was about to rescue him.

'Stan?' queried Bree, looking between the two of them.

Molly was apprehensive as she wasn't sure how Bree was going to react to Stan's death, knowing they were close. But right at that minute the conversation was steered in another direction as George appeared in the doorway and ran towards Molly, who attempted to hoist him up on her hip, 'Nope! I can't lift you up. You are too big now! In fact, I think you have grown since I've been gone.'

George looked chuffed and giggled.

Molly popped a noisy kiss on his cheek. 'George, why don't you take Bree through to the living room, get warm by the fire and I'll make us all a drink.'

As soon as Bree was out of sight, Molly slid her arms around Cam's waist and looked up at him. 'We are so lucky. I found that poor wee girl wrapped in a blanket in the church. She'd slept there last night. I can't even begin to imagine how cold and lonely she must have felt.'

'I can't imagine either but she's here now. Though I'm not sure we can get her to the shelter in these weather conditions…'

'I know, but can she stay here today?' Molly looked up at Cam, who didn't hesitate.

'Of course she can. I need someone to teach us how to bake chocolate slabs. I need some inspiration. I have a competition to win.'

Molly's eyes widened in delight. There he was, the old Cam was back and fighting. Molly was impressed.

'I've been thinking about it and we have to carry on as normal. I have to think positive and focus on what I do best…' He looked down at his chocolate-splattered apron. 'Even though that is debatable.'

They laughed as they hugged. 'I'll go and break the news to Bree about Stan and then maybe we could get everyone involved in the baking to take her mind off things.'

'Sounds good to me.'

As Molly walked out of the bakery, she glanced behind her. 'I really do love you.'

'Back atcha,' replied Cam, giving her a wink.

Walking towards the living room, Molly could hear George chattering away. 'I'm not allowed out in the snow because it's that deep it's going to come right up to my chin.'

Bree was laughing where she was sitting on the rug in front of the fire, holding her hands out towards the flames.

'George, could you just go and help Daddy in the kitchen?'

George saluted before he zoomed out of the living room at top speed. As soon as Molly heard their voices in the bakery kitchen, she took a seat in the battered old armchair next to the fire. She was staring at Bree, who was waggling her toes in front of the fire.

Feeling a wave of sadness knowing she was going to have to break the news to Bree about Stan, Molly swallowed.

'Bree, I have some sad news to share with you.'

Wide-eyed, Bree looked up hesitantly.

Molly took the plunge. 'I'm really sorry to say Stan passed away last night.'

Bree didn't speak. She wrapped her arms tighter around her body, turning her gaze back towards the log fire, and began to slowly rock back and forth. Molly watched a tear slide down her cheek, which she wiped away with the back of her hand. Molly's heart was breaking for her. The cards that life had dealt her were so unfair.

'Are you okay?' asked Molly tentatively.

'Stan was a good friend. He was always kind to me.'

Molly reached for the box of tissues on the dresser and placed it next to Bree.

'If this is life, I'm not sure it's for me.' Bree's voice cracked. 'It's so unfair.'

Molly placed a cushion on the rug and sat next to Bree. She crossed her legs and stared into the fire. 'You have your whole life ahead of you,' she reassured her. 'You've just had a shaky start.'

'I'm really scared, Molly. Really scared,' she repeated.

Molly reached out and took her hand.

'I barely sleep, I don't want to eat. There's a continuous tightness in my chest. Sometimes I feel like my heart is just going to stop beating.' Bree took a breath. 'I have happy memories swirling around in my thoughts, then those thoughts turn to sadness. Life isn't the same without my mum.'

'Grief is a reaction to loss. At times you will feel comforted, other times in shock and disbelief.'

'When will these feelings stop?' asked Bree, looking at Molly.

'Grief comes in waves. It takes time for reality to sink in. It doesn't mean forgetting that person, it's just about finding ways to remember our loved ones and adjust to life without them present. I know exactly what you are going through, though I was a little older when I lost my parents. Sadly, it doesn't make it easier but at least I had my own security of a job and a home.'

'Everyone I get close to leaves me.' Bree's voice was shaky and she blotted away the tears that were blinding her eyes. 'Why? Why me? I walk around the streets day after day and walk past families who are laughing and joking. Dads giving their kids a piggyback ride, mums and daughters out having lunch. Why couldn't I have all that? What is going to happen to me?' Bree took a sideward glance towards Molly. 'Me and Stan, we had a pact.'

'A pact?' queried Molly.

'If neither of us made it to the shelter then the next place we would go would be the church.' Bree smiled. 'There's been many times when Stan and I have ended up in the church overnight. He'd push open those heavy oak doors with a smile on his face and we'd have a party for two. We'd make a bed out of the pew cushions, which I have to say is comfier than some of Sam's mattresses. There's a small room at the back of the church with a kettle and usually a packet of biscuits. I'd make the tea and Stan would often plug in the organ; he was a brilliant musician.' Bree took a breather. 'He didn't make it to the church last night, I just thought he'd gone to the temporary shelter.'

Molly was shaking her head. 'He was discovered on the mountain pass.'

'What was he doing on the mountain pass in that weather?'

Molly shrugged. 'I really don't know, Bree.'

'And now I've not even got Stan… Loon moon,' Bree murmured under her breath.

Molly turned towards Bree and stared at her, the hairs on her arms standing on end. 'What did you just say?'

'I said I've not even got Stan now.'

'No, not that. What did you say about the moon?'

'Loon moon.' Bree was smiling through her tears. 'It's something I remember from my childhood. If Stan and I weren't taking cover in the same shelter, or were somehow apart, wherever we were, we used to look up at the sky and pray that each other was safe. Last night, I couldn't see the moon. The sky was dark and heavy with snow so there wasn't a chink of light to be seen. I prayed for Stan and wished him goodnight.'

The words were washing over Molly. 'Loon moon,' she whispered under her breath. The memory that flooded back to her in that moment was so clear it felt like yesterday. Immediately, Molly was transported back to the dingy flat in the past. She was standing on a blue crate, her mum standing beside her. Through the grimy window her mum was pointing to the stars and the moon. 'You are as lovely as the moon … loon moon.' Molly gave herself a little shake. She squeezed her eyes shut trying to remember. In her mind, she heard the door slam in the stairwell, footsteps thudding as her mum would hurry her to the mattress in the corner of the room. Her mum encouraging her to pretend she was asleep as the flat door swung open.

'A childhood memory, you said?' asked Molly, her heart beating fast.

Bree smiled and nodded. 'Mum used to say I was as lovely as the moon. She used to say if we were ever apart then I should look up at the moon and I would know she was always with me. Stan and I did the same.'

Molly could feel the thump in her heart race faster. She cradled her stomach then realised her hands were shaking. She knew she was staring at Bree but couldn't help it.

'And your mum used to say that?'

Bree nodded.

In a daze, Molly stood up. 'I'll get us a drink.' Walking into the kitchen, Molly took a deep breath and shut the door behind her. With her pulse racing she placed her hands on the Belfast sink. 'It's not possible,' she murmured. Her thoughts were spiralling out of control. Was this a coincidence? Trying to compose herself, Molly made Bree a drink and plated up a sausage and bacon sandwich from the Aga.

'Are you having anything to eat?' asked Bree, when Molly handed her the plate.

Molly shook her head. 'I'm just going to nip out, I won't be long. After you've finished eating, have a bath, I'll leave you some towels and one of my own tracksuits in the bathroom, so you've got something clean and warm to change into.'

'Thank you,' replied Bree, watching Molly heading out of the living room.

Five minutes later, Molly's stomach was performing a double somersault as she fastened her coat and pushed her feet back into her snow boots. Winding her scarf around her neck she popped her head into the bakery kitchen and smiled. George was standing on a small stepladder so he could reach the worktop and was wearing Cam's hat as he scooped out chocolate from the bowl with a spatula.

'Look at you pair.'

Cam looked up from kneading a loaf and swiped his hands of flour. 'Where are you going?' he asked, noticing Molly was wearing her coat.

'I've just got to nip out.'

'Again? Its freezing out there. The Met Office aren't issuing weather warnings for no reason.'

'I won't be long.' Molly didn't elaborate as she was having trouble trying to process her thoughts, never mind trying to explain what she thought she could possibly know.

She pressed a kiss to his cheek. 'I won't be long, promise.'

'Is it important?'

'Possibly. Bree is having a bath and I've left her clothes to change into. I'll explain later.'

Puzzled, Cam narrowed his eyes at Molly, but before he could say anything else, the bakery door had shut behind her.

In no time at all, Molly was trudging through the snow. Running on adrenalin, she barely noticed the bitter cold stinging her cheeks and within minutes she was back standing in front of the wrought-iron gates of the churchyard. The graveyard was still deserted and Molly hadn't passed a soul on the way to the church, which she was grateful for as her insides were twisting and she didn't want to make polite conversation with anyone. For a brief moment she looked up at the sky and with jumbled thoughts she pushed open the gate. Passing Bree's mother's grave, she paused, then, taking a deep breath, she walked into the church.

Out of the corner of her eye Molly spotted the vicar standing in the vestry along with Florence, his wife, who was holding the largest bunch of colourful artificial blooms that Molly had ever seen. Hearing footsteps they both turned and Molly was met with a warm smile.

'It's been cancelled,' said the vicar. 'But any tombola prizes you can leave in the back room of the church.'

'Oh, the Scout fundraiser, I wasn't here for that. Do you by any chance have a moment?'

'There is a God!' he joked as his wife playfully swiped his arm. 'You've just rescued me from … actually that doesn't matter. What can I do for you?' The vicar gestured towards a room at the back. 'This way, it's warmer in there.'

Molly peeled off her gloves as she followed the vicar towards the small room at the back of the church, his traditional robe floating behind him as he walked. There were various candles lit around the room and Molly took in the aroma of incense. The electric fire in the corner was emitting a lovely warmth that Molly was grateful for, and though the room was small it was impressive. Books lined the shelves of one wall and the stained-glass window was a beautiful feature, letting in the light just in front of his desk.

'Have a seat,' the vicar said, gesturing to a chair as he sat down behind the desk. 'What can I do for you?"

'I'm looking for a dead person,' Molly blurted, then realised exactly how that sounded.

'Well, I think we can safely say, you've come to the right place.' The vicar gave a little chuckle. 'I've got a graveyard full of them. Any particular dead person?'

'That I am a little unsure of,' admitted Molly. 'Do you hold records for each burial plot?'

'The local county record office does, but in this weather it's likely closed. I'm not even sure the bridge is open for you to travel there.'

'Is that the only record?' asked Molly, knowing she couldn't wait that long to answer the question she so desperately needed answering.

'Or there's the computer.' The vicar gestured towards the computer in front of him. 'Everything these days is computerised but I really don't like technology. I'm all about the simple things in life, pen and paper.'

'I can find what I'm looking on the computer without travelling into town to the county offices?'

'Yes, it's simple. All you need is the deceased's full name and it will tell you what plot they are buried in and then…' The vicar got up and walked over to a large chest. He elevated the lid and Molly watched as he lifted out a leather-bound folder. The vicar sat back down and cleared a space on his desk. He carefully took off the band that bound the book together and opened up what looked like a map. He tapped it. 'Then I can tell you exactly where they are buried.'

Molly was staring at the prehistoric-looking map in front of her, which had numbers written all over it and the churchyard drawn in fountain pen. The paper looked fragile and old.

'Free plots are still available, but not many. Look out for the January sale, you buy one and can get one free.'

Molly raised an eyebrow. 'I'll bear that in mind.'

'Make sure you do, because people are dying to get in here.' The vicar laughed at his own joke. 'The old ones are still the best.'

'What if I don't know the deceased's name?'

'Then that is a little trickier. I'd need the name to locate the plot.'

Molly sighed. 'Somehow, I thought you were going to say that.' Molly was kicking herself for racing up here so quickly. The easiest thing would have been to ask Bree her mother's name but she hadn't been thinking straight.

'Is there no headstone?' continued the vicar.

'Unfortunately not, but what if I know where the plot is?'

The vicar pondered for a second. 'That's different, we just need to work backwards. I can locate the plot number on here and see who is buried in there...'

Molly brightened. 'Fantastic. I can show you where the plot is.'

'I'm intrigued, who exactly are you trying to find?'

Molly exhaled. 'Possibly my mother.'

Chapter Eleven

The vicar looked confused. 'I may be a little long in the tooth but my memory is still going very strong, unlike my knees; those steep stairs into that vicarage can be a little challenging at times... But I know exactly where Di and Doug are buried, and you do too. I see you tend to the grave.'

'I was adopted.'

The vicar processed the information. 'Well, I never. I always said to Doug you were the spitting image of him.' He looked amazed.

Molly smiled. 'He would have been so chuffed with that. Di and Doug were wonderful to me and so I've never had any real desire to look up my biological parents before now. I've been so happy with my life and I couldn't have wished for better parents.'

'Well, they were lovely people and you were a lovely family. Always had the time of day for the church. But what

I don't understand is why you think your biological mother is buried in this churchyard.'

'Call it a hunch. I may be way off the mark but it's something I just need to keep to myself for the time being.' Molly pointed to the plan of plots. 'It's in this area, near to the bench. The whole area is covered in deep snow so I'm not entirely sure which it is, but it's definitely one of those.'

The vicar adjusted the spectacles on the end of his nose and stared at the place where Molly was pointing. He nodded. 'And you do not know your biological mother's name?'

Molly shook her head. 'I know that sounds daft but I was a little girl when I was adopted and I only ever called her "Mummy". Di and Doug are really all I have ever known and though they never hid from me the fact I was adopted, they also never talked about who or where I'd come from and so I never really gave it much thought. But I keep getting flashbacks to the time I was around four or five years old, and it's made me wonder about where I came from.'

'I best get my coat. There are a few in that area with no headstones so it would help if you could pinpoint the plot outside for me. If you could excuse me for a moment.'

The vicar left the room and Molly took a closer look at the map. There were a few plots dotted in the area where Bree had hovered. Molly didn't know what she was about to uncover but was filled with excitement mixed with trepidation. When the vicar returned, she followed him back through the church towards the heavy oak doors.

He held the door open for her and Molly shivered as she stepped outside. 'It's going to be like this for the rest of the week,' she said.

'Yes, all sermons are cancelled until further notice. There's only one place to be in weather like this and that's indoors, in front of the fire.'

They took a few steps down the snowy path and Molly pointed to the bench. 'It's one just over there, but I'm not sure which one,' she admitted.

The vicar pointed. 'That's a family plot, belongs to the McDonalds, that one is Mr Jones and the one just there ... the name escapes for the moment. But the funeral was a small affair. I can remember a young girl – the deceased's daughter. That's plot 1507.'

Molly gave a sharp intake of breath. 'That's my birthday, the fifteenth of July.' Was that just another coincidence? She stared at the untended grave. It was just a mound covered in snow and Molly felt saddened.

'Come on, let's go and see if we can track down the name.'

Back inside the church, Molly watched as the vicar hung up his coat then walked over to the magnificent bookcase on the far side of the room. There were rows and rows of leather-bound books, statues of Jesus and donation boxes. The vicar pulled a red leather-bound book off the shelf. 'Like I said, I'm not a fan of technology and even though I shouldn't, I still record everything the old-fashioned way. This one should contain plot 1507.'

The vicar sat back down in the chair and placed the

book on the table. Molly's heart was racing. Was this the right time to go delving into the past? Was she ready to hear this name? The name of the person buried in that plot could have a major impact on her life.

The silence hung in the air as the vicar began to slowly turn the pages; Molly's eyes were fixed on the motion. Then the vicar tapped the book. 'Here it is.' He glanced towards Molly.

'Go on…' she encouraged. 'I'm ready.'

'The plot is occupied by one Lilian Allen. Died age forty-six of a coronary.'

Molly gave a short intake of breath. 'Lilian Allen.' Her head was whirling as she said the name out loud.

'Does that ring any bells with you?' asked the vicar.

Molly shook her head. As much as she tried, she'd never heard that name before, but her mind was still calculating the years between her and Bree. It was absolutely possible that they could have shared the same mother if Lilian had conceived Molly as a young teenager.

'And that's all I have,' said the vicar, shutting the book.

'Do you know anything else about Lilian? Was she one of your congregation?'

The vicar shook his head. 'No, she wasn't but thinking back…' He looked towards the book. 'I can remember the wee girl coming to visit me. She had a letter… Yes, I can remember a letter.'

'A letter?' queried Molly.

'Her mother's wish. The girl discovered the letter in her mum's personal belongings and in it she requested to be buried in this graveyard. They weren't from the village but from, I believe, the town of Tutbury, about half an hour from here on the train. I'd never set eyes on the girl before...'

'Bree, her name is Bree,' cut in Molly.

'That's right, Bree. And it was a sad set of circumstances. She lost her home when her mother passed and I believe she ended up on the streets. She spends a lot of time sat on the bench near to where her mother is buried. I have to say she's always a polite girl and I do know she has slept in the church numerous times.' The vicar pointed up to the CCTV camera in the corner. 'She has been no trouble though, and I now deliberately leave the church unlocked overnight and extra blankets on the front pews, especially with the weather being like this and Sam having had to move the shelter temporarily whist the heating is being fixed.'

'That is so kind. It breaks my heart to think of anyone out on the street in this weather. It was so sad to hear about Stan too.'

'It was,' replied the vicar.

'Do you know why Lilian requested to be buried at this particular church?'

'I've no idea but like I said, the young girl had a letter in her possession, maybe she could tell you more. And you think Lilian is your mother?'

Molly blew out a breath. 'I'm not entirely sure. There's just been a bizarre set of circumstances and I was hoping to find out a little bit more before I approached Bree. Is it possible ... could we keep this between ourselves, for now?'

The vicar nodded. 'Of course. I'm not too bad at keeping secrets; some of the confessions in this village would make your hair stand on end,' he joked, smoothing down the little hair he had whilst he chuckled.

'Thank you, and thank you for your time,' said Molly, standing up. 'I'll see myself out.'

As Molly walked back through the church and out into the freezing cold, she paused to stand in the front of the grave. For all of her life, Molly had assumed her mother had been dealing with addiction or in a violent relationship and that's why she'd put Molly up for adoption. The mother that Bree was describing wasn't at all like that though. Maybe she was overthinking it all. 'Loon moon. Happy birthday, Lilian Allen,' she murmured as a Robin Redbreast flew and landed on top of the snowy mound for a moment. Molly brought her hands up to her chest, knowing that robins symbolise visits from the dead. 'Lilian,' she said, a lump forming in her throat.

Her thoughts suddenly turned to Martha. She had predicted Molly's unborn child was going to be a girl and her name would begin with "L". Surely that was just another coincidence?

Chapter Twelve

With her thoughts tumbling all over each other, Molly slowly walked back to The Old Bakehouse mulling over the information the vicar had shared with her. She wasn't sure what she was going to do with it yet but decided that before she did anything she was going to go back to her old house and finally look through the old suitcase of documents her parents had left her, to see whether it provided any further clues.

Relieved to be finally back in the warmth, she pushed open the bakery door and was met by George running his toy car up and down the counter.

'What can I get you today?' he said in a posh voice, making Molly laugh.

'What do you recommend?' she asked, peeling the coat from her back.

George shrugged. 'Everything!' he said with a grin. 'I'm playing shopkeeper.'

'And playing it very well,' replied Molly, placing her cold hands on his cheeks and making him squeal. 'Where's Daddy?'

George pointed to the bakery kitchen then jumped off the stool and slipped his hand into Molly's as they walked into the hallway. While she took off her boots George ran off towards the living room.

'I'm home,' Molly shouted, heading towards the bakery kitchen and popping her head around the door. 'How's business been?' she asked.

Cam and Bree were on either side of the baking table looking over a large piece of paper. Bree, who was now clean, fresh and dressed in Molly's old tracksuit, had an apron tied around her waist and a black felt-tip in her hand.

Molly did a double-take. 'You remind me of me stood there.' She smiled.

'I've already said that,' said Cam, tapping the paper then turning back towards Bree. 'Go on, illustrate how this is meant to work, because I'm not sure I understand it yet.'

Molly stepped up to the table. 'What are you pair up to? You look as thick as thieves.'

'Plotting and experimenting,' replied Cam. 'Bree is talking me through her mother's magical recipe – chocolate slabs with secret layers.'

'They sound fabulous,' exclaimed Molly. 'Chocolate slabs with secret layers,' she repeated.

'Layers Treats,' confirmed Bree. 'My mum always had aspirations of her chocolate slabs becoming a national phenomenon, with her very own recipes being sold across the whole of Scotland.'

'And as it's Bree's mum's birthday, we thought we'd give it ago,' added Cam. 'This session may provide a little inspiration for my entry for the competition.'

'And…' George appeared in the doorway with a cheeky grin on his face, 'I'm going to be chief judge.' George had been upstairs and pulled out one of Cam's white shirts from the wardrobe. He'd put a waistcoat over the top and attempted to tie a bow tie around his neck.

'And don't you look the part.' Molly straightened his bow tie. 'I'm in need of a hot drink, then do you mind if I join you in the kitchen?' she asked. 'I would love to watch you pair bake.'

'The more the merrier. If this slab of chocolate is anything like the bread Bree made, we are definitely on to a winner. I've got a feeling no one will have anything like this.'

Molly noted the enthusiasm in Cam's voice. She wandered into the kitchen to make a cup of tea. As she stood by the sink filling the kettle, Cam walked in. 'Thank you,' said Molly.

'What for?' asked Cam.

'Keeping Bree occupied, especially with today being her mum's birthday.'

'She has some really good ideas, and you were right … the best thing is to keep focused and keep going. The bakery has been quiet today so why not use this time to perfect my entry for the baking competition? I've decided I am definitely going to enter.'

Immediately, Molly stood on tiptoe and kissed him hard on his lips. 'Good decision!'

'If I get kisses like that maybe I should have made that decision a while ago . . . but never mind me, where have you been? You seem a little preoccupied, like you have something on your mind.'

'I have, but not now. It'll keep. Let's talk later.'

'Is it anything I should be worried about?'

Molly shook her head. 'No, but I need to go back to the old house as soon as possible.'

'You aren't going anywhere in this as there are no vehicles getting across that track until the snow has thawed. I've rung Sam too. There will be no extra delivery to the shelter for the next couple of days.'

'How is she?'

'Broken-hearted over the loss of Stan but she was relieved when I explained Bree was staying with us until we can get her to the shelter.'

Molly's smile widened. 'Really? You're saying she can stay here?

'Yes, really. I'm not having another night like last night with you in the spare room and me not getting a wink of sleep worrying about where she is in this weather, but as soon as the shelter opens...'

'I know,' replied Molly, throwing her arms around Cam's neck and hugging him tight. 'You are simply the best.'

272

'Now, what is it you aren't telling me? Why do you need to go back to the other house?'

'I need the suitcase from the loft.'

'What suitcase? You aren't thinking of going on holiday, are you?' joked Cam.

'My parents' suitcase, the one full of important documents. I need to properly look at what's in it. I was too grief-stricken to do it in the days after I lost them.' She placed three mugs on a tray and juice for George.

'Maybe the best time to swing past the other house is on the way back from my hospital appointment; hopefully the track will be driveable in a couple of days' time. What do you need with the suitcase?'

'I'll fill you in later. For now, let's not leave Bree in the bakery by herself. I think she's in need of good company today.'

'But everything is okay, isn't it?'

Molly nodded. 'It is.'

As they wandered back into the bakery, they saw Bree had set out numerous bowls on the worktop alongside the utensils.

'I've written down the ingredients my mother used to use.' Bree was smiling, clearly enjoying every second of being in the kitchen.

'This looks pretty good to me,' observed Cam, looking over the recipe. He reached up and took the weighing scales off the shelf.

'Call yourself a baker? We won't need them. My mother

taught me the best way to bake is by estimating the ingredients.'

'That's a talent right there. Then that's exactly what we do. And I've not even asked you, what's your mother's name?' Cam asked curiously.

'Lilian Allen, baker and creator of Layers Treats. Her chocolate bars were the best.'

'Tell us all about your mum, I want to know everything,' encouraged Molly, as she sat up on the stool and watched them get to work.

'She was the loveliest, most caring person in the world . . . and thank you for this.' Bree gestured towards the baking. 'I didn't think I would ever feel strong enough to bake her recipes without feeling a twinge of sadness but I'm excited to share her fabulous recipe and I hope her creations will live on.'

'Okay, let's do it Lilian Allen's way,' said Cam, disposing of all measuring equipment and quickly glancing over the recipe that Bree had penned.

'An original S'mookie ... a layer of marshmallow and chocolate filling sandwiched between two milk chocolate cookies then dipped in an indulgent layer of creamy Belgian milk chocolate. Wow, this sounds amazing.' Cam was impressed and smiled up at Molly.

'You could melt this bar a little and eat it with a spoon,' shared Bree. 'This was the type of chocolate bar we used to make on a day like today – a cold winter's day. But today let's start off with the brownie and cookie creation.'

'Let's make Lilian Allen proud,' said Cam triumphantly.

'Today my kitchen is your kitchen and you get to tell me what to do.'

Molly watched as Cam took the baker's hat off the peg and handed it to Bree.

'I couldn't possibly wear that,' she exclaimed, beaming.

'You can and you will. I'm learning from you today,' insisted Cam.

As Bree put the hat on her head her smile was wide. 'Let's get this show on the road.'

Cam winked at Molly, who was lapping up the jovial atmosphere in the room. There were so many questions she wanted to ask Bree, but first she was itching to get over to her old house and delve into the suitcase to see if there was anything of interest. She sat on the stool and watched as they worked together creating the chocolate bar. Bree was in her element, her eyes sparkling, her smile wide.

'The Belgian chocolate needs to be melted at forty-two degrees, gradually cooling to twenty-nine. Do you have any polycarbonate moulds?' asked Bree.

Molly jumped off the stool and retrieved the moulds from the cupboard and placed them on the worktop next to Bree.

'Perfect.' Bree looked over them and pointed. 'This one.' She passed the mould to Cam. 'We're going to make two slabs of chocolate so to start we need to dispense a layer into the mould and wait for the chocolate to cool and shrink. Then we are going to make chocolate brownies and cookies. Once everything is cool, we take the chocolate out of the mould and then leave a 3mm edge around the bar, drizzle with caramel, add the brownies and cookies, along with a sprinkle of The Old Bakehouse secret ingredient, and layer it all between to the two slabs of chocolate.'

'The Old Bakehouse secret ingredient... Which is?' asked Cam

'Exactly that, a secret,' replied Bree with a chuckle. 'Top with a drizzle of white chocolate and marshmallow and once more let it cool. This will be our starter bar and from here we can play around with other fillings in the chocolate slab if you don't want to use brownies for your entry.'

'Can I be chief taster?' asked a wide-eyed George, peering over the counter.

'You certainly can,' replied Bree. For a second Molly noticed a flicker of sadness in her eyes and wondered what had prompted it. Perhaps she always used to be 'chief taster' when it was just her and Lilian?

'You are so lucky to have such a wonderful family,' added Bree.

'It sounds to me like you were too, so let's bake and do Lilian proud,' replied Molly with a smile. 'And with not many weeks to go until this one is born' – she patted her stomach – 'I best eat my body weight in chocolate because I'm not going to get away with it much longer.'

Bree laughed as she straightened the hat on top of her head. 'Let's bake!' she trilled.

Molly watched Cam and Bree closely as they set to work. What exactly would happen next if Molly discovered she and Bree had the same mother?

Chapter Thirteen

Cam's jaw dropped open as he and Molly sat in bed with fresh cups of tea later that night. His head was spinning with the information that Molly had just shared with him.

'And you think there's a possibility you have the same mother just because she made a comment about the moon. Does Bree have any idea this is what you're thinking?'

'You think I'm mad, don't you?'

'I'm not sure what to think. Is it even possible?'

'It is. I've been doing the sums. If Lilian had a baby at sixteen – me – and she had Bree at thirty-one, it's very possible.'

'Indeed, possible, but a little…'

'I know what you're thinking, but since Bree came across my path, I've begun to have flashbacks to my own past with my mother.'

Cam blew out a breath. 'Flashbacks? What sort of flashbacks?'

Molly told Cam all about the visions that had been coming to her more frequently. 'Meeting Bree triggered something. It's strange.'

'Do you think you've been repressing these memories?'

'Possibly. Maybe I didn't want to know the truth about the past because my present was always so happy.' She shrugged. 'I never really thought about being adopted because Di and Doug loved me so solidly. I never felt I missed out on being raised by my biological parents because Di and Doug *were* my parents.'

'And now?'

'I'm curious. I was under the impression that my mother's past was dark – that maybe there was addiction involved – but this doesn't add up to the picture that Bree has painted of her mother. I mean, you heard her this afternoon when we were all baking together.'

'I did notice the way Bree came to life when she talked about Lilian. It didn't sound like they had much money but they spent a lot of quality time together. Lilian was clearly a hard worker with the number of jobs she had, and what a baking talent she must have been. Was it Tutbury where they lived? Maybe Google would throw something up, you never know.'

'I'll take a look tomorrow. It was lovely when you lit the candle and placed it on top of the chocolate slab. I could see the tears welling up in Bree's eyes when we sang "Happy Birthday" to Lilian. It was a nice touch.'

'George seems to like her too. I'm sorry I misjudged her initially.'

'You had a lot on your mind,' replied Molly.

Cam took Molly's tea from her hand and placed it on the bedside cabinet. He then stretched his arms out and Molly snuggled in close and looked up at him. 'There's just one thing I can't get out of my head. I remember my biological mother saying "loon moon" as clear as day. Is it something you've ever heard before?'

Cam shook his head. 'Never heard it before in my life.'

'And that's what I mean. It means something. I'm sure of it.'

'Are you going to talk to Bree about it?'

Molly shook her head. 'Not yet, I want to see if there's anything in the suitcase that proves Lilian is my mother, and even if I do find proof, what am I going to say? I have to remember she's only young.'

'She may be young but that chocolate she made was a clear winner, I'm certain of it. I've saved a slab for my grandmother to sample. I need her opinion on it.'

'Good idea, because no doubt Dixie would have sampled all of Ted's practise bakes for the competition. Her opinion will be worth its weight in gold.'

'Just going back to the previous conversation,' said Cam, 'what if the suitcase doesn't throw up any further answers?'

'I'll have to cross that bridge when I come to it. Talking of bridges … has the track been cleared? We need to get to the hospital for your appointment in a few days.'

'Funnily enough I received a message from Drew saying

he and Fergus are going to get the snow ploughs out tomorrow and attempt to clear the track. They were asking for volunteers. I was thinking I'd bake a little stock for the shop tomorrow morning, then pop in and see Grandmother with the chocolate slab, then, if you're able to mind the shop, I could help the lads to clear the track.'

'Of course! We also have another helper tomorrow. Did you see how Bree thrived sharing the chocolate ideas? We could maybe ask her if she would like to work in the bakery for a couple of hours, and pay her?' Molly looked hopefully up at Cam.

'Okay, we can ask. And I have to say I'm intrigued to discover more about Lilian Allen because if she could bake like that...'

Molly gave him a little squeeze. 'I'll think she'll jump at the chance. And it's not as though she's going to be tired – she went to bed at eight-thirty p.m.' Molly gave a little chuckle. 'I think it's the novelty of sleeping in a huge, soft bed.'

As Cam leant across and switched off the bedside light, Molly snuggled down under the duvet.

It wasn't just Cam who was intrigued to discover more about Lilian Allen. Who exactly had she been and was it possible she was Molly's birth mother?

Chapter Fourteen

Molly heard muffled laughter from the hallway as she sat up in bed and stretched. The space next to her lay empty as she took a glance at the clock and she was amazed to see it was a little before nine a.m. She couldn't believe she'd slept in this long! Pulling Cam's faithful sloppy sweater over her head she padded downstairs and was greeted by the aroma of sizzling sausages. The table was set and as Cam stood at the cooker preparing breakfast, Molly couldn't help thinking how utterly gorgeous he was. She slipped her arms around his waist.

Cam glanced over his shoulder as he stirred a pan on top of the Aga. 'Here she is. Good morning, sleepy head!'

'I can't believe I've slept this long, but if it means waking up to a full Scottish breakfast then I might just attempt more lie-ins.'

'Good luck with that, because very soon I think someone

will be having different ideas. How are you feeling this morning?'

'Big,' replied Molly with a smile. 'It's getting to the point where I'm finding it difficult to put on my socks.' She looked down. 'In fact, I can't even see my feet.'

Cam laughed. 'That's all about to change,' he said, kissing the top of her head. 'I've baked numerous loaves and pastries this morning just in case any villagers want to brave the freezing temperatures but it's unlikely the shop is going to be busy.'

'Where is everyone? It seems very quiet.' She looked over her shoulder towards the hallway.

'George has gone to have breakfast with Dixie, and Bree is in her element minding the shop so I thought I'd cook you up your favourite and we could eat together.'

'You old romantic, you. I really could get used to this.'

'You better believe it. There's tea in the pot on the table so go and take a seat and I'll dish up. Oh, but first take a look at the email opened up on the laptop.' He gestured towards the small table in front of the log fire.

Molly sat down on the armchair and balanced the laptop on her knee. 'Oh wow! Decision made.' She was thrilled to see the confirmation from the baking competition that Cam would be competing for the title of Baker of the Year.

'I'll book the train tickets this evening, but I've hung fire on booking a hotel because I'm not sure what you want to do, as we are going to be quite close to the due date. Do you want to travel there and back in one day? Will that be easier? You need to make a decision on what's best for you and George.'

'I'll have a think. Have you broken the news to Dixie that you are definitely taking part?'

'I thought I would break the news in person when I take her the chocolate slab after breakfast.'

'I'm coming, I want to see her reaction!'

Cam placed two plates of the cooked breakfast down on the table and poured them each a glass of orange juice.

'I feel a little guilty eating this with Bree out in the shop,' Molly said between bites.

'I already cooked her a breakfast before you woke up, so no guilt necessary.' He smiled. 'As I mentioned last night, I'll walk over to the track after collecting George from Dixie's. If we can clear the snow, hopefully it will be a smooth journey to the hospital tomorrow.'

'How are you feeling about that?' asked Molly. She was trying to be supportive and put on a brave face whilst inside there was a huge knot in her stomach every time she thought about it.

'I'm trying to keep it from the forefront of my mind until tomorrow and then we will know more. But I'm not going to mention it in front of Dixie.'

Molly reached across and squeezed his hand. 'It'll be okay.'

'I hope so,' he replied, squeezing the brown sauce from the bottle, which erupted in a rude noise. 'Nothing like a comedy sound to lighten the moment.'

Molly rolled her eyes and laughed. 'I've contacted the

tenants at my old house to let them know we will be calling in tomorrow. They are currently away, so getting the suitcase down from the loft will be easy enough.'

'Tomorrow is going to be a bit of a day, isn't it?' Cam raised an eyebrow.

That very thought had just crossed Molly's mind.

Twenty minutes later, when breakfast was finished, Molly quickly got washed and changed whilst Cam cleared up the dishes, then she wandered into the bakery to see Bree standing behind the counter chatting to Ash on the other side. Molly couldn't help noticing how relaxed they seemed in each other's company, as Bree threw back her head and laughed at something Ash had said.

'Good morning! Thank you for holding down the fort whilst I was treated to breakfast. I was just going to ask if it would be okay if we popped next door to collect George from Dixie, but as Ash is in no hurry to get on with his rounds,' Molly teased, 'I'm sure he'll keep you company.'

There was a crimson blush on Ash's cheeks, and a huge beam on both his face and Bree's.

Cam breezed in then, slipping his arms into his coat and hoisting it up onto his back. 'We won't be long as we're just off next door; maybe twenty minutes or so.' He looked towards Bree and Ash then paused. 'You look a bit flushed in the cheeks there, Ash, are you coming down with something?' he said, causing the crimson on Ash's face to deepen.

Molly pushed Cam towards the door. 'He is absolutely fine,' she said. Cam looked bemused, not really understanding what was going on.

'Why are you pushing me out of the door? What did I say?'

'He's lovestruck, not poorly.'

Cam looked back towards the door. 'Really, those two?"

'Possibly,' replied Molly. 'Is that the chocolate slab in the bag for Dixie to taste?'

'It is. I can't wait for her to try it. I have to say I thought it tasted divine.'

'I second that,' replied Molly.

'If my grandmother thinks this is the way to go for the competition, then we are halfway there.'

'As long as Bree is okay with you replicating her mother's recipe.'

'I've already asked that question and she said she would be honoured. I had a look through Great-Uncle Ted's recipes this morning to get a proper idea of his winning entries and these chocolate slabs would be right up his street. I could even mix up the different fillings.'

Molly smiled as she opened the garden gate of Bumblebee Cottage. 'It's nice to see you so enthusiastic about it.'

The second they knocked on the door, Darling woofed and could be heard frantically sniffing on the other side.

'Come in, it's open,' came Dixie's voice from the living room.

Stepping inside they took off their boots and Molly scooped Darling up in her arms as she sniffed frantically at the bag in Cam's hand. 'That is definitely not for you,' she said, tapping Darling lightly on her nose.

The log fire was roaring and Dixie was sitting with a blanket over her knee, reading a book, whilst George was on his knees, leaning against the coffee table, attempting to piece together a jigsaw.

'This looks very cosy,' said Molly, hovering by the doorway. 'Should I make us all a cup of tea?'

'You read my mind.' Dixie smiled. 'That would be perfect.'

Five minutes later, having brought in a pot of tea, three mugs and a plate for the chocolate slab, Molly positioned herself on the sofa next to Cam and gave him a little nudge.

'I sense something is going on between you two. What am I missing?' Dixie didn't miss a trick.

At first, Cam's wide grin wasn't giving anything away. 'We've got something to show you and we want your professional opinion.'

Dixie sat up straight. 'I'm intrigued.' She watched Cam as he reached for the white paper bag.

'What we want to know is, in your professional opinion,

would this be in with a chance of winning the Baker of the Year competition?'

Immediately, Dixie let out a tiny gasp and brought her hands up to her chest, her eyes teeming with happy tears. 'Are you serious? Is this actually happening? You're going to compete for the title?'

'I am, and I've had a little help from my friends with this creation. But as I've never competed before and you have inside information on the competition, we would like your professional opinion. Are you ready?' asked Cam.

'Ready,' replied Dixie.

Sliding the scrumptious-looking chocolate slab onto the plate, Cam presented it to Dixie.

'Ta-da! Let me introduce you to The Old Bakehouse's new chocolate bar, which we have called "Layers Treats".'

Dixie was silent as she took the plate from Cam and stared at the slab of chocolate, making no attempt to taste it. Her eyes widened and a strangled noise came from her throat before her jaw dropped wide open.

'Dixie, are you okay?' asked Molly.

'Grandmother, what's wrong?' asked Cam, his expression worried.

Dixie pointed to the plate. 'Where did you get this recipe from? Because I know it's not in your Great-Uncle Ted's recipe book.'

Confused, Cam and Molly looked at each other then back towards Dixie.

'How have you heard of Layers Treats?' asked Cam, stringing the words out slowly. 'I don't understand.'

'And I don't understand how you have baked a similar recipe to the one which caused all the controversy back then.'

'Controversy? Grandmother, I'm completely lost here. Back when?'

Without saying a word, Dixie stood up, walked to the decanter on the dresser and poured a large glass of sherry. She swigged it back, took a deep breath and sat down again.

'It was the scandal of all scandals in the baking world. It was splashed all over the tabloids and the TV news and the story spread like wildfire.'

'Go on,' encouraged Cam, before taking a sip of his tea.

'It must have been at least fifteen to sixteen years ago when she disappeared.'

Molly's eyes widened. 'When who disappeared?'

'Ted's faithful assistant,' replied Dixie. 'He trained her up for ten years. The business was going from strength to strength, and then boom … she disappeared overnight. And when I say disappeared, that's exactly what I mean. She left with no word and no forwarding address – absolutely nothing, it was bizarre – and we never heard from her again. And after all Ted did for her. Why, he never even charged her rent in all those years.'

'Rent?' asked Cam.

'She lived in the spare room at The Old Bakehouse as it was easier for the early morning starts. I would even go as far as saying she became one of the family. Ted was devastated. He'd trained this girl and they'd built up a good friendship and working relationship. He taught her everything he knew.'

'And then she vanished?' said Cam.

Dixie nodded. 'Ted was overcome. He'd taken her off the streets, given her a chance, and to leave with no word ... we couldn't make head nor tail of it.'

'Great-Uncle Ted took her in off the street?' asked Cam, casting his mind back. He must have come across her working in the shop in his youth.

'He did. She initially started turning up night after night for the leftovers. She had no family, looked a bit bedraggled, and Ted gave her a chance, offered her a job as his apprentice and they became an excellent, unstoppable team.'

'So how is her disappearance linked to a baking scandal? I'm not sure I'm following,' Molly said.

'Ted and his apprentice were always creating new recipes and not just at competition time. The two of them perfected a recipe with a chocolate element that Ted sat on for nearly seven years after she disappeared. Then, once again, the gold sealed envelope arrived inviting the top three bakers in Scotland to compete for the title and the special element was chocolate. Ted was over the moon as he had been waiting for this.

'This is when all hell broke loose. That year, there were two bakers who baked similar recipes and when I mean similar recipes, I mean they were nearly exactly the same. The other baker involved in the scandal claimed that Ted was a cheat, that Ted had copied him somehow, which was impossible. Maybe it was just a strange coincidence, maybe their creative brains were just similar, God knows. But it nearly ended in fisticuffs with each baker discrediting the other. The judges had no option except to disqualify them both from the competition, yet they both still claimed it was their own original idea.' Dixie took a breath. 'Ted knew he had done nothing wrong but Barney Miller – the other baker involved – went to the local press and from there the story spread nationally. You could never imagine how it affected Ted. He thought his reputation was in tatters and wanted to close The Old Bakehouse and move away, but I talked some sense into him and reminded him that he had a clear conscience, that's all that mattered.'

Cam was silently racking his brains. He recognised that name … and then it came to him. 'Barney Miller is one of the judges in this year's competition.'

Dixie rolled her eyes. 'That should be interesting,' she stated.

'And what exactly did they both bake?' asked Cam.

Dixie held up the plate with the chocolate slab. 'This. Layers Treats chocolate slabs. They even used the same name for it.'

'Woah! How is that even possible?' asked Cam.

'That's what we couldn't fathom out,' replied Dixie.

'Did Ted and Barney know each other, move in the same circles?' probed Molly.

Dixie was shaking her head. 'They only came across each other when they were competing. It was all just pure madness.'

'How could anyone come up with the same recipe and the same name if their paths had never crossed?' Cam picked up the plate and stared at the slab of chocolate. 'That's an unbelievable coincidence.'

'I absolutely agree, especially when it was Ted's assistant who came up with the name. I was there the moment she did; I heard it with my own ears.'

Cam was still looking at the slab of chocolate as Molly gripped his leg. She was staring at Dixie.

'Ted's assistant. What was her name?' asked Molly, her pulse beginning to race.

'Lilian ... Lilian Allen.'

Molly brought her hands up to her heart and swallowed.

'Lilian was blooming brilliant at baking the chocolate slabs. Her Easter Eggs were also off the scale and my personal favourite was the lemon drizzled cake bar. There was even talk that we could possibly turn this front room at Bumblebee Cottage into an extension of The Old Bakehouse, making it into a chocolate shop of the same name.'

Molly and Cam were now just staring at each other.

'What I'm not understanding,' said Dixie, breaking the slab of chocolate in half, 'is how you found the recipe, as I know Ted ripped it out of his book after all the controversy. How have you stumbled across it?'

Molly was still in a state of shock as she blew out a breath. 'You aren't going to believe this.'

'Bree – the homeless girl – showed me how to bake this,' shared Cam.

'But I don't understand. How would Bree know all about Layers Treats?' asked Dixie, looking confused yet intrigued as she sat forward on the edge of the chair.

'Because Lilian Allen was her mother,' replied Molly.

'And that's not all,' continued Cam. 'Molly thinks that Lilian Allen could possibly have been her biological mother too.'

Shock was written all over Dixie's face. 'Christ on a bike,' she spluttered. She stood up and walked straight to the dresser. 'I need another drink.' Then she turned back around. 'How... Why... And you just said you think she could have possibly been your birth mother? Been?'

'Lilian has passed away,' shared Molly.

'Jeez. I need a double sherry,' confirmed Dixie, pouring a large tumbler full. 'Tell me everything.'

'There's so much to take in,' Molly said, not knowing where to start. Surely there was no way Bree knew that her mum had once worked at The Old Bakehouse and that that was where she had been trained by the best baker in the land? Surely, she would have mentioned it if she did?

Molly had quickly done her sums. If Lilian had left around sixteen years ago, then that was either at the time she was pregnant with Bree, or just before. But why would she run from the people who had offered her the world? It just wasn't making any sense to Molly.

'I'm just thinking aloud here, but if Barney Miller is one of the judges at this year's competition, what's going to happen if I bake this?' He pointed to the chocolate slab.

'He's going to work out that I'm related to Ted and then think I've baked this to stir up trouble or prove a point.'

'Do it!' encouraged Dixie. 'Ted was as honest as the day is long. There was no way on this earth he copied anyone. That recipe was created by Ted and Lilian together.'

Cam was unsure what to do. He needed to think this through, but if he wasn't going to use the recipe, he needed to think quickly about what he was actually going to bake. 'What do you think, Mol?' he asked.

But Molly didn't answer as she was lost in thought. Why had Lilian Allen disappeared that night? There had to be more to this story than met the eye.

Chapter Fifteen

T he next morning, Molly and Cam were leaning against the radiator in the nursery with their arms folded, looking around the room. The past twenty-four hours had been more than an eye-opener for the pair of them and Molly had been kept awake by Cam tossing and turning all night wondering whether he had the guts to enter the competition with his Great-Uncle Ted and Lilian's recipe if it had caused that much controversy before.

'Are we going to be bold and give the nursery a lick of pink paint?' asked Molly, looking around the neutral yellow room that had been untouched for nearly four years since George had moved into the bigger bedroom.

Cam's eyes widened. 'On Martha's say-so? Are we really that brave?' he asked, unsure whether that was the right thing to do.

'She's been right about everything else so far! What Dixie revealed yesterday was more than a scandal. A baker disappearing overnight, two more bakers somehow pinching each other's recipes. You couldn't write it, could you? And then I've got the two words that Bree said going round and round in my brain, but even I know it's far-fetched thinking we might have the same mother.'

'I have to admit, I've noticed you do have similar mannerisms,' replied Cam. 'But Dixie wasn't aware that Lilian had any children. You'd think that if Lilian was so close to Great-Uncle Ted and was one of the family, that might have come up in conversation over the ten years she worked at the bakery.'

'Would it though, if that child had been adopted? Would you bring up the past if you had made a fresh start?'

Cam thought about what Molly had just said. 'Maybe, maybe not,' he admitted.

'You must have met Lilian at some point.'

'It was during my teenage years. I'd discovered girls by then and hanging out at your grandparents' house was a little uncool,' he remarked with a glint in his eye.

Molly swiped his arm.

'I'm joking. I was a shy boy. I probably said hello but didn't stick around in the bakery as I preferred to be out on my bike or fishing,' he added, redeeming himself.

'What I don't understand is why – if Lilian had a roof over her head, a good job and security after being thrown a life-line to pull her up from street life – would she up and leave in the middle of the night, with not a word to anyone?'

'I've no idea,' replied Cam.

They stood in silence for a moment before Molly turned to Cam. 'Are you ready? We do need to leave for the hospital in the next ten minutes.'

He nodded.

'How are you feeling?' she asked tentatively.

'Scared out of my wits. My stomach is in knots and I feel like I could throw up at any minute, but it has to be done.'

'It does,' she said, standing in front of him, wrapping her arms around him and squeezing him tight.

Walking downstairs, they found Bree standing behind the counter looking proud in her apron. 'I think there night be a few more customers today as the snow is beginning to thaw a little.'

'You might be right. Are you up for the challenge?'

'I am and I can't wait,' she replied, straightening the delicious-looking pastries in the glass cabinet.

'George is with Dixie, but if things get too busy and you need help, ring her and she'll be right over,' said Cam, handing her Dixie's number on a piece of paper.

'I won't let you down,' she relied. 'I've got this.' The beam on her face was huge as she walked towards the bakery door and opened it wide. 'Now don't worry about a thing while you're out. Are you going anywhere nice?'

Molly and Cam looked at each other and hesitated. Molly had already swerved the very same question that morning when she dropped off George at Dixie's so she told Bree the same thing she'd told Cam's grandmother. 'Just a couple of meetings,' she replied, holding out the van keys to Cam. 'Come on, otherwise we'll be late.'

As they set off towards the track that took them over the bridge into Glensheil, they drove in silence. Though there was still snow almost everywhere, Drew and the boys had done a brilliant job of clearing the road, and the bridge was now open, thanks to the wind dropping. As soon as they hit the main high street in town, Molly noticed the colourful Christmas lights draped from one lamppost to the next, and standing next to the clock tower a huge Christmas tree that looked magnificent. Christmas was one of Molly's favourite times of the year. Inspired by Jamie Oliver, Cam had taken over the cooking for the past few years, dishing up the most succulent, mouth-watering turkey with homemade cranberry stuffing and all the trimmings, and George had an annual tradition of polishing off most of his chocolate for breakfast. This Christmas would be even more special with another baby added to the mix, and it couldn't come soon enough for Molly.

———————

The drive to the hospital was quite straightforward despite the terrible weather of the last week and with no delays they sailed through the rush-hour traffic and arrived at the hospital twenty-five minutes later. Taking a ticket from the machine at the side of the barrier, Cam pulled the van into a vacant space in the parking garage and breathed deeply.

Molly placed a supportive hand on his knee and gave it a little squeeze. 'It's going to be okay. Whatever the scan reveals, we are in this together,' she reassured him. Cam looked at her and nodded.

They located the unit from the specifics in the letter and hand in hand headed off in the right direction, following the arrows on the signs down the long white corridors. Cam checked in at the desk and after the receptionist confirmed his personal details, a nurse took him through to a separate room. Managing a wobbly smile of encouragement before he disappeared, Molly sat patiently in the waiting room. She couldn't even begin to imagine what was going through Cam's head and she was trying to think of everything and anything that was positive – filling her head with George's face, his smile and his voice – to keep herself distracted.

Meanwhile, the nurse handed Cam a gown and asked him to undress from his waist down. She pulled the curtain around on the rail, turning the corner of the room into a cubicle, and asked him to let her know when he was ready.

Cam was nervous and his hands slightly shaking as he untied his shoelaces, slipped off his shoes and removed his jeans and pants, which he folded up neatly and placed on the trolley beside him. Taking another deep breath, he managed to call out, 'I'm ready.'

The nurse pulled back the curtain and took him through to another room where he was met by a technician who was colour co-ordinated with the clinical white room right down to her clogs. She gave Cam a reassuring smile and asked him to take a seat while she explained that she was going to undertake a scrotal ultrasound scan. She reassured him that it was a painless procedure that used high-frequency sound waves to produce an image of the inside of his testicle, which would be the main way of finding out if the lump was harmless or not.

She asked Cam if he had any questions but he just shook his head. He wanted this over and done with as soon as possible.

Trying to think about anything other than what was going on in this room, he thought about Molly and his mood swings in the last few weeks. He was angry with himself for keeping the news of the scan from her for so long and he was glad she was waiting for him in the other room because he couldn't imagine getting through today on his own.

Before long Cam was back behind the curtain and reunited with his jeans and pants, thankful that the procedure was over with.

Molly was still sitting on her chair as Cam slid into the vacant one next to her.

'Everything okay?' she asked, placing her hand on his knee.

'Yes. She said I just have to wait until the consultant looks over the scan.'

The next hour was excruciating as Molly and Cam sat in silence until his name was finally called. They followed the nurse into another room and sat down on the plastic chairs in front of the desk. Cam was fiddling with his watch strap, trying to keep his emotions in check – trying to stay as strong as possible – but he wasn't finding it easy. His palms were sweating, his head was throbbing.

The door slowly opened and the consultant sat down at the desk. He checked over Cam's details before taking one last look through the results of the scan. Cam had no idea what the diagnosis was going to be.

'You did exactly the right thing by checking yourself,' said the consultant. 'I can't urge you enough to keep doing that.'

Cam swallowed. His heart was pounding as he waited to hear the next words.

'The scan shows that there is nothing sinister going on at all. It's just a build-up of fluid, which I will be able to drain for you if it is causing you distress.'

Cam closed his eyes and breathed out as relief flooded through his veins. 'So you're saying I'm okay? I'm not going to die?'

The consultant smiled. 'I can confirm you are not going to die from this.'

Cam flung his arms around Molly, who had happy tears leaking from her eyes.

'Thank you,' said Cam, looking back at the consultant, who nodded.

'Let me talk you through the procedure for draining the cyst,' continued the consultant.

Thirty minutes later they'd left the hospital. The return journey was upbeat. Cam and Molly were smiling, relief written all over their faces as they sang along to the radio whilst driving towards Molly's old house.

'It's a right rollercoaster of a day, isn't it? The unknown, the known, and now we are back to the unknown. How are you feeling about this suitcase?' asked Cam, glancing at Molly as he indicated right and turned into her old road.

'I'm not sure why I didn't open it up at the time. I suppose everything was just too difficult to deal with when the grief was so new. It might throw up absolutely nothing and if so, I keep thinking: do I tell Bree about my mad thoughts?'

'Possibly mad, possibly not. A DNA test would sort out that niggle.'

'Bree is only a child and I've no idea how she would react to my musings. But if I had some concrete evidence, it would be a lot easier. And then say we were sisters – half-sisters? – could we really let her go back to living in a shelter?' Molly was thinking aloud. 'I've no clue who my own father is and where is hers? The more I think about it, the more confusing and impossible it all seems.'

'What about your birth certificate? You must have needed that at some point.'

'You'd think so, wouldn't you, but this house was bought by my parents so I've never had to arrange a mortgage. The vet's surgery and hospital originally belonged to my dad's good friend and when he retired, my dad bought it off him, lock, stock and barrel, and I paid him back through my savings and wages.'

'But you have a driver's licence. Please tell me you are not driving illegally.'

'Of course I'm not, but I passed my test aged seventeen and again my dad sorted out the paperwork. Which I was quite happy about, because that meant he was going to pay.'

'I think that's every teenager,' replied Cam, parking the car outside Molly's old house. He cut the engine as she rummaged in her bag for the keys, then followed her up the path.

She placed the key in the lock, opened the door and stepped inside. 'It seems strange I once lived here; I feel like I'm trespassing,' she whispered.

'Why are you whispering?' asked Cam in a low voice. 'There's no one here.'

Molly shouted, 'Hello,' at the top of her voice, causing Cam to jump out of his skin. 'I'm just checking no one is home.' She grinned.

'Jeez,' he said, bringing his hands up to his thumping heart.

'I'll just check around—'

'Have a nosey, you mean,' interrupted Cam.

Molly rolled her eyes. 'It's my house.'

'You haven't lived here for nearly five years.'

'There is that,' she replied, lightly pushing Cam towards the stairs. 'The loft is that way. You'll have to go up as I'm not going to fit through the hole.' Molly chuckled, patting her heavily pregnant stomach.

'So that's the real reason you brought me,' he replied in jest as he climbed the stairs.

'I'll follow you up in a sec.'

Five minutes later, Cam's voice echoed down from the loft space above, 'My God, you're a fireman's worst nightmare! How could you have accumulated so much stuff in such little time? It's rammed to the rafters.'

'It's not that bad. I've only kept important stuff,' Molly bellowed back up into the hole that gaped above her head.

Cam's head appeared, amusement written all over his face. 'You've only kept the important stuff, eh? What's this?' He disappeared then reappeared with a big black curly wig on his head and dangling a blue sequinned jumpsuit.

Molly giggled. 'That's my ABBA fancy-dress outfit from talent night at the Grouse and Haggis maybe eight years ago. I'll have you know, me, Isla, Drew and Fergus came first.'

With his eyebrows raised he scooted out of sight. 'At least give me some idea where you think this suitcase is.' He reappeared in a straw hat with red tinsel draped around his neck.

'Towards the left, right at the back,' Molly instructed.

Cam disappeared again, and after a few seconds Molly heard the dragging of the suitcase. 'I think I've got it.'

'Excellent.' Molly raised her hands to steady the suitcase as Cam began to lower it down from the loft hatch.

'Be careful, Molly, it's quite heavy.'

'I've got it,' she said, lowering it on to the landing.

The ladder creaked as Cam climbed down and closed up the hatch. He swiped his hands and shook his head. 'I feel so dusty.'

Molly was staring at the suitcase then peered up at Cam anxiously. 'Do we open it here, or back at home?'

'It's up to you, whatever you think is best.'

Molly thought for a moment. 'Let's head home.'

A few minutes later, with the suitcase stored in the back of the van, they set off.

'What are you thinking?' Cam asked, slowly following the line of traffic towards the junction at the bottom of the road.

Molly took a breath. 'I'm not really sure. That case might provide all the answers or none at all.'

'There's only one way to find out,' Cam replied, giving Molly a sideward glance.

Chapter Sixteen

After they pulled up outside The Old Bakehouse, Cam took the suitcase around to the back door whilst Molly stepped into the shop. Bree was in place behind the counter and Molly looked around in surprise. There was hardly any bread left in the baskets. 'Woah! You've been busy,' said Molly.

'Run off my feet and I've loved every second of it!' Bree beamed. 'And not one single problem except maybe there weren't enough pastries for all those that wanted one.'

'The villagers must be venturing out again now those cold winds have dropped.'

'Did you have a good meeting?' asked Bree.

'We did,' replied Molly. 'But is it possible for you to hold the fort for maybe another thirty minutes?'

'It'll be my pleasure.'

Molly walked down the hallway and peered into the

living room, which was empty. Then she heard Cam's voice from the top of the stairs. 'I'm up here.'

Quickly taking off her coat and shoes Molly arrived at the top of the stairs, where Cam ushered her into their bedroom. He quietly closed the door behind her. The suitcase was lying in the middle of the bed.

They both perched on the bed, and Cam pulled the suitcase towards them. 'Are you ready?' he asked.

'Ready as I'll ever be.'

Feeling emotional, Molly watched as Cam undid the buckle then unzipped the suitcase. He pushed open the lid and Molly gave a tiny gasp – lying on the very top was her mum and dad's wedding photograph. She leant forward and picked it up. 'Look at them there, they look so young. My mother is so beautiful and my father was so handsome. I've often said that I think finding your one true love is luck. They were indeed very lucky.' Molly's voice faltered as she laid the photograph on the bed.

'Indeed they were,' agreed Cam. 'Just like we are.'

Taking a deep breath, Molly began to look through the stuff. There were photographs from when her parents moved into their first house. Photographs of Molly's sports days at school alongside all of her school reports.

'"Molly is a joy to teach! Her kindness towards others never goes unnoticed. A caring and dedicated child,"' teased Cam, reading from one of the reports.

'Behave!' Molly swiped his arm. 'I can't really see much of any interest,' she said, shifting through her parents' memories.

'What's that?' Cam pointed to a blue plastic folder that was sticking out from underneath a pile of nativity pamphlets from Molly's primary school.

She picked it up then opened it. Her heart began to beat fast when she saw exactly what the official document was. With a shaky hand she handed it to Cam. 'My birth certificate. I can't look. Can you look for me? I feel like my heart is going to pound out of my chest.' Molly closed her eyes briefly and took a deep breath. 'Does it say who my mother is?' She clutched Cam's knee and stared straight in front of her, trying to prepare herself for what Cam was going to say.

He nodded. 'It does ... but it's not Lilian Allen. The name on your birth certificate says your mother is Bethan Williams, your father is unknown.'

Molly exhaled and turned towards him. 'It's not Lilian Allen?'

Cam was shaking his head. 'Here, take a look.'

Molly gazed down at the birth certificate. 'Bethan Williams. I've never heard that name before.'

'How are you feeling?' asked Cam tentatively.

Molly was still staring at the name. 'I've no idea. Maybe ... a little disappointed? I suppose I had this romantic notion that it would be Lilian, and I was about to be reunited with my long-lost sister ... that I didn't know was lost. I thought everyone was going to live happily ever after together. Honestly, I was convinced. I just thought the fact that Bree sparked my flashbacks was some sort of sign.'

Cam lightly tapped the birth certificate. 'And what about Bethan Williams?'

Molly shrugged. 'It's a lot to take in.'

'Aren't you just a wee bit curious?'

'I honestly don't know. I can't get my head around it all, probably because I wasn't expecting this.' Disappointed, she placed the birth certificate back in the folder. 'And that's it. There's nothing else.'

Cam shook his head. 'What are we going to tell Bree about her mother? After all, once upon a time she seemed to be a huge part of this place,' he said, placing all the items on the bed back into the suitcase.

'I think she'll be chuffed, over the moon even, to learn about Lilian's involvement in The Old Bakehouse and...' Molly paused, her eyes widened. 'Those old video tapes that Dixie gave you ... Lilian has got to be on those, especially if she was here for ten years! Bree could see footage of her own mother, that would be lovely for her.'

'It would,' agreed Cam. 'I'll check with Dixie and maybe tonight we could have a film night. After today's events I think we need to relax, maybe open a bottle of wine.'

'Sounds like a good plan for you.' Molly patted her stomach and smiled. 'It won't be long until I can join you. How are you feeling after the hospital visit?' she asked.

'Relieved, without a doubt. I know us men don't like talking much about personal stuff but we do need to check ourselves.'

'You do. I'm just glad it's all going to be okay.'

For a moment they sat quietly, lost in their own

thoughts. Cam was thanking the Lord that everything was okay for him whilst Molly was feeling a little disappointed that her birth certificate hadn't thrown up a different name.

Should she just let sleeping dogs lie? After all, she had the perfect life and family as it was.

Cam broke the silence, looking around the room. 'It's strange to think that Lilian actually lived here for all that time. She's sat in the living room watching TV, cooked meals in the kitchen...'

'I know. But why would she choose to give all of this up? It sounds like she had one hell of a baking talent and could possibly have won any baking competition in her own right if she had kept going.'

'I've no idea . . . and I'm not sure we're ever going to find out why.'

Molly leant towards Cam and kissed him on his cheek. 'Come on, we best check on the shop and collect George from Dixie's.'

'You stay with Bree and I'll check with my grandmother about that video footage. Maybe she would like to come and watch it with us tonight. We could order a takeaway now the roads are little clearer?'

'That sounds like a plan, I've got so much heartburn with this little one already that a takeaway can't make it any worse,' said Molly, standing up and placing the suitcase in the corner of the room.

'Mol...' Cam paused and Molly sensed he wasn't sure whether to ask her whatever was going through his mind.

'With the road open, when is Bree going to go back to the shelter?'

Molly knew that question was coming and she'd already had the answer mapped out ... but then the name on the birth certificate changed everything. Instantly, she felt her eyes welling up at the thought of Bree sleeping in a hall, and she really couldn't bear the thought of it. But the bottom line was, they weren't related and Molly had no responsibility for Bree whatsoever. Yet deep inside, she still had a niggle that she couldn't brush off and she didn't know why.

'Just one more night, for film night?' said Molly, reluctantly.

Cam nodded.

Taking her chance, she asked, 'How would you rate Bree in the bakery? You've been impressed with all of her baking and were prepared to use her recipe for the competition... Wouldn't she solve all our problems? We wouldn't have to advertise, and it would help Bree to get back on her feet and give her a purpose.' Molly was looking at Cam with hopeful eyes, and her fingers crossed in hope behind her back. Unfortunately, she knew Cam and could have predicted what he was going to say.

'Hygiene, Mol. I can't have someone turning up to the bakery who has slept goodness knows where. Bree's clothes wouldn't be clean, and she might not have even showered.'

Cam had a fair point, but surely there were ways around it. 'Your Great-Uncle Ted gave Lilian a chance, took her off the street.'

Cam was quick to reply. 'But Great-Uncle Ted rattled about this place all by himself. We have a family and another child about to arrive at any time.'

'Would it have made a difference if the name on the birth certificate had been Lilian's?'

Cam thought for a moment. 'Possibly.'

Molly sighed. 'All she needs is a chance. She's a blooming good baker, young and enthusiastic. Imagine if she could follow in her mother's footsteps at The Old Bakehouse. Maybe there are other options...' Molly's thoughts were racing.

'What are you thinking now?'

'What if there was a free van to rent up at Foxglove Farm on a more permanent basis? I know Isla rents out the vintage vans to holiday makers but if there was the possibility of long-term rent... I could ask. Then Bree would have her own little place. Or what about Dixie?'

'What about Dixie?'

'There's plenty of room next door, at Bumblebee Cottage. That would be the perfect solution and Bree would never be late for work.'

'My grandmother might not even want a lodger.'

Molly tilted her head, her eyes wide as she flashed a hopeful smile at Cam.

'I'll think about it ... okay?'

'That's all I ask,' she replied with a huge beam on her face. Cupping her hands around his face she planted the biggest kiss on his lips. 'But I'm still intrigued to know what caused Lilian Allen to flee in the middle of the night.'

'Maybe we should ask Martha,' joked Cam.

'Maybe we should ask her what recipe you're going to bake for the competition.'

'I've been thinking about this and I think I'm actually going to enter the Layers Treats recipe. Let's see what reaction we get from Barney Miller, especially when he realises who I am.'

'Very controversial,' replied Molly.

'But I don't think Bree needs to know about the baking scandal from the past. It's our business.'

'Agreed,' said Molly. 'And let's get George to bed tonight before we tell Bree about Lilian.'

'Sounds like a good plan; she might be a little emotional.'

Indeed, Molly was already feeling somewhat emotional herself on Bree's behalf, picturing her watching films and photographs of her mum that she'd never seen before.

'Cam, I don't like the thought of Bree going back to the shelter. She just fits in so easily here. Please, let's ask Dixie what she thinks about having a lodger.'

'I've told you I'll think about it.'

'But if there's no need for her to go back to the shelter … and she's already proved she has the skills to bake…'

Cam surrendered and held up his hands in defeat. 'As you say, there's no harm in asking Dixie, see what she thinks…'

'I love you,' Molly exclaimed, flinging her arms around his neck.

'She might say no.'

That was something that Molly wasn't even going to think about. She skipped towards the door.

'Where are you going?'

'To ask Dixie.'

Molly's footsteps could already be heard pattering down the stairs.

'I thought *I* was going next door? I'll take over the shop, then, shall I?' Cam bellowed after her but there was no answer. He heard the back door slam before he finally got up off the bed.

Chapter Seventeen

'I don't want to go to bed. It's not fair!' George stamped his foot and looked around the room. 'I want to stay up with the grown-ups.'

Molly smiled at George. 'I promise you, you can stay up as late you want when you are a proper grown-up.' She placed her hands lightly on his shoulders and guided him towards Dixie. 'Now give everyone a kiss and Daddy will read you a story.'

'He's so cute when he's grumpy,' remarked Bree, watching George with amusement as Cam lifted the boy clean off the floor and swung him over his shoulder. George was now dangling down the length of Cam's back towards the floor, giggling uncontrollably as Cam made his way up the stairs.

'I'm going to bring the drinks and nibbles in,' declared Molly, disappearing into the kitchen and then returning with her hands full and placing everything down on the coffee table.

'What are we watching?' asked Bree, looking at the carrier bag at the side of Dixie's chair.

Dixie glanced at Molly and the look didn't go unnoticed by Bree.

'What is it?' she asked.

Molly shuffled towards the edge of her chair and took a deep breath. 'We've got something really nice to share with you but it may be something you already know.'

'Share away,' replied Bree with a huge beam on her face.

Molly smiled back. 'Did you know that your mum used to work here, at The Old Bakehouse?' she asked, and noticed the surprised look that flashed across Bree's face as soon as the words left her mouth.

'Here?' Bree pointed to the floor. 'My mum worked here?'

Molly nodded. 'Lilian was Ted's apprentice. He trained her and crafted her into a brilliant baker.'

'She lived here, at The Old Bakehouse,' added Dixie. 'I knew your mum well.'

Bree was speechless, her mouth opening and closing as she gathered her thoughts. 'No, I didn't know that. No way, are you serious?'

'Yes way,' replied Dixie with a nod. 'Absolutely she did. Ted taught her to bake and they worked together for over ten years. He gave her a job and a home.'

'She actually lived here?' Bree repeated, struggling to process the news.

Molly smiled. 'Yes, she did. Just like you did today, your mum used to stand behind that counter and help Ted bake the bread and the pastries, and she minded the shop when he was making his deliveries.'

'He used to say they were the dream team,' added Dixie. 'And recently I've been having a big clear-out and discovered numerous photographs from back then.'

Bree's bottom lip trembled. 'Have you any pictures of my mother?'

Dixie nodded. 'We have, but not only that...' Dixie reached down towards the carrier bag. 'We also have some video footage.'

Bree let out a tiny gasp. Her eyes had welled up with tears and her tiny body was shaking.

'Come and sit here,' said Molly, her maternal instinct taking over as she patted the empty space next to her.

Bree stood up and sat down next to Molly on the settee, hugging her knees tightly.

Molly pulled her in for a hug. 'Would you like to watch the video?' she asked gently.

'If that's okay?' replied Bree.

Molly gave her knee a little squeeze as she stood up and took the videotape from Dixie. 'It's amazing we still have this old video player; it was here when we moved in.' Molly switched on the TV and pressed a button on the control. After she inserted the tape it clunked then whirled as the TV screen burst into life.

Cam slipped into the room just then without saying a word and sat down.

Everyone watched the screen eagerly.

'Look at Ted,' exclaimed Dixie. 'He never aged, always looked the same.'

'Maybe a little less hair,' chipped in Cam. 'So why was he filming this?'

'Would you believe this was for a documentary? They wanted to follow Ted for a few days. I can remember they arrived around four-thirty a.m. Ted and Lilian hadn't gone to bed much before midnight as they scrubbed the bakery from top to bottom, not that it needed it. There was a buzz in the village in the days leading up to the filming and the villagers were camped out on the green, watching everything that was going on. Ted and Lilian claimed they felt like famous film stars.' Dixie gave a little chuckle. 'Ted wasn't too keen on having his make-up done,' she revealed. 'Honestly, he made such a hoo-ha about it, whereas Lilian loved it.'

Cam pointed at the TV screen. 'Look at The Old Bakehouse. It looks the same yet everything seems different. Great-Uncle Ted did pack those shelves full.'

'He did.'

'And what's that?' asked Cam, noticing the small cart that had been wheeled into the shop.

'That was the chocolate stand ... Layers Treats, chocolate barrow. Those chocolate slabs didn't even last until mid-morning. Believe me, they were famous around these parts.'

'My mum's chocolate slabs were famous?' Bree was amazed.

'They were,' replied Dixie.

At that moment Ted appeared behind the counter with Lilian at his side. Bree immediately sat up straight then moved from the settee and crouched down on the rug in front of the TV, rocking gently. Dixie leant forward and passed Bree a tissue. There was no denying Lilian lit up the screen. Molly couldn't take her eyes off her. Goosebumps prickled her skin. She was beautiful, her skin flawless, her brunette hair trailing the length of her back. She was slim, with the most gorgeous smile, and Molly thought she wouldn't look out of place on the cover of *Vogue*.

Even though the name on her birth certificate was not Lilian's, Molly couldn't shake off the feeling that she knew her. There was something very familiar about her, something about her eyes. Maybe it was because Bree was the spitting image of her.

Molly caught Cam's eye and he mouthed, 'You okay?'

She nodded before looking back towards the screen, where Ted and Lilian were serving the local residents.

'There's me,' said Dixie, recognising herself on the screen. 'Oh, and there's my George. He looks so young and so, so gorgeous.' Dixie brought her hands to her chest as she watched through bleary eyes.

'He was a very handsome bugger,' said Molly, reaching across and touching Dixie's arm before looking back at Bree, who was dabbing her cheeks with her tissue.

Next, Ted and Lilian were filmed in the bakery kitchen as they baked bread and pastries. Their onscreen presence was amazing, their laughter infectious, and you could see they were the best of friends.

Then, as the video came to an end, Lilian looked directly into the camera and said, 'I wouldn't change working with Ted for the world, he's just the best.' She winked into the camera and Ted could be seen rolling his eyes in jest in the background. Then the screen went black and the video ejected from the machine.

Bree was still staring at the TV, her chin resting on top of her knees. Molly awkwardly crouched down next to her on the rug. 'Your mum was beautiful.'

Bree swallowed. 'It seemed so real. Mum looked so young, carefree, happy. It felt like she was still here. I miss her so much.' Her voice wavered.

Molly extended her arms and hugged her tight. 'She was a very special person.'

'She was,' replied Bree as she pulled away slowly then dabbed her cheeks with the tissue again.

Cam leant forward and switched off the TV before turning the lights up while Dixie placed a handful of photographs on the coffee table. 'There's a picture of your mum on her first day of work at The Old Bakehouse.' Dixie pointed to the picture and Bree picked it up. In the image, Lilian was standing next to Ted in the doorway of the bakery. Each was wearing a pristine white apron embroidered with the words 'The Old Bakehouse'. Lilian looked so proud.

'I can't get my head around the fact that my mum actually worked here. I thought that we'd talked about everything but why wouldn't I know that this is where her career started? Why was Ted never mentioned? I just don't understand.'

'I'm not sure,' replied Molly. 'Maybe in time this place became a distant memory. Your mum had moved on and was working in other jobs.'

Holding numerous photographs, Bree sat back on the couch. After flicking through the photographs, she turned towards Dixie. 'On that video, you could see that my mum loved it here. Why would she move on?'

The question hung in the air.

'Is there something I should know?' asked Bree, sensing that something wasn't quite right.

Molly looked towards Dixie for guidance. 'We honestly don't know, Bree.' Dixie took a breath, knowing that the next words to come out of her mouth would sound somewhat dramatic. 'Your mum disappeared in the middle of the night.'

Bree looked confused. 'What do you mean?'

'I mean exactly that. Ted told me she was watching a film and everything seemed very normal when he said goodnight – it had been just like any other day. The next morning, his alarm went off at the usual early hour and after a quick shower he went down to the bakery to begin baking the bread. Lilian usually appeared half an hour later but time ticked on with no sign of her. Ted thought she must have overslept so after an hour had gone by, he went up to her room, gave a knock on the door, then a little shout, but still there was nothing. He finally opened the door, thinking something might be wrong, or she'd fallen ill, but she'd gone. The bed was made and her clothes were no longer hanging in the wardrobe.'

'Did Mum not leave a note or anything? And when was this?'

'There was no note, and no one saw or heard from your mum again. Ted was devastated, heartbroken. He wracked his brains thinking maybe he'd done something wrong but he couldn't think of anything. It was an absolute mystery. As to the timing, it was about sixteen years ago.'

'Just before I was born,' said Bree, thinking out loud.

'After Lilian left, Ted threw himself into work and refused to look for another apprentice. He did everything himself and I helped out as much as I could.'

Bree was perplexed and flicked again through the photographs in her hand. 'That just doesn't sound like Mum. I couldn't ever imagine her leaving in the middle of the night for no reason and without a word. Where would she go?'

Dixie shrugged. 'I've no idea, but she was sadly missed – not just by us but by the villagers as well. Lilian had become a huge part of the community. The Old Bakehouse felt a little lost for a good while.'

'Do you know anything about your mum's life before you were born?' asked Molly.

'The only thing I know is that she spent some time travelling around, moving from pillar to post. She once said that she didn't really know where she belonged as she had no real roots that she could call home ... but you're telling me something different. This place sounded like her home, so why give it all up?'

'That may be something that we'll never find out,' said Cam as he sifted through the rest of the photographs on the table.

'I do know that my mum spent some time on the streets.' Bree wiped a tear with the back of her hand. 'It was only when I was older that she shared that with me. I was a little taken aback because even though we didn't have money for extravagant things she was a hard worker – kind, caring and loyal – and I couldn't see how that could possibly happen. Of course, I didn't know the circumstances as that was something she never shared with me, but maybe she would have at some point in the future.'

Bree placed the photographs down on the table. 'It was good to see her today.' She looked at the TV screen before standing up, walking towards the windows and pulling back the curtain. Molly knew exactly what she was doing. She was searching for the moon.

'Mum loved the moon. She said it guided her when times had been tough and if there was a time we were never together, then if I looked at the moon she would be looking at it too. In the whole of our lifetime together we'd never spent a night apart until she...'

Bree didn't finish her sentence and sat back down. 'When did you realise that my mum was the same Lilian Allen that worked and lived here?'

'When Cam took the chocolate slab to Dixie earlier

today, she instantly recognised the Layers Treats. That recipe was one Ted and your mum used to bake together.'

'And there was something about those words you said to Molly – "loon moon",' Cam added, standing up. 'I'm just going to get myself a beer.'

Bree watched Cam walk out of the door. 'What does Cam mean?'

'When you said those words I had a flashback to maybe the only thing that I remember my own biological mother ever saying to me. For a few hours I even considered it might be possible that we could have the same mother. I know it sounds daft but I went up to the church to find out your mother's name. The vicar told me – and I hope you don't think he was talking out of turn – that your mum asked to be buried at Heartcross and it made me wonder about her ties to this place.'

'She did,' replied Bree. 'That's how I ended up sleeping rough in these parts. I just wanted to be close to her.'

'Do you know why she asked to be buried here?' asked Molly.

'The letter stated that she wanted to be buried here because once you arrive in Heartcross you never want to leave. And I suppose after what you've just said about Mum working here, she probably wanted to be buried here because this was the place she felt was home. But I don't think it was daft that you thought we had the same mother, because I also got a strange feeling the first moment I saw you outside the shelter. It just felt like I knew you from somewhere. There was something familiar about you that I just couldn't shake off,' she said, picking up her drink from the table and taking a sip.

'You did?' quizzed Molly.

'I suppose the connection is this place,' added Bree. 'Maybe the universe crossed our paths because my mum had a connection to this place. Who knows.' She shrugged.

'I was convinced there was some sort of connection but I dug out my birth certificate – my adoptive parents had stored it away in a suitcase full of documents – and the name wasn't the same.'

'Had curiosity never got the better of you before?' asked Dixie.

'Not until I bumped into Bree. I'm not sure what I'm going to do with my findings but that's a thought for another day. At least after seeing it I now know that my adoptive parents kept my Christian name and my surname was changed from Williams to McKendrick. My mother's name was Bethan Williams.'

The glass of water that Bree was holding slipped out of her hand and bounced on the carpet. She was staring straight at Molly. 'Sorry … sorry, but say that again.' Bree's face had paled.

'My mother's name was Bethan Williams. What is it, Bree? Do you recognise that name?'

Bree managed a nod and stuttered, 'My bag, where's my bag?'

'In the hallway.'

Molly and Dixie exchanged glances as Bree disappeared and returned holding her bag. After rummaging inside she pulled out a plastic bag, which held a crumpled, dirty envelope that looked like it had been through the war. She handed it over to Molly.

'What's this?' asked Molly, taking the envelope from her and straightening it out. With a thumping heart she looked at the bold lettering in black biro on the front of the envelope, which read 'MOLLY WILLIAMS'. 'I don't understand,' Molly said, confused.

'Lilian Allen – my mum – was also known as Bethan Williams. I found this letter in her things after she passed away.'

Molly's jaw dropped wide open. She couldn't think straight. Stammering, she asked, 'Did you know your mum had another child?'

Bree nodded. 'I did. Mum told me that she changed her name to escape an abusive relationship and that I had a sister somewhere out there. I've carried this letter around with me every day since I was made homeless. I've kept it in a plastic bag in the lining of my bag, hoping I'd find my sister one day.'

'Oh my God' were the only words that Molly could manage.

'Does this mean you really are my sister?' asked Bree.

'Well, I never,' exclaimed Dixie, who was sitting in the edge of her seat. 'Come on, open it up. What does it say?'

Just at that moment, Cam walked back into the room with a beer in his hand. 'What have I missed?' he said cheerfully, sitting down and taking a huge swig from the bottle.

'I've got a letter from my mother.'

'Huh?' replied Cam, suddenly noticing the strange atmosphere that had flooded the room.

Molly held his gaze and repeated, 'I have a letter from my mother.'

Chapter Eighteen

M olly stared at the envelope for a while longer. Everything seemed surreal. Bethan Williams had changed her name and reinvented herself to escape an abusive relationship, which made a lot of sense to Molly. Cam moved from the chair and perched on the coffee table in front of her. Surrounded by silence, Molly opened the envelope carefully and pulled out a sheet of white paper. She stared at the words on the page, but found it hard to focus.

Cam touched her arm and Molly jumped. 'Would you like me to read it?'

Blinded by tears she nodded and handed the letter over to Cam, her thoughts swinging like a pendulum between apprehension and excitement. All eyes were on Cam. He swallowed then began to read aloud.

My Dearest Molly,

I'm struggling as how to begin this letter and I'm not even sure you will ever read it. You were a wee girl when we were parted and since then, you have always been in my head and my heart. Not a day has passed without me thinking of you.

It was the hardest decision I've ever made to put you up for adoption, but my life had spiralled out of control. After my own parents had passed away, I found life incredibly difficult and along the way made some bad decisions, which included a toxic relationship with a man – your father. Things were going from bad to worse and I knew my main priority was to make sure you were safe. I met with Di and Doug on numerous occasions before the adoption was finalised and they seemed so lovely. I hope your life with them has been a happy one.

Cam looked up at Molly to see tears streaming down her face. 'Do you want me to go on?'

Molly nodded. She didn't trust herself to speak.

Your father was a drug addict and as much I loved him I feared for my own safety so I planned my escape with the help of a woman from the women's shelter. She gave me clothes and food and I stayed at the shelter when I left him. This is when I decided to change my name and make a fresh start so I took a risk and moved from the safety of the shelter to the small village of Heartcross. I didn't have a job or anywhere to stay but a kind man called Ted Bird gave me a chance at life. My best days were spent at The Old Bakehouse learning how to bake and more importantly being a part of a family I truly loved.

'I still don't understand why Lilian would leave after we welcomed her into our family,' murmured Dixie.

'I think I'm coming to that,' said Cam, looking from Molly to Bree, whose eyes were fixed on him.

After getting my life back on track I can't believe what I am about to write: not only did I let my good friend Ted down, I also let myself down. After some years your father tracked me down. He walked into The Old Bakehouse as bold as brass. I'd escaped for nearly fourteen years and there he was standing in front of me. I was shocked and scared.

He claimed he was clean and that he did it for me and all he wanted was his family back. I fell for his chat and his charm and even after everything that had happened, I agreed to meet him that evening. Which I did. He'd organised a picnic at Primrose Park and pulled out all the stops, including champagne. The sun was shining and everything seemed quite relaxed. We shared a moment and soon after, while we were lying on the blanket under the stars, he told me that all he'd ever thought about for the last ten years was us. He wasn't aware you had been adopted as I'd escaped his clutches the day after you left. When he was talking, I noticed a figure by the bandstand and when he excused himself I watched him go over to speak with the stranger and realised that your father wasn't clean as he handed over money in exchange for a package. I was engulfed with fear. I didn't want to go back to that life and I was stupid to have agreed to meet him.

Soon after, I made my excuses and left, promising I would see him again but knowing I wouldn't. When I arrived home, I put on a film and after Ted went to bed I knew I needed to take the opportunity to run again. That man would have brought a lot of trouble to Ted's business and to me and I was frightened of what he would do, especially when he realised that you were no longer with me. So I left in the dead of night without a word to anyone. I had to start again and hope he wouldn't find me.

It is just over eight months later now and here I am writing this letter to you while lying in a hospital bed after just giving birth to your sister, Bree Allen. She is as gorgeous as you were.

I have no idea how to finish this letter, but I hope it's not the end, just the beginning and that one day we will all be reunited. Your sister and I would love to meet up with you soon.

Keeping looking at the moon until we can be reunited. Loon moon.

I love you,

Lilian x

Molly's head was whirling as Cam finished reading. She was never going to be reunited with Lilian but sitting next to her on the couch was her sister, and not just a half-sister. Even though there was a terrible sadness in the room that Lilian wasn't here for this moment, Molly knew she had been brave to hand her over for adoption for her own safety. It had been the right thing to do in the circumstances.

'Lilian must have been scared witless to give up her life again and run from everything that had made her feel so safe,' said Dixie.

'And you really didn't know anything about Molly when Lilian started working here?' asked Cam.

'Absolutely nothing, and if Ted did, he never breathed a word to me,' Dixie replied.

Molly took the letter from Cam and her eyes flicked over it quickly. Then she turned towards Bree. 'You're my sister,' she said, her voice cracking with emotion.

'I am,' replied Bree. 'I know you will never see Mum again but she was one in a million, and I'm so sorry she isn't here for this.'

Molly's eyes searched Bree's.

'Mum must have discovered she was pregnant with me soon after leaving here,' Bree added.

'Yes, and we still have no idea who our biological father is. The letter doesn't even give a first name,' said Molly.

'Do we care though?' replied Bree. 'I'm not sure I do. Always looking over her shoulder must have been a huge burden for Mum.'

'For sixteen, you are a very clear-headed young woman who knows her own mind,' Molly said, her admiration clear in her tone.

'I had a good teacher.' Bree picked up the photograph from the table. 'Our mum. I do wish she was here with us, right at this moment.'

'Me too,' replied Molly as she stretched her arms out. Bree fell into them as tears of joy started streaming down both their faces. 'Pleased to meet you, little sis. I always wanted a sister.'

'Me too,' replied Bree, her voice barely a whisper.

Chapter Nineteen

'How do I look?' asked Molly a couple of weeks later, looking down at herself then at the pile of maternity clothes thrown on top of the bed. Nothing fitted. Molly felt like she was going to pop at any moment and she knew she was taking a risk travelling to Edinburgh, but there was no way she was going to miss Cam competing in his very first Baker of the Year competition.

'I'd say blooming gorgeous,' replied Cam, who was packing Great-Uncle Ted's toque at the top of his rucksack.

'You have to say that,' Molly said with a smile.

'No, I don't at all. Give me a twirl!' He took her hand and turned her around then pulled her in close and kissed her softly on the lips.

'And how are you feeling?' she asked, looking down at the hat that had won many a competition for Ted.

'Have to admit, the adrenalin is kicking in. I'm excited to see what the competition is and nervous to come face to face with Barney Miller, especially if he recognises the recipe.'

'I'm in no doubt that he's going to recognise the recipe given you've named your entry "Layers Treats", but Dixie is adamant that Ted and Lilian came up with that recipe together and Dixie is sticking to her guns. She also knows Barney from old and is willing to give him what for if needed. I have to say, as much as I love Dixie, I wouldn't like to get on the wrong side of her,' added Molly, grinning.

'My grandmother can be so feisty,' replied Cam, giving Molly a squeeze before picking up his bag. 'I think I've got everything: change of clothes, my apron, Great-Uncle Ted's lucky hat—'

'And you don't mind that we aren't staying overnight?' interrupted Molly, feeling a twinge of guilt that Cam had changed his plans for her.

He smiled at Molly. 'Of course I don't mind, and I cleared it with the organisers that I didn't have to be there until a few hours before. Thankfully, Flynn is helping to transport us in style and so we only have to get ourselves to Starcross Manor.'

'Isn't it nice to have friends in high places that own planes, trains and every type of automobile? George and Bree are going to love travelling in the helicopter.'

'They are but are you going to be okay?'

'I'm going to be perfectly okay, as long as I don't go into labour in the air.'

'Don't say that – you know that I'm worried sick about exactly that.'

'What are the chances that I go into labour just as we are soaring through the sky?' she teased, pretending to suddenly have a little twinge and glancing at the small overnight pack by the door, which was ready to go to the hospital with her as soon as she went into labour.

'You are not funny.'

'Sorry, sorry,' she said, holding up her hands. 'Only joking! Now come on, let's go and win the Baker of the Year title.'

'Where are the others? They should be here by now.'

'George, Bree and Dixie are ready and waiting, don't you worry about that.'

As they walked into the bakery, Molly pointed towards the window. 'Come and take a look.'

Cam swung a glance that way and couldn't believe his eyes. 'Well, I never...'

The villagers had lined the edge of the snowy green, most wearing baker's hats, waving flags and holding up banners wishing Cam all the luck in the world for today's competition.

'All these people have come out just for me?' Everyone he knew was standing on that green.

'Of course they have. They're your friends,' replied Molly, linking her arm through his. 'They're here to wave you off just like the community did each time your Great-Uncle Ted went off to compete. Grab your coat.' Molly opened the bakery door wide as Cam pulled on his coat and lifted up the overnight bag. As soon as he stepped outside loud cheers erupted. Despite the cold it looked like the whole village had come out to celebrate.

'Honestly, I feel like an international superstar. This is amazing.' Cam waved and smiled at his friends, then he spotted George running towards him followed by Dixie and Bree. He scooped him up in his arms. 'What do you think of all this?' asked Cam, placing George back on the ground.

'It's going to be so much fun.'

'You make the most of it, little fellow, as the school will be reopened on Monday,' said Dixie.

'And how's your new lodger?' asked Molly, smiling at Dixie then Bree.

'Not bad,' replied Dixie with a glint in her eye. 'I need to teach her how to make a decent cup of tea but apart from that she'll do.' Dixie gave Bree a cheeky wink as the younger woman raised her hands in mock protest. 'Are we heading over to Starcross Manor now?' Dixie asked.

'There's no need. Look!' Molly pointed up into the sky.

'Woah! Look at those!' exclaimed George, his hands cupping his eyes as he tilted his head up to the sky.

Two navy-coloured helicopters whirled above them with Flynn Carter's initials in bold gold lettering on the side of each. The noise was getting louder and the villagers began to move to the pavement opposite the green.

'Are they actually going to land on the green?' asked George, still looking up at the sky.

'What it must be like to be a multimillionaire...' murmured Cam.

'And a gorgeous friend to boot,' added Molly.

They watched as the two helicopters landed, one at each end of the green, and then Cam waved to the crowd and took hold of Molly's hand. The villagers shouted their good luck messages and Cam waved above his head once last time. Dixie and Bree held on to an excited George's hand as he eagerly pulled them towards the helicopters.

Molly turned back around. 'Bree, George, you're coming with me. Dixie, you ride with Cam.'

'Are you sure?' asked Dixie.

Molly nodded. 'Of course you need to arrive with your grandson. If you hadn't encouraged him to follow in Ted's footsteps then we wouldn't be here. Let's go and make Great-Uncle Ted and Lilian proud. We'll see you when we land,' she said, kissing Cam's cheek.

They made their way towards one of the helicopters and were helped inside by the pilot. Once they were all seated and strapped in, the pilot shut the door and passed them each a pair of headphones. 'Here, put these on.'

Molly could see the excitement written all over George and Bree's faces as they looked out at the crowd of villagers, who were still frantically waving from the pavements.

'This is something else, I actually feel like royalty!' exclaimed Bree. 'Never in my life did I think I was ever going to ride in a helicopter. It's out of this world.' She turned towards Molly. 'Thank you … and I don't mean just for this. Thank you for my job and a home with Dixie.'

'You don't need to thank me; that's what families do and Cam is lucky to have such a talented apprentice. I'm not sure who is teaching who more.' Molly gave Bree a warm smile.

'I'm just a little sad Mum never got to see us together . . . and Stan would never have believed me if I told him I was riding in a helicopter. He had a good send-off yesterday.'

'He absolutely did,' replied Molly, thinking back to Stan's funeral. She had never seen the pews so full in the church with all his friends from the shelter there to say goodbye to their trusted friend. There wasn't a dry eye in the place when Sam got up to say a few words and another resident played Stan's favourite tune on the church organ. He was going to be sorely missed.

Just at that moment the pilot turned towards them. 'Are you ready?'

George squealed with excitement.

'I think that's a yes,' replied Molly, squeezing George's hand.

Within seconds, the helicopter began to slowly rise as the blades spun round and the machine lifted effortlessly off the ground. They waved to the villagers who were flapping their flags in the air, and watched as they began to get smaller and smaller. Up in the blue sky above Heartcross Mountain, the view stretched for miles. Molly smiled, noticing that Bree had taken George's hand and was pointing out all the different landmarks. They never took their eyes from the window.

Molly couldn't wait for them all to arrive.

Before long the helicopter began to descend into the grounds of Crossley Hall Manor, home to the elite baking competition for many years. Molly was already in awe of the place, having seen magnificent images of it online.

'Just look at this place. It's grander than Heartcross Castle,' said Bree admiringly.

'Crossley Hall Manor is a Grade I listed country house built in 1670 and largely renovated in the 1840s. There's over 50,000 acres of land,' Molly supplied, having read up on it extensively.

'It's like something off the TV,' added Bree, jumping down from the helicopter.

Molly and George were helped down by the pilot. Cam was smiling as he walked through the snow towards them. He looked gorgeous in his duffle coat with his tartan scarf wrapped around his neck. 'Absolute breathtaking,' he said, tilting his head towards her.

'Me or this place?' joked Molly as they stared at the splendid building in front of them.

'You, of course,' replied Cam, noticing that Molly was rubbing her stomach. 'You're okay, aren't you, no twinges?' He looked at her with concern.

'I'm just fine. Come on, let's get inside. I'm dying for a cuppa.'

She watched as Cam chased George across the snow-covered lawn towards the path that led to the entrance of Crossley Hall Manor. Molly knew she hadn't been entirely honest with her answer. For the last thirty minutes, she'd felt a couple of tightenings across her stomach. She recognised the familiar pains, but she was putting them down to false contractions – Braxton Hicks. She knew her body was getting ready for the real thing but as this was her second pregnancy Molly wasn't going to make the same mistake as last time and text all her friends to say she was in labour only to be sent home from the hospital an hour later.

'This is it,' said Dixie. 'I never thought I would be back here. I'm so proud of him.'

'Me too,' replied Molly. 'I'm so proud I could actually burst.'

'Do not be doing any bursting until this competition is over and we are safely back home and in driving distance of the hospital,' ordered Dixie, laughing before turning to Bree. 'Lilian came here with me a number of times over the years to support Ted. We didn't fly in a helicopter, mind.'

'I can't believe I'm here,' said Bree, her eyes firmly fixed on the old manor house.

'Cam would never have known about the Layers Treats if you hadn't turned up at The Old Bakehouse.'

As they approached the entrance a doorman dressed in a smartly cut black suit and wearing a top hat and gloves opened the door and welcomed them to Crossley Hall Manor. They stepped onto a red carpet, which led into a grand foyer that reminded Molly of footage she'd seen in a documentary on Buckingham Palace.

'Just wow! It's beginning to look a lot like Christmas!' exclaimed Molly, looking all around. To the side of the reception, a beautiful winter-wonderland scene had been created, the floor laden with fake snow surrounding an enormous real Christmas tree, which towered over them and sparkled. They moved further into the lavish foyer. The ceilings were painted with wonderful artwork, there was a crystal chandelier, and the marble floor stretched to a regally arched staircase.

They were approached by a professional-looking woman dressed in a pinstriped suit and wearing the highest of heels, which echoed on the floor. 'Are you here for the competition?'

Cam nodded. 'Cameron Bird. I'm competing today.'

'You are indeed.' She smiled, striking his name off her list. 'You are the last to arrive. If I can whisk you away to the competitors' suite, you'll have a couple of hours to prepare yourself before the competition begins.'

'Eek!' Molly grabbed hold of Cam and hugged him tight. 'Good luck, don't be nervous. We'll be cheering you on from the audience.'

'This is it – my first ever baking competition! I'll see you on the other side.'

'Hopefully with the first of many trophies. Good luck,' said Dixie enthusiastically, clapping her hands then squeezing Cam's cheeks just like she usually did to George.

'Grandmother!'

'You are never too old to have your cheeks squeezed.'

Cam shook his head as he high-fived George and Bree.

'And the family room is that way,' the woman said to Molly and the others while gesturing to a doorway on the left. 'The doors to the auditorium open in an hour and' – she checked her clipboard – 'you are in seats A5 to A8, right at the front,' she informed them, gesturing. 'In the meantime, there's complimentary food and drinks in the family room.'

They watched as Cam was led off through the foyer, waving as he disappeared around the corner.

'This is it. He's up against the best bakers in Scotland. I'm feeling so nervous for him,' shared Molly.

'Ted would be so proud. The next generation of Bird bakers waving the flag for The Old Bakehouse. It'll be you next, George.' Dixie ruffled the top of his head.

'Look at this place.' Bree was turning around in circles, staring at the magnificence of it all.

'Come on, let's go and get a drink,' said Molly, who began to walk towards the door then suddenly stopped in her tracks. She took a deep breath. 'Ooh, this little one is taking my breath away today.'

Dixie narrowed her eyes. 'Are you having twinges? Please tell me you're not…'

'No, I'm not in labour, it just feels a little uncomfortable, that's all,' Molly replied, trying to brush over the fact that her stomach had tightened so much that it had taken her breath away. 'Honestly, I'm okay.'

She carried on walking and they all sauntered into an impressive room where waiters circulated with free drinks and a buffet was laid out on a long trestle table. After they'd helped themselves to drinks from a passing tray, Molly's eyes swept the room, which was packed with the families and friends of the competitors. George had run off to a set of large burgundy velvet curtains at the far end of the room and was beckoning Bree over.

'Behind there is where the competition takes place,' pointed out Dixie.

Molly too peered behind the curtain, which revealed another room with rows and rows of chairs laid out in front of a stage. The set on stage looked like three proper kitchens as each workstation was equipped with its own sink, baking trays, utensils, bowls and a mixer. On the back wall huge hanging letters spelled out the words 'Baker of the Year Competition'. There was a line of pastel-coloured American-type fridges at the side and numerous pans hanging from the wall underneath the sign.

'It all looks so real.' Molly was amazed to think that it had been purpose-built just for this competition.

'Is that where Daddy is going to bake?' asked George, pointing towards the stage.

'Yes, and see that that table there? That's where the three judges sit. And we are sitting right at the front so you'll be able to see everything,' replied Molly. 'Come on, let's get a bite to eat before it begins.'

An hour later a loud gong sounded and everyone's heads turned towards the curtains. 'Welcome to you all. The auditorium is now open.' The curtains were drawn back and there were a few gasps around the room as other members of the audience saw the room for the first time.

'Dixie Bird, is that you? What are you doing here?'

Dixie spun round to see her old friend William Hartley, the manager of Crossley Hall Manor, standing beside her. Immediately a huge smile hitched on her face as she leant forward and kissed him on both of his cheeks. 'It's me all right,' she replied.

'You are looking beautiful as usual, but what are you doing here?'

'My grandson is following in the footsteps of Ted and competing.'

'Cameron Bird, why didn't I put two and two together? I know I shouldn't be biased but Ted was always the clear winner.' William gave her a wink. 'We must meet afterwards for a drink.'

'That would be lovely,' said Dixie, and quickly introduced the rest of the family.

'It's lovely to meet you all, but it's time to take your seats. I'll find you after the competition. Your favourite gin is still stocked behind the bar, Dixie. It's been awaiting your return.'

'Good man,' replied Dixie as William touched her arm before walking off towards the auditorium.

'If I didn't know any better, I'd say he has a soft spot for you,' Molly teased as she cocked an eyebrow.

'What can I say? He is a man of good taste.' Dixie chuckled as she took George's hand and they all began to walk towards the front row.

Soon after they were settled William walked onto the

stage and switched on the microphone. The whole room hushed and all eyes focused on him.

'Welcome, welcome, welcome, to Crossley Hall Manor. My name is William Hartley and I am the owner and manager of this wonderful establishment. We are all here today to crown this year's Baker of the Year!'

There was a ripple of applause around the room.

'I'm sure you all know that this competition has been running for nearly thirty years and our team of experts trail every inch of Scotland looking for the best bakers to invite to compete for this elite title. This year's special element is chocolate and our wonderful bakers can bake any recipe as long as it's an original creation. So, without further ado, please welcome into the kitchen … Cameron Bird all the way from Heartcross, Paul Hughes from Edinburgh, and Graham Lewis from Newton Stewart.'

The audience erupted into applause as the three competitors walked onto the stage.

'There's my daddy!' shouted George, standing up and waving madly at Cam, who gave him a quick thumbs-up and a massive smile before he went to stand behind his workstation.

Proud tears were running down Dixie's face and Molly quickly passed her a tissue. 'Look at him standing there, wearing Ted's hat and apron.'

Molly too came over all emotional. She could tell Cam was nervous by the way he was fiddling with his watch strap.

William continued. 'Now, please welcome to the stage our judges, who know exactly how our three competitors are feeling right at this very second because at one time or another they have each been standing behind these very workstations. Welcome Mary Smith, Tom Newey and Barney Miller.'

The audience cheered and clapped and each judge waved as they walked onto the stage and took their seats behind the judges' table.

'What are we looking for today?' asked William, directing the question towards Barney.

'Individuality. A unique recipe involving chocolate that shows your skill as a baker.'

'How long do the bakers have?' William held the microphone towards Mary.

'Two and a half hours,' she replied.

'And Tom, you've been in this position before, what advice would you give the bakers standing here?'

'Keep your cool and don't get distracted.'

'The judges will be wandering around asking questions and watching the competitors' techniques and of course tasting the finished dish! We wish you all the best of luck and may the best baker win. Your time starts ... now!' he called as the digital clock on the wall began the countdown.

'Here we go! Good luck, Cam!' shouted Molly, clapping her hands.

William went over to talk to the judges whilst the three bakers on stage got to work and Molly watched Barney closely. She wondered if he even realised that Cam was related to Ted but there was no evidence of that yet. He was acting very professionally in his position of chief judge. He took off his jacket and placed it on the back of his chair, then, taking the microphone, he walked over to the far workstation and began chatting to Graham, who introduced his unique recipe while Barney nodded with enthusiasm.

Next up was Cam.

'If he hasn't realised who Cam is, there's a possibility the penny is about to drop,' Dixie leant in and whispered to Molly.

Molly felt anxious; she had no idea how this was going to play out. Would Barney even remember that this was the recipe that had caused the controversy many years ago? Both Molly and Dixie sat up in their seats; neither of them was going to miss a second of this introduction. Barney was now standing at the edge of Cam's kitchen.

Swiping his hands on his apron, Cam shook Barney's hand with a smile. Barney looked at Cam's name on the plaque that was hung at the front of his workstation. 'Cameron Bird from Heartcross.' Barney strung the last word out as he quickly did a double-take at the name then swiftly glanced towards the front row where his gaze fixed straight onto Dixie.

'There it is,' uttered Dixie under her breath.

All eyes were on Barney as he rolled up his sleeves and asked Cam to introduce his recipe.

'My recipe is all about the best slab of chocolate you will ever taste ... guaranteed,' said Cam with confidence. 'Creamy Belgian milk chocolate filled with chocolate brownie and toffee sauce, topped with a Belgian white chocolate drizzle… It's all about the layers.'

Barney had narrowed his eyes. 'And what have you named your creation?'

'Layers Treats,' replied Cam, holding Barney's gaze without faltering.

It was at that very moment that Molly felt a different tightening in her body. She glanced down at her arm to see that Bree had grabbed hold of her. Bree's eyes were still fixed on the stage but she was digging her nails into Molly's arm and looked ghastly white.

Molly turned sideward. 'Are you okay?' Something wasn't right, Molly could feel it in her bones.

'I'm not sure.' Bree began to stutter. 'I know him. He's the man with the scar on his arm.'

'What man with a scar on his arm?'

'Barney, I know Barney. That man was a huge part of our lives. He knows our mother.'

Molly's eyes widened. 'What exactly do you mean?'

'Barney Miller is the man my mother used to work for. She used to take me to his bakery with her every Saturday.'

'You're kidding me?'

Bree was shaking her head. 'I saw that man every Saturday up until the age of seven and I can remember quite clearly when that changed.'

'When?'

'They had a massive row just before Christmas. I'd never seen an argument like it before. My mother ushered me into the café part of the bakery so I couldn't hear most of it but five minutes later, she didn't have a job and I never saw him again … until now.'

'Are you sure it's the same man?' asked Molly.

'Same man, same name, same scar.'

Molly's eyes flickered back to the stage to see Barney was looking at Bree inquisitively. Or was it just her imagination?

Chapter Twenty

All eyes were on the stage, where Cam's confidence oozed out from his workstation. There were cameras dotted all around that panned in and projected images onto the screen at the back of the stage, showing all three competitors as they worked briskly to finish their creations.

The judges flitted from workstation to workstation asking questions and joking with the competitors. Barney could be seen standing at the side of the stage talking with William; then Bree noticed him slip through the door. 'I'm just nipping to the toilet,' she said and hurried out of the auditorium.

Moments later, she was standing in a grand hallway, the bright lighting illuminating the royal blue walls and a long line of gold-framed pictures of the previous winners of the Baker of the Year competition. She noticed Barney at the bottom of the hallway talking on his mobile phone and knew this was her chance. Bree hadn't wanted the toilet; she wanted answers. Seeing him standing in front of her on the stage was a shock and now she wanted to know: what exactly did happen all those years ago?

Bree's pulse quickened as she began to walk towards him. She really wasn't sure what she was going to say, but she knew she had to say something. She could barely breathe as he hung up his call and looked in her direction. Barney had once been a huge part of her and her mum's lives and now he was a complete stranger. Bree tried to keep her emotions under control as the full enormity of what she was about to ask him struck her. Could he possibly be her father? The letter that her mother had left for Molly suggested they had the same father, and the man standing at the end of the hallway was someone she remembered being very close to her mother. He'd also shown Bree a lot of care, taking her out to feed the ducks on a Sunday, or going with her to the park.

Her mother had run from him after that huge row had erupted and Bree needed to know what had been so bad that they had needed to move on again.

Barney had begun to walk back towards the door at the side of the stage and she knew it was now or never. 'Barney,' Bree called.

Barney paused and simply stared at her. 'Can I help you?'

'Barney. Hi, do you remember me? I think you knew my mother … Lilian.'

'Lilian,' he repeated.

'Lilian Allen.'

Lilian's name hung in the air as Barney stared at her. 'Bree?' he whispered.

She nodded.

'Wow, you've grown. How are you? Is Lilian here?' He took a swift glance up the corridor.

Bree shook her head. 'Mum passed away.'

It took Barney a second to process those words and when he did he looked grief-stricken. He raked a hand through his hair and blew out a breath. His eyes had welled up with tears. 'I wasn't expecting that... How? When?'

Bree could see that Barney was hurting and told him briefly what had happened.

'I can't believe you're here. I thought the world of Lilian and I missed you both when you left. I thought she would just turn up again after all the controversy had settled.'

'What controversy?' asked Bree.

'I hope there isn't going to be any trouble, Barney Miller. Cam is taking part in this competition fair and square.' Dixie was now standing behind them both.

Barney looked a little puzzled. 'Dixie, how are you? How do you know each other?'

'Bree is Cam's apprentice.'

'Really? You're a baker too? Just like Lilian. She would have been so proud of you.'

Now it was Dixie's turn to be confused. 'How do you know that Bree's mum was a baker?'

'Because she worked for me for over seven years. She was the deputy manager of my bakery and she used to bring this one into work most days as a baby and then on Saturdays when she started school.'

'Lilian Allen worked for you?' Dixie couldn't believe what she was hearing. This whole situation was getting more bizarre by the second.

'And what controversy?' Bree repeated, wondering what Barney was talking about.

Barney stretched his hand out towards Dixie. 'No trouble, Dixie. Just an apology, which I hope you and your family will accept on behalf on Ted. He was an honest man. I know that now.'

'That's not what you were saying at the time.' Dixie was taking no prisoners.

'How do you two actually know each other?' Bree was looking between them. She was so confused now.

'Barney Miller, here, and Ted both competed here for Baker of the Year with the same recipe, each claiming that it was their original recipe. It came to fisticuffs and they were both disqualified for cheating. Their names appeared all over the press as a certain someone' – she looked pointedly at Barney – 'sold their story to the papers and magazines trying to discredit Ted and put him out of business.'

'And I am sorry for that,' replied Barney, sounding genuine.

'How is it even possible that you both came up with the same recipe?' asked Bree.

Barney checked his watch. 'I really do need to be back on stage.'

'Not before you've explained, because I really want to hear this explanation,' demanded Dixie.

Barney turned back towards Bree. 'We came up with the same recipe – Layers Treats – because of Lilian. That argument you asked about – that's what we were arguing about. I arrived home from the competition and was fuming about the whole situation and the fact I'd been disqualified because Ted had baked a similar recipe and called it by the same name. Lilian never said a word. It was only weeks later she came clean and told me that she used to work for Ted at The Old Bakehouse and that he'd trained her. When she began working for me, she had never shared that information – she'd made up a story about moving from Glasgow, and never even mentioned Heartcross – so we argued and she left.'

'But why would Mum lie?'

'I later learned she was frightened about an old boyfriend tracking her down and so she'd made up the story to cover her tracks.'

'Was that my father?'

Barney nodded. 'Lilian started all over again when she got to my bakery. She fabricated a story of past employment and I didn't check it out properly. It was only six months after taking the job that she told me she was pregnant with you. I supported her the best I could. Lilian was a hard worker and I could see that having a youngster around the place kept me on my toes. I quite enjoyed it.'

'So why the argument? Why did we never see you again?'

'Because Lilian never told me that she and Ted had come up with the original idea together when I asked her if I could use it for the baking competition and she said yes. I thought I was going forward with a completely unique recipe and I couldn't believe it when Ted baked a similar chocolate slab. When Lilian came clean, we rowed, but I didn't expect her to up and leave. I thought she would turn up again for work on the Monday after she'd cooled off, but she didn't. I was incredibly saddened that I didn't see her again ... or you.' He paused. 'I really am sorry, Dixie. If I had known I would never have used the recipe.'

Dixie nodded her appreciation. 'Past is past. You are lucky I am a woman of forgiveness.'

'Much appreciated,' he replied.

'And Cam?' she asked.

'Cam will do his Great-Uncle Ted proud and the Layers Treats recipe deserves to live on.' Barney looked at Bree. 'I hope we can catch up after the competition?'

'I'd like that,' she replied.

'Dixie, would it be possible to talk later?' He touched her arm, she nodded and then Barney walked back through the door onto the stage.

'Well, I never,' said Dixie. 'Wait until Cam and Molly hear all this.'

'What the hell are you doing? Come on, you're missing so much. Cam is hilarious on this stage,' Molly shouted up the hallway towards Bree and Dixie, who immediately hurried back towards the auditorium. 'Where have you both been?'

'We'll explain later,' replied Dixie, taking her seat.

The competition was drawing to an end. Molly could hardly believe it. It had flown by so fast and the bakers had provided great entertainment.

As soon as the gong sounded all three bakers threw their hats up into the air to the sound of rapturous applause. Cam looked pleased as he clenched his fists and grinned at Molly. The Layers Treats chocolate slab had been baked to perfection, with a lot of love and a sprinkle of magic from Heartcross and The Old Bakehouse.

Cam waited nervously as he presented his creation to the judges, praying he'd done enough to make Great-Uncle Ted proud.

The judges took thirty minutes to make their decision and all three bakers who'd been waiting backstage were then brought back out onto the stage. The atmosphere was tense as William handed the microphone to Barney, who made his way to the centre of the stage.

'It is a great honour to announce this year's Baker of the Year,' he said as the room fell silent. 'In a unanimous decision, the judges have decided the winner of Scottish Baker of the Year is ... Cameron Bird with his creation Layers Treats.'

Molly was up on her feet and cheering at the top of her voice as soon as Barney said Cam's name. She glanced towards Dixie whose eyes were streaming with proud tears.

'He did it! Baker of the Year!' She clapped furiously as Cam walked over to Barney and shook his hand, the two of them sharing a few whispered words. Cam then proudly took the trophy and thrust it up in the air.

Cheers and applause surrounded him as George ran onto the stage and straight to Cam, who quickly gave the trophy to William as he scooped his son into his arms and placed his baker's hat on George's head. The hat promptly slid down over his eyes, making the audience laugh.

At that very second there was a loud 'pop' and Molly clasped her stomach as she looked down at the stream of water that was soaking through her tights. Her waters had broken.

'Dixie ... Dixie...'

But Dixie couldn't hear because of all the noise in the room. Molly glanced towards the stage, where Cam was taking the microphone from William and was just about to make his speech.

Cam looked overwhelmed as he blew out a breath. 'I did it— *We* did it,' he corrected himself. Cam was beaming as he gathered his thoughts and the audience hushed. 'My Great-Uncle Ted won this award for many years on the run and when he passed away, I took over The Old Bakehouse. I never dreamt I would be standing on this stage, holding this trophy and winning prize money of fifty thousand pounds. It's thanks to Ted and my family – Molly, Dixie, George and Bree – and to Lilian Allen, who is no longer with us. Lilian was Ted's right-hand woman and invented the concept of

Layers Treats, a recipe I've adapted for today's competition. I've been thinking a lot about expanding The Old Bakehouse and I think opening a chocolate shop called "Layers Treats" in the village of Heartcross is now a given.'

He smiled at Bree, who had her hands clasped. She couldn't believe how her life had turned around in a matter of weeks.

'And I hope you will all come and visit.' Cam held the trophy high in the air. The room erupted into further applause as Cam handed the microphone back to William and everyone stood and watched as all the competitors and judges waved and walked backstage.

'A chocolate shop in Heartcross. The children will love that,' said Dixie, looking towards Molly who was doing everything in her power not to cry out in pain.

'Molly, what is it, you look…'

Dixie followed Molly's gaze to the floor. 'Bloody hell. William … William…' Dixie bellowed over to William who was standing at the side of the stage. Quickly, she turned towards Bree. 'Grab George and take him through to the other room. Get yourself a drink and some food. The baby is coming!'

'Oh my God, no way! Eek! Good luck! Is that what you say? I've no idea!' Bree was grinning, her eyes wide with excitement.

William appeared at Dixie's side. 'We need Cam but more importantly we need an ambulance,' stated Dixie. 'Molly is in labour.'

'I think it may be too late for an ambulance.' Molly was taking in deep breaths.

Immediately, William rang the reception. 'We have a spare bedroom just up this hallway. Let's get you comfortable. Cam is on his way.'

Dixie took hold of Molly's arm and they pushed through the crowd of people gathered around the doorway. 'Woman in labour, let us through,' announced Dixie as the crowd hurriedly stepped to the side.

Cam was running up the hallway clutching his trophy, and he kissed Molly's head once he reached them.

'I'm so sorry, I shouldn't be stealing your thunder.' She stopped walking and took in a sharp breath.

'I can't leave you alone for a second,' he joked, taking her hand. 'You've really picked your moment, haven't you?'

'Here, this room.' William held a card against the keypad and it swung open. 'The ambulance is on its way. Can I get you anything?'

Cam looked towards Molly. 'Towels, we need towels. I've seen that in the movies.'

'Pain relief, I need pain relief.' Molly was overcome and let out a high-pitched squeal.

'I'll go and look after George and Bree.' Dixie gestured for William to leave the room then touched Molly's shoulder. 'Good luck!'

Molly sat down on the bed and took off her cardigan. She was clutching her bump in agony, the contractions becoming more frequent. It was obvious to Cam that Molly wasn't going to hold on to this baby for much longer and that trying to move her to the nearest hospital would be too complicated. It was probably too late anyway. He helped her to lie down on the bed and she raised her knees and clutched Cam's arm tightly.

'I need to take off my tights and you need to take a look at what is going on down there.'

Cam looked petrified but didn't protest. Molly was breathing heavily now and she wasn't the only one. Cam helped her out of her tights and her pants then she lay back down. Panic-stricken, she yelled, 'Can you see the head?' as another contraction took over. She squeezed Cam's hand so tight that he started to lose feeling in it.

Cam willed the ambulance to hurry.

'It's coming, I want to push,' Molly panted.

'Try and keep calm and push through the contractions,' Cam encouraged her calmly, even though he felt far from calm. He didn't even know if that was the correct thing to say. 'You're doing really well.'

Molly was pale so Cam quickly ran a hand towel under the tap and wiped her brow.

'This goddamn hurts,' she shouted.

'Not long to go,' he said, wishing with all his might that the paramedics would walk through that door and take over.

'I can feel the head,' screamed Molly.

Cam took a quick look. 'And I can see the head.'

'I need to push again.'

'This baby isn't hanging about, is it? My guess is it's nearly here. With the next contraction push as hard as you can.' Cam knew the contraction was coming by the pain in Molly's face. 'One last push.'

She nodded, and despite the pain in her eyes, gave it everything she had. 'I need pain relief.'

'It's a little too late for that now. PUSH!'

Molly gave a scream and with one last push a beautiful baby girl slid straight into Cam's arms. He quickly placed the baby on the bed, grabbed a handful of tissues from the bathroom and wiped away the mucus from the baby's nose and mouth. The baby let out a cry. The relief in hearing that sound was instant.

Molly was worn out, tears running down her face, as she asked, 'What do we have?'

'A beautiful baby girl,' replied Cam, giving Molly a kiss on the top of her head. 'You did brilliantly.'

With a hasty knock on the door the paramedics arrived, stepping in to help Cam cut the cord and wrap the baby up in a towel so she could be passed to Molly.

'She's absolutely beautiful,' she murmured, unable to take her eyes off her daughter.

'Do we have a name?' asked the paramedic.

Molly and Cam held each other's gaze and Cam nodded. He knew exactly what Molly was thinking.

'Lilian,' she replied. 'Lily for short.'

They both gazed at the baby. Molly couldn't quite take in the fact that she was holding her daughter in her hands. She was perfect.

Just then the door was flung open and three pairs of eyes peered into the room.

'Lily, let me introduce you to your older brother George, your great-grandmother Dixie and your Auntie Bree.'

George was soon by Molly's side stroking Lily's head gently. 'You don't think she will pinch my cars, do you? Because they're my favourite.'

Everyone laughed.

'I think it'll be a while before you have to worry about that,' replied Cam, ruffling George's hair.

'And you've called the baby Lily? After Mum?' asked Bree.

'After Mum,' replied Molly with a warm smile. 'I think she would be proud of all of us.'

Molly looked around the room, feeling so lucky to be surrounded by her family. Her heart swelled with happiness.

Hearing Dixie chuckle, Molly looked up. 'Martha predicted right again: a letter, a death, scandal and new beginnings.'

'And a baby girl whose name begins with "L",' added Molly, glancing out of the window. 'Bree ... look!'

All heads turned towards the window, through which the moon was visible in the late afternoon sky.

'Loon moon,' Molly and Bree murmured together.

'Mum's watching over us,' Molly said quietly. Tears caught in her throat and a feeling of warmth flooded her body as she held her baby close. Gently kissing Lily's cheek, she glanced up at Cam, her heart dancing with joy.

'I have to say, this has been one of the best days of my life. Making Great-Uncle Ted proud, winning Baker of the

Year and now we have a brand-new wee pudding that has arrived.' Cam kissed the top of Molly's head. 'I love you.'

'I love you too,' she replied. She nodded quietly towards George, who had slipped into a chair in the corner of the room and was biting into the winning Layers Treats chocolate slab.

'Hey!' joked Cam.

George looked up sheepishly then grinned. 'I'm not sharing,' he replied, taking another huge bite whilst keeping one eye on baby Lily.

Everyone laughed.

Acknowledgments

I can't quite believe my sixteenth book has been published. It's so surreal!

There is a long list of wonderful folk that I need to thank and first up is Charlotte Ledger, an encouraging boss who captains a great ship! I am so grateful to you for turning my stories into books – thank you.

Writing is a huge team effort and even though my name might be on the cover a lot of hard work goes on behind the scenes. Thank you to my editor Laura McCallen and all the team at One More Chapter. You work so hard making my books the best they can be and helping them to fly in the big wide world. You rock!

Biggest thanks go to my children, Emily, Jack, Roo and Tilly. They are my greatest achievement with my books coming a close second.

Much love to my two pesky loons Woody (my mad Cocker Spaniel) and Nellie (my bonkers Labradoodle). Most days you drive me insane but both of you are just the best writing partners-in-crime.

Love to my BMITWE, Anita Redfern. You are my epic friend, a friend like no other. Simply the best. Can't fault you!

A massive thank you to Julie Wetherill. Roses are red, violets are blue, I'm so lucky to have a friend like you!

A special mention to Karl Ladley – you are not funny!

High fives to the team at Radio Northwich especially Kim Smith, John Thompson and Matt Cat. All three of you champion and flag-wave my books at every opportunity and it is very much appreciated – Thank you.

Much love to Kim Smith (2nd mention!) Sam Newey and Ashley Costello. You are three amazing women who encourage and champion everyone in your community. All three of you were the inspiration behind this story and thank you for that weekend of support when I needed you all most.

A big thank you to Tom Newey who is the creator and owner of the chocolate business Layers Treats. Tom kindly allowed me to use his name and chocolate business in this book. Obviously, the storyline is completely fictional and doesn't bear any resemblance to Tom's personal life except he does own the best delicious treats and desserts business in the whole of Cheshire – fact!

A special mention to Jacqui and Colin Fletcher who are the best neighbours in the world.

Group hug to a lovely bunch of authors Bella Osborne, Glynis Peters, Deborah Carr and Terri Nixon. Thank you for all the texts, chats, RT's and shout outs – I appreciate you all.

A virtual group hug to all my readers, the wonderful bloggers and reviewers, retailers, librarians and fellow authors who have supported me throughout my career. Authors will be lost without you, and I'm so grateful for your support.

I have without a doubt enjoyed writing every second of this book and I really hope you enjoy hanging out at The Old Bakehouse with Molly, Cam, Bree and Dixie. Please do let me know!

Warm wishes,
Christie xx

Don't miss *The Hidden Secrets of Bumblebee Cottage*

**The next heartwarming instalment in the Love Heart Lane
series by Christie Barlow!**

Where friends are there for you no matter what…